REESE GOLDEN MYSTERIES, BOOK TWO

DIAMONDBACK REVENGE

Cindy Keen Reynders

**CAMEL
PRESS**

Kenmore, WA

PRESS

Camel Press books published by Epicenter Press

Epicenter Press
6524 NE 181st St. Suite 2
Kenmore, WA 98028.
www.Epicenterpress.com
www.Coffeetownpress.com
www.Camelpress.com

For more information go to: www.Epicenterpress.com
Author's website: www.cindykeenreynders.com

Diamondback Revenge

ISBN: 9781684920556 (trade paper)
ISBN: 9781684920563 (ebook)

LOC: 2022936030

Printed in the United States of America

Dedication

As always, thank you to my husband and my family for their patience and understanding when I go into my office and disappear for hours. They appreciate my writing addiction and for that I will be eternally grateful.

Also, a huge thank you to my editor Jennifer McCord, who believed in this story and my ability to write it.

Acknowledgments

Thank you to the Greater Power that has blessed me to have my way with words. Also, I appreciate that Coffeetown Press has allowed me to join the ranks of their authors.

Chapter One

A breeze cooled Reese Golden's flushed face as she hiked along a winding Devil's Tower trail. Bright summer sun filtered through an emerald canopy of leaves, highlighting patches of blue sky.

Her friend Kiki Morningstar walked beside her as they made their way around the russet, vertically ridged rock monolith, also known as Bear's Lodge by local Native American tribes.

Standing 867 feet from base to summit, it remained a sacred spot for tribal members who had attached colorful prayer bundles of red, yellow, and blue on tree trunks and suspended them from branches.

The reverence of the display was not lost on Reese, and she was glad Kiki had urged her to leave her house in order to enjoy spending some time outdoors. Reese's mom had brought her and her younger brother Jesse here when they were kids, but she hadn't understood the significance of the landmark back then.

Her heart twisted when she recalled their car accident. Her grandparents had taken her in and raised her afterward, but all these years later, they, too had passed on.

The surroundings took her breath away—the mossy boulders scattered across the forest floor, birds chattering in the trees, chipmunks scurrying through wildflowers. In the distance, grassy prairie displayed the blue, snaking Belle Fourche River.

Reese pressed a hand to her perspiring brow, then brushed aside a fly. The end of summer brought baking heat to cowboy country and right now, the temperature must be soaring.

"Sheesh," she said as she came to a standstill. "I think I'm melting."

"Come winter, you'll be griping about shoveling snow." Kiki also stopped walking and batted away another insect. She pushed strands of her frizzy dark hair back under a wide pink headband. Her black hiking boots, tight black leggings, and a crop top enhanced her knockout figure.

"I'm sure you're right," Reese agreed. "Still, right this minute it is hot as, well, you know."

Because this wasn't a heavy-duty trail, Reese wore a pair of hiking sandals. Her lightweight clothing consisted of a khaki shirt and shorts, along with her grandfather's straw cowboy hat. It was old and sweat stained, but it brought to mind fond memories of the man who helped raise her, his involvement in her life like that of a father.

"Surely you don't miss living in Denver, because it's like an oven in summer, too," Kiki pointed out. "You're not regretting your move back home, are you?"

"No, I'm not," Reese admitted.

After a 10-year career with the Denver Police Department, and being shot while on duty, she'd resigned and moved back to her home in Meadowlark Valley. The town held a population of around 40,000 inhabitants, which made it big enough to offer the necessities of life plus a few more perks. It wasn't too big, and it wasn't too little—it was just right.

A little over six months ago, she'd taken up residence in her grandparents' old bungalow, which they had gifted to her in their will. Since she intended to use her law enforcement skills to help others, she'd launched a private investigator business in the converted garage.

Initially, she adhered to conducting federal background investigations—a lucrative business she'd gained the confidence to do well. On occasion, she strayed from that and handled random cases brought to her through the local police department or private citizens.

"Hello! Earth to Reese," Kiki said, interrupting the monotonous hum of buzzing insects. "You're supposed to be taking it easy. What are you doing?"

"Trying to catch my breath," Reese said.

"Come on, let's go. We're almost back to the parking lot." Kiki resumed walking. "We can get a soda out of the cooler, then head home."

Reese trotted up beside her friend and fell in step.

"You sure you don't need any more smudging sticks or chakra crystals for your holistic shop?" Reese asked. "Maybe some colored feathers or bells?"

"Nope. I found everything I needed when we stopped at the Bright Crow Trading Post."

"Awesome." Having caught her second wind, Reese jogged ahead of Kiki and made a beeline toward her old Bronco. She didn't want to wait any longer than she had to for that drink. By now, her mouth had a dry, cottony feel that she very much disliked.

"Hey, no fair! Wait for me," Kiki called out.

With a chuckle, Reese increased her pace, feeling the burn in her leg muscles. As a wise person once said, time waits for no one.

This is crazy, Reese thought, to be traveling on a scorching day like this with the truck's air conditioning on full blast. Kiki didn't seem to care about that. Sound asleep, head pressed against the passenger seat headrest, she let loose a snort and then settled into regular snoring.

"Sweet." Reese turned up the old cassette tape featuring her favorite country music and sang along with the tunes. The uplifting, encouraging words were exactly what the doctor ordered to finish out the road trip.

Unaffected, Kiki only snored louder.

Noting the red needle on the gas gauge heading toward E, Reese slowed down and began watching for a gas station where she could refuel. Around these parts, those were pretty far and few between, so she kept her eyes peeled.

About 10 miles out of Meadowlark Valley, she spotted a sign directing her toward a gas station named Barking Squirrel Gas & Oil. She smiled. Wyoming natives knew that barking squirrels were prairie dogs—chubby rodents that dug potholes across the prairie big enough to swallow a horse. Not really, but sometimes it seemed that way.

They were cute things, but also a huge nuisance. Her grandfather had cussed out the critters when he regaled her with tales of his childhood on his family's ranch. The acres had been sold after her grandfather grew up and moved away, but the lifestyle he'd experienced had gifted him with plenty of stories.

She sailed the Bronco, restored by herself and her grandfather, down the exit and toward the stop. Betty, Reese's nickname for the truck, fit perfectly beneath a red metal awning and into a slot beside the gas pump. Curiously studying the device, she decided it was most likely a relic from the 1970s.

Scooting out of the driver's side, Reese removed the gas cap and began pumping regular. Wind whipped dirt devils around the parking lot, depositing nasty grit in her mouth. A couple of tumbleweeds bounced past and on down the road. A wide swath of prairie surrounded the gas station, with pine-covered mountains rising along the horizon like stately lookouts.

Finished fueling and ready to pay, she glanced at Kiki who still slept, amazingly unaware the Bronco had stopped moving. Shaking her head at her friend's dead-to-the-world condition, Reese walked over beside the truck and rolled down her window so Kiki would have fresh air. Then she headed inside the Barking Squirrel gas station, which was housed inside a creepy, crumbling stone building that had seen better days.

Chapter Two

Inside the store, Reese sneezed as a musty odor assailed her nostrils. She blinked as her eyes made the transition from bright sunlight to dim interior. Leather and saddle soap fragranced the air. Strains from a radio broadcast vintage country music.

She took note of the shelves stocked with convenience store items—gum, candy bars, chips, and miscellaneous staples like bread and cookies, crackers, and cans of nonperishable food.

Not-so-typical objects included cans of smoked rattlesnake meat, metal racks displaying rattlesnake-themed T-shirts, rattlesnake leather belts, and even a few rattlesnake plants with spiky green leaves sporting a two-tone pattern reminiscent of the reptile.

Bicycle chain rattlesnake sculptures covered a corner shelf, along with rattlesnake Christmas ornaments and even packages of pink gummy rattlesnakes.

Faded and ripped posters plastered the walls. One was titled, *Rattlesnakes of North America*, another was titled, *Venomous Snakes of Wyoming*—the prairie rattlesnake and the midget faded rattlesnake. Yet another was titled, *Southern Fried Rattlesnake*, complete with the recipe.

Reese winced, and her stomach did a flip-flop. She didn't think she'd be interested in learning to cook that delicacy. Not unless she was starving. Only under those circumstances would she reconsider.

Tastes like chicken, she heard in her mind.

"Sure," she murmured.

Three large tanks filled a corner. Each held sand, cactus, and driftwood. Snakes dangled from tree branches and slithered through their desert dioramas, making Reese's skin tingle.

She was not a fan of the cold-blooded critters, yet she had a healthy respect for those who did. As they say, to each his own.

Her gaze rested on a glass display case brimming with earrings, rings, bracelets, brooches, and necklaces. The glittering jewels were crafted into all manner of snakes, serpents, and other bedazzled, slithery creatures.

One large cupboard sat empty; the glass front shattered with jagged shards sprinkled across velvet-lined shelves. The damage looked fairly recent, and Reese gave a low whistle. After studying it for a moment, she continued on.

The Barking Squirrel gas station wasn't all that far from Meadowlark Valley, and she wondered why she'd never noticed it. Of course, she hadn't lived around here for years, so perhaps someone had brought it back to life during her absence.

"Is there something I can help you with ma'am?"

Reese spun around, finally noticing the elderly man in a black felt cowboy hat, a red flannel shirt, jeans, and suspenders. Long gray hair fell to his shoulders, and he sported a giant, bushy mustache. His beard seemed large enough to fill an entire zip code.

"Sorry, I didn't see there," she said. "I need to pay for my gas."

"Sure, let me help you," the man said as he strode behind a register that rested on a smooth wooden counter.

She edged up to where he stood and told him which pump, she'd used. After he rang up the charge, she handed him a credit card.

"Cash only," he said. "Sorry. I believe in good, old-fashioned greenbacks."

"No problem," Reese said. "In fact, wait a second while I pick up a couple of things."

"I'm not going' anywhere," he drawled.

Reese stepped over to the T-shirt display, selected a desert brown, medium size top featuring a coiled rattlesnake. She might not care for the reptile, but the top looked fun and would be a great addition to her comfortable wardrobe. Reaching for a package of gummy snakes, she decided munching on them would break up the monotony during her final driving stretch. She also liked supporting small, local businesses.

As she placed the items on the counter, the store owner met her gaze.

"You sure you don't want to add a package of them barbecued rattlesnake bites?" He grinned and his eyes sparkled with mischief. "They're mighty tasty."

"No, thanks. I'll pass," she said with a chuckle.

"Not too many folks care to indulge." He rang up the extra items and gave her the new total, then slid everything into a brown sack emblazoned with the store's name.

Reese handed him the exact amount of bills and change. "Have you operated this store for long?"

"The building was here, but it was run down and falling apart. I bought it a while back after I retired."

He handed the purchases to Reese.

"That explains why I've never seen it. I just moved home to Meadowlark Valley from Denver a short while ago."

He rubbed the back his neck as he studied her. "How do you like what I've done with the place?"

"It's… interesting."

"That's all?" He gave her a crooked grin.

"There's probably a story behind your rattlesnake theme, but I don't want to be nosy and ask what that might be."

"It's no secret. As a kid, one of those suckers bit me clean through my leather boot when I was out fishing' with my pa." He chuckled. "Same damn thing happened years ago when I was out jade hunting with a friend. Riled me up both times I got bit, but now I'm sort of fixated on snakes."

"I see."

"If you don't mind me asking, what in the world took you away from the big city and drew you back to the armpit of Wyoming?"

"That's a long, boring story," she said.

"Sounds like something happened that made you gun-shy. After serving in the war, I know what that's like."

"Yeah, something like that," she said.

A phantom pain shot through her right shoulder. Memories of the shooting incident from her days as a cop flashed in her mind, and she pushed it away. Dwelling on it wasn't healthy.

"Meadowlark Valley's a sleepy little town. How do you get by, if you don't mind me asking? I sense you're not the type to wait tables at the local greasy spoon."

People here made friends quickly, Reese thought, and the guy asked lots of questions. But what the heck. She could tell he was just being hospitable—something she loved about her neighbors.

"I was a police detective in Denver," she told him. "I decided to move home and start my own private investigator business."

He snapped his fingers. "No wonder you seem so familiar. I saw your photo in the newspaper when the Meadowlark Valley Chronicle ran an article about you. How's it going, if you don't mind me asking?"

"So far, so good," she said.

She remembered visiting with the Chronicle reporter and the subsequent published piece. Being interviewed was one of her least favorite activities, but it was free publicity. No way she could complain about that.

The man clucked his tongue. "Good for you. Running your own shop isn't for everyone. You work long hours for few rewards and it's not always easy to make a living."

"I've been lucky," she said.

"Still, it's impressive," he insisted.

"I know it's cliché, but someone once told me I'm like a dog with a bone," Reese commented, remembering the police officer who'd said it—Jeremy Savage. She'd worked with him on a previous case, and he'd recently moved to Meadowlark Valley for a job with the local police department.

"By the way, my name's Ford Presley," he said.

"Reese Golden," she shot back, realizing he probably remembered her name from the article "Thank you for your service. What conflict did you serve in?"

"The Vietnam War. I was young and dumb and didn't have

any real prospects, so I joined up." He reached out and they shook hands over the counter. "Glad I'm no longer caught in the thick of the action, except for the war in my mind."

He tapped his wrinkled forehead.

Reese sympathized with him, understanding how troubling memories could keep you awake at night with anxiety, enough to nearly drive you bonkers. His last name, Presley, seemed familiar. Then she remembered why.

"By any chance, are you related to Bella Presley?" she asked. "I went to high school with her."

"She's my daughter," he said in a sad tone. Ford looked down at his hands, then back at her, tears glimmering in his eyes. "God help me, for a minute there, I forgot what's been going on. Bella is, well..."

Reese instantly wished she hadn't mentioned her former schoolmate. Local radio and TV stations had been buzzing about Bella drowning yesterday during a whitewater rafting trip with her church group. Rescue workers scouring the river still hadn't recovered her body. They feared her lifejacket snagged on undergrowth and she'd been trapped beneath the water.

"I'm so sorry," she said.

"My old ticker can hardly stand this," Ford said, a catch in his voice as he placed a hand over his upper chest.

"Please know you have my deepest sympathies."

Reese thought of her family members who had passed away, and how much she missed them. Parent to child ties ran deep, and she could see that Ford was having a hard time letting go. And no wonder.

"Then last night, some jerk broke into my shop," Ford said, his nostrils flared.

"That's terrible," Reese sympathized. Ford had lost his daughter yesterday, then there was a break in at his place that evening? Her heart went out to him.

"They stole the snake diorama Bella gave me," Ford continued. "It was a Christmas present one year. We joked about how it represented all the snake bites I'd survived. Now it reminds me of the good times the two of us shared."

Reese frowned, still upset by her lousy judgement of mentioning Bella. Poor Mr. Presley. No one expects to outlive a child and she could tell he ached from the loss.

"I need a favor from you, young lady."

"Yes, sir. What can I do?"

"Call me Ford."

"Okay."

"I want to hire you to find my diorama." He slid his wallet from his back pocket and opened up a plastic sleeve that contained Bella's senior photo. She stood next to a massive, gnarled cottonwood tree, her dark, curly hair tumbling down her back. "It would mean a lot to me."

Reese didn't expect that. Her job performing background investigations kept her busy enough and paid the bills, so she didn't need the income. Honestly, she didn't feel ready to take on anything beyond her regular work load. Yet, that picture of Bella tugged at her heartstrings.

Their senior year of high school had been so carefree and full of promises for the future. Not a single individual in their senior class could have foreseen the inevitable difficulties clouding their futures.

Ford must have seen the reluctance in her expression, and his eyes twinkled.

"I'll make it worth your time," he said.

"It's not about the money," she assured him. "Did you call the police this morning and report the theft?"

"Yes, but I don't think they really care." Ford shook his head. "Cops around here are about as useful as a three-legged hunting dog. Meaning no offence, of course, since you are a former police officer and all."

"Was there anything else stolen?"

He shrugged. "Some junk food. Chips and candy bars. And some cheap snake jewelry."

"I'm sure the police will do all they can to recover your diorama," Reese advised Ford in a reassuring tone, though she knew from her experience, stolen property rarely made its way home again.

"Maybe, maybe not," Ford muttered.

"You had insurance, right?"

"That's not the point," he said, his voice trembling. "Money can't replace my diorama. I need it back. It's a matter of, well, just help me find it, will you please?"

"Yes, of course," Reese responded quickly. "I apologize if it seemed I wasn't taking the theft seriously enough."

For Pete's sake, she felt like she just kept putting her foot in her mouth and making matters worse. She couldn't blame Ford for being upset. He'd just lost his daughter. Now someone had stolen an item that held sentimental value. Reese maintained many keepsakes for similar reasons.

She, of all people, got it.

"You noticed that broken display case, didn't you?" Ford inclined his head toward the back of the store where it stood in its disheveled condition.

"Yes, I did." Reese glanced over at it, taking stock.

"That's where I kept it. It was a gaudy thing covered in diamonds."

"Real jewels?"

"No, no, nothing like that." Ford shook his head. "They were simply shiny."

"Probably rhinestones," Reese suggested. But if it looked expensive, the thief or thieves must have believed they could sell it for big money.

Ford sighed. "It was just window dressing for the store. I liked looking up at it when I was working because it reminded me of my girl…"

He trailed off and Reese noted the anguish lining his face.

"As a precaution, you ought to add extra deadbolts and locks on your windows and doors so nothing else turns up missing."

"Yeah, sure. Will do." Ford met her gaze, concern glimmering in the depths of his eyes. "What do you say, Reese?"

Reese wanted to tell him no, but the entire situation was a gut wrencher. It wouldn't hurt to do some investigation work for Ford.

Footsteps echoed on the floorboards.

"Take the job, Reese," Kiki urged as she eased up beside her and patted her arm. "I think you need to help. Bella was my lab partner in my sophomore biology class. I made her dissect the frog while I took lab notes."

Everyone chuckled, then sobered.

"That girl is fearless," Ford said, then added, "uh, was fearless."

Reese realized it wouldn't take much to ask the local police department's newest detective, Jeremy Savage, what he thought about Ford's break-in. She could follow a few leads and put Ford's mind at ease. Unfortunately, she feared the snake diorama was probably long gone by now.

She smiled at Kiki. "Why didn't you stay in the truck, sleepyhead?"

"Because, it's like a gazillion degrees out there and I needed a pit stop." She glanced down the hall at the ladies' room sign featuring a carved outhouse.

On a deeper level, Reese envied Kiki's ability to expertly appeal to people and their human nature. Kiki had missed her calling. She should have become a therapist—not a holistic shop owner. Perhaps the services Kiki offered at her place were a subtle form of therapy.

Reese reached into her purse and handed over one of her business cards. "Call me if you have any questions, Ford. By the way, do you have any pictures of the diorama?"

"No, no." Ford smiled, revealing chipped, tobacco-stained teeth. He reached into his cash register, removed some bills and with a trembling hand, held them toward Reese.

She noticed several Benjamins in the stack of currency, and frowned. It made her feel guilty to take any payment, because that wasn't why she'd agreed to help.

"Let me check into the matter first and see what I come up with," she suggested. "I'm doing this as a favor."

"Nope. I insist. Bella would want me to pay for your time."

Reluctantly, Reese took the money and slid it into a pocket in her purse. She'd find a way to give it back to Ford at a later date down the road.

Ford stared out of the store's front window toward the rolling prairie landscape, his gaze reflective. "You know, I come from a long line of folks who settled in Wyoming..."

Chapter Three

Ten minutes later, Reese had heard a complete retelling of Ford's life story. She sympathized with how sad he must feel right now, considering his recent loss. If talking with her helped alleviate his sadness, she could at least listen.

He told her he'd been born and raised in Medicine Bow, Wyoming, the only child of a father who had worked for the Union Pacific Railroad. His mother, a hairdresser, had died of cancer when Ford was 10.

After high school graduation, Ford said he'd enlisted and served in the Vietnam War, explaining he'd been nothing more than a "grunt with a gun." His tales about the jungle conflict chilled her, for example, the time he'd nearly been captured, the terrible firefight where he'd carried a wounded buddy on his shoulders to safety, and the awful exposure to Agent Orange.

"That's the chemical that treated me to such a sweet grin," he commented, pulling his lips back to give her a good look at his crumbling teeth.

"You sure had a rough time over there," Reese said, truly humbled by his experience.

"We all did," Ford said. "After 'Nam, I trained to become a truck driver. I drove long-hauls with a big rig for another twenty years and delivered goods all over the country."

"I bet you've seen some beautiful places," Reese commented.

"The best is Wyoming and her rugged hills, prairies, and rushing rivers."

"We do have a great state," Reese agreed.

"Of course, my family has lived here for generations, so I'm partial. I didn't marry until I was in my 40s. I kind of had to when I accidently got Bella's mom, Charlene, in the family way." He grinned, then continued. "She passed soon after Bella was born. A while later, I met Naomi, my current wife, and she helped me raise Bella. Bella was six when her little brother Ian was born."

Reese found Ford's story heartwarming, but she wanted to get back home and make plans to start looking for his diorama. She shot a glance over at Kiki, who was pawing through a box of polished stones, holding one up toward the light now and then to examine it.

"Ford, tell me what your snake diorama looks like," she pressed.

"I'm getting' there, young lady," he drawled. "Hold your horses."

Well, that was a mistake to try and interrupt his thought process. By regaling his past, Ford was possibly trying to deal with Bella's drowning. Reese quashed her impatience.

"Where was I?" Ford stared at the ceiling. "Oh, that's right. After I retired from the truck driving business, a buddy of mine introduced me to jade prospecting. That's one helluva fascinating hobby and it kept me busy. One time when me'n Dutch were traipsing around in the Laramie Mountains, I stumbled over a rattlesnake. Little bastard bit me right through my leather boot, just like it happened when I was a kid out fishing with my pa. Dutch drove me directly to the hospital to be treated."

Reese recalled her recent encounter with a rattler when she'd traveled up to an old ghost town. She'd been helping to clear landslide debris off of a road when a bone-chilling rattle told her she'd uncovered one of the slithery creatures. Thankfully, a friend had scooped it up with a shovel and pitched it into a ravine.

"For some reason, that blasted snake really got to me," Ford continued. "That's when I started collecting snake paraphernalia. Boots, belts, jewelry—you name it. I opened up this place as a retirement gig and I stocked it with my treasures."

"You have quite a collection," Reese said, ready to get down to business, and hoping Ford wouldn't object if she prodded him in that direction again. "I want to start looking for your diorama right away. Can you describe what it looks like?"

Ford scratched the side of his head, brows furrowed. "Sorry for rambling."

Reese reached inside her purse to fish out a pencil and a notepad. "I'll sketch a thumbnail, though I warn you, I'm not very good at drawing."

Ford held his hands apart. "It's about yea big."

Narrowing her gaze, Reese tried to judge how large "yea big" would actually be, which wasn't easy. "I'm envisioning it must be about two feet long," she suggested. "Would you agree?"

He nodded. "Sounds right."

"It's got snakes on it?" Reese tapped her pencil on the notepad.

"That it does."

"How many? And what kind of snakes are they?"

"Rattlesnakes. There are two, I think. No, actually there are three."

Reese tried to create an image in her mind of the diorama, but failed. "What are the snakes doing?" she asked.

He rested his age-spotted hand on the counter. "As I recollect, they are all posed in some way."

"That's good. What else?"

"The snakes have real shiny eyes," he added.

"The taxidermist must have filled them with rhinestones," Reese suggested.

He nodded. "Probably. Their rattles are covered with 'em, too. Tiny clusters of them."

Encouraged, Reese asked, "What do you think the base is made out of?"

"It's wood," Ford finally said. "It's painted brown and gray and is covered with sagebrush and sticks and grass. There are two large snakes and a smaller one—a baby. One's in a striking position, the other's all coiled up and the baby is coming out of a cracked shell in a nest of eggs. It also has a brass plate with a name—*Diamondback Revenge*."

He took a deep breath, and added, "Like I said, this thing is very important to me. If I've lost it forever, I don't know what I'll do."

Reese swept her hand across the page, drawing as she recalled Ford's description. She wasn't the world's greatest artist, that was for sure. Finally, she'd managed to render a representation. She handed him the notebook.

He took it, flipping it in all directions, then left it upside down, his brows drawn together.

He studied it so long that Reese wondered if he really was seeing it. He seemed lost in memories again. Gently, she pried the notepad from him and turned it right side up.

"This is the way to look at it," she said.

"Hmm, no, the snakes are closer," Ford decided.

Reese erased some of the markings and sketched in a couple of changes.

Curious, Kiki eased up beside them and studied the drawing.

"The little feller is mostly out of the egg shell." Ford frowned. "You can barely see its head the way you've got him."

Once again, Reese made adjustments. "What do you think now?"

"The bigger snake that's ready to strike needs his backside draped over a piece of driftwood."

Reese erased some of her scratches and penciled in what Ford had described.

"That looks good," he finally said. "My mind isn't what it used to be and I've forgotten the details."

Reese examined her sketch of a wood base diorama with two adult rattlers and a baby rattler coming out of a nest of eggs. She'd adorned it with buffalo grass, sagebrush, and driftwood. To emphasize that the snake eyes and rattlers were encrusted with rhinestones, she'd etched small stars around them.

Rubbing her brow, she absorbed the details. From that sketch, she would begin her search. Her goal would now be to find the diorama and return it to Ford, along with the cash he'd given her.

Ford rubbed his hands together. "How soon do you think you can find it?"

"All I can promise is that I'll do my best."

Chapter Four

Driving into Meadowlark Valley, Reese headed downtown to Kiki's place, a lovely old home where she also had her shop. After going inside to drop off Kiki's luggage, they discussed Bella's death, along with Ford's diorama.

Both she and Kiki were shocked and saddened to hear their high school friend had drowned. What should have been an exciting wilderness adventure had turned into a nightmare.

"It's such a tragedy," Reese said.

"If I can help you search for that diorama, let me know," Kiki said. "I want Bella's dad to get back the present Bella gave him. It obviously means a lot to him."

"I'll tell you if I think of anything," Reese said.

She drove the next few blocks to her house, steered the Bronco under the carport, grabbed her stuff and went inside. Yawning, she tossed her duffel bag and purse on the couch.

Mr. Bojangles, her black cat, wandered up to her and started his meowing pleas. She loved how he always greeted her, but she knew he had ulterior motives.

"Hey there chubs. I bet you want dinner, right?"

He looked up at her with steady green eyes.

"Nice, gooey wet cat food full of salmon and chicken?"

He meowed and wound his sleek, furry body around her legs again.

"You little mooch," she said with a chuckle. "You need a twelve-step program to get you weaned from wet food. You gobble down way more than the vet recommends."

He skittered along at her feet as she entered the kitchen, opened a can of wet stuff and spooned some into his dish. Mr. Bojangles was needy, but he kept her company and she appreciated having him around the house in case a mouse or two decided to take up residence. A proficient hunter, he kept them away.

He'd originally belonged to her grandfather, and when he passed, the cat went to stay with Mrs. MacGillicuddy, who lived next door. When Reese moved into her grandparents' house, she'd claimed him and he'd quickly become loyal to her. Mrs. Mac usually didn't mind watching Bo if Reese went out of town more than a few days.

She scratched behind Bo's ears, after which he arched up and meowed, telling her how much he enjoyed the attention. Her stomach growled, so she put together a bologna sandwich. Lowering into a chair at her small kitchen table, she chowed as she watched the counter TV. As usual, the world was in turmoil—whether it was from protests in the streets or from harsh political rhetoric.

Even worse, just south of here, beetle-kill deadfall and ancient trees in the rugged terrain of Medicine Bow National Forest had caught fire. Firefighters were having a dreadful time dousing the flames. The stories saddened Reese.

Changing channels, she landed on a vintage black and white movie. She watched until her eyes grew heavy. Though the kitchen was flooded with twilight, and her typical bed time was hours way, Reese decided to hit the sack. The so-called vacation she'd just taken had wiped her out.

She switched off the boob tube and headed into her bedroom. Stripping down to her underwear, she stretched across the covers and felt herself drifting into dreamland. A soft thud on the mattress meant Bo had joined her. She fell asleep to the soothing sound of purring.

Sometime in the wee hours, she dreamed of being surrounded by people while riding a raft that splashed down the river. When the watercraft hit rough rapids, it overturned and everyone fell out. As others flailed in the waves, Reese felt her foot catch on something and under she went, sucking brackish water into her lungs.

Then she saw Bella in the murky blue distance. Bella held up a hand as though waving. She seemed to be speaking, and Reese didn't understand how she could manage that since they were underwater.

"Help me, Reese!" she said. "I'm in trouble, and I don't know what to do."

Reese began swimming toward her, but Bella disappeared in an explosion of iridescent, foaming bubbles. Frightened, Reese thrashed around looking for her. She fought her way past schools of fish and searched behind rocks, tangled weeds and other floating shrubs.

Opening her mouth to call out, water rushed in and slid down her throat. She couldn't breathe. I'm drowning like Bella, she thought. Her life flashed before her eyes, and she considered all the things she still wanted to accomplish.

Desperation swept through her.

Awakening with a start, Reese sat upright, her skin prickling. She clutched her throat and coughed, still affected by the dream.

Poor Ford and his family. And poor Bella. Hopefully the search and rescue workers would find her body soon so they could have closure.

Coming to the conclusion that it would be impossible to get back to sleep, Reese got up, dressed in jogging gear and went for a run through the park. The sky lightened as sunrise, nestled in pinkish orange clouds, lifted over the eastern horizon. Unfortunately, a haze of smoke blanketed the air, clogging the atmosphere.

Ignoring the condition of the sky, Reese swept her gaze across the trees, shrubs and flowers, which were bursting with late summer exuberance. A quiet hush had descended, save only for a few twittering birds.

Warmth seeped into Reese's body, and she assumed it would be another sweltering day. Since it was late August, she hoped the heat wouldn't hold out much longer. In this part of the country, summer usually didn't linger.

Before long, autumn would arrive and encourage the trees to shower lawns with orange, yellow, and red leaves. Hopefully, moisture would soon pour from the heavens to douse the infernos rampaging through the southern mountains.

Energized from her run, Reese headed home. After a shower, coffee, and a couple pieces of bacon, which she nuked in the microwave, she put on a touch of makeup, dressed in jeans, a sky-blue summer top, and her old boots.

People might have questioned her choice in wearing the footwear she'd inherited from her grandfather, but she didn't care. Gramps hadn't stood much taller than Reese, and his feet had been about her size, so the old leather fit perfectly. The boots weren't in the best shape, but they were worn in and comfortable.

Above all, they held sentimental value.

It occurred to her that's probably how Ford felt about his snake diorama. He seemed desperate, just as she'd felt in that strange dream. When Bella had mentioned being in trouble, it had shredded her nerves. Conjuring an image of her high school friend, she recalled a tall girl with brown hair and large brown eyes. She'd been a student in one of Reese's math classes and also in her AP English class their senior year.

During high school, Bella had mostly kept to herself and Reese didn't recall her having many friends, but she was exceptionally bright. Like Reese, she'd attended college at the University of Wyoming, where she'd maintained her straight A's. She'd continued excelling in art and had won awards for her work. Just as she'd done in high school, she'd been a champion swimmer on the college swim team, which was ironic since she'd drowned.

Ford grieved her loss, and she couldn't blame him. In lieu of his daughter's actual presence, he longed to have her gift. No doubt he'd have preferred for his daughter to be alive, but at least the diorama represented her spirit.

"I need to get busy," she told herself. Scooting out the door, she walked toward the main part of Meadowlark Valley where the police station stood. Blue and white squad cars lined the parking lot in front of the white cinderblock two-story building.

Reese recalled that when she was a kid, the lower floor had held Red's Butcher Shop, and the upper floor held an apartment where Red lived with his wife and two kids. A decade or so ago, the building had been renovated to hold the offices of Meadowlark Valley's finest.

The roots of a cottonwood tree had broken the sidewalk out in front of the station. Reese's boots crunched on tiny chunks of crumbling cement as she strolled past two poles bearing a United States flag and a Wyoming flag. She opened the glass entrance door and walked inside the cool interior.

A waiting area with a black leather couch, a couple of mauve chairs, and an artificial Ficus tree sat to the right. To her left, beyond the half wall, several office workers sat at desks concentrating on computer screens. TV monitors hung on walls. Filing cabinets, printers, and bookshelves jam-packed the area. From above, fluorescent light fixtures illuminated the scene with harsh light.

A young man at the front reception area smiled at her. He had short, spiky hair like a Marine recruit, and wore a dark blue polo shirt emblazoned with the Meadowlark Valley Police Department logo. The engraved nameplate sitting on the edge of his desk said, Steve Daniels, Administrative Coordinator.

"May I help you, ma'am?" Steve asked.

"I'd like to speak with Detective Savage about a robbery," Reese said.

"Detective Savage?" Daniels gave her a blank look.

"Yes, Jeremy Savage," Reese said, remembering when he'd called to let her know he was moving to town. "He's been on the job about a month."

"That's right," Steve said, slapping his right palm against his forehead. "Sorry for the brain glitch."

He grabbed the phone receiver, then punched in a number on a black handset. After touching base with Jeremy, he met her gaze again.

"He'll be with you shortly. Take a seat if you'd like."

"Thanks." Reese plopped on the couch and pulled out her cell to catch up on Facebook posts, which consisted of pictures of babies, puppies, current events and Kiki's new ads plugging a sale on herbal hand lotion.

In the back of her mind, she considered Jeremy's move here, and what that meant. For him, it was definitely a plus since his promotion was a strategic career change. She hadn't decided what it meant for her.

The two of them got along well and she enjoyed his company. Together, they made a good crime-solving team. The jury was still out on whether their relationship would go any further. Bottom line, it would be worthwhile to have a law enforcement pal to give her the police viewpoint on cases of her own, as well as those the department hired her to help with.

As far as anything else went, only time would tell.

It wasn't long before Jeremy, wearing crisp dark jeans, a blue button-down shirt, and a tweed jacket with leather elbow patches entered the waiting area.

She stood, grinning, as she looked him up and down. "You look very detective-ey," she said.

"Is that good or bad?" he asked with a chuckle.

"I'm accustomed to seeing you in your Sage Police Department uniform. This is different."

Jeremy crossed his arms over his chest. "Steve here says you want to talk to me?"

"Yes." Reese slipped her phone into her purse. "Ford Presley, who owns a gas station named the Barking Squirrel Gas & Oil just outside of town, had a break-in last night."

His brows furrowed. "I heard about that from the officer he reported it to. No one was hurt, right?"

"Right, and only some snacks were stolen. But the culprits ripped off a snake diorama that has sentimental meaning. Ford hired me to try and find it."

"Good move on his part," Jeremy said. "We've got a lot on our plates here, and you'll have more time to look for it."

"I went to high school with Ford's daughter, Bella Presley, so this is kind of personal to me."

"You mean Bella Northwood? The lady who drowned in the Trout River?"

Reese nodded. "Yes, Northwood is her married name. I can't believe her body hasn't been found."

"River rafting's a dangerous sport. People go missing all the time, unfortunately."

"I'm just sick about it," Reese said.

"Come on back to my desk and we can discuss this more." Jeremy motioned for Reese to follow him down a hallway.

"How's your new place, by the way?" Reese asked.

"It's nice. Thanks for recommending Birch Gate Apartments," Jeremy said.

"My friend, Lance Bonneville, is the manager," Reese said. "He lives on site, so he's easy to work with if you have a problem."

"In this heat, I'm really enjoying the pool. The club house will come in handy if I decide to have buddies over for some beers."

"Peachy." Reese envisioned Jeremy and a few other guys hunkered over a table, smoking cigars as they stacked poker chips, their throaty laughter radiating throughout the room. She recalled seeing a picture of dogs playing poker, and squelched a snigger.

Jeremy glanced over at Reese. "How'd you hear about the complex?"

"Huh?" Reese asked, her mind having wandered. Quickly, she reined in her thoughts. "Oh, right, I lived there for a couple of months while a contractor made renovations on my house."

"You must have had a lot done."

"Believe me, my grandparents' place needed plenty of upgrades. I ordered new flooring, new carpet, new cupboards, granite counters and some other things. It also needed repainting inside and out."

"Did the repairs come out good?"

"Yep, and they were worth every penny."

Jeremy opened a door for her and stood so she could enter a room that held a sea of desks. A few uniformed officers leaned over stacks of papers, studied their computer screens or talked on the phone. Other desks sat empty, as no doubt, the owners were out on patrol.

Jeremy stepped around a wall of room dividers and sat down in a chair behind another desk, this one larger than those arranged in the outer area. His black engraved name plate sat on the wooden surface, covered by a snowstorm of papers. A Wyoming Game & Fish Department calendar had been tacked to a wall, with his framed bachelor's degree diploma located beside it.

"Have a seat," Jeremy said, pointing to another chair wedged across from him.

Reese sat down as Jeremy fiddled with his computer keyboard, adjusted his screen, then looked at her.

"I'm sorry to hear about Mr. Presley's break-in," Jeremy said. "Darned kids trawling around getting into trouble and wreaking havoc during the summer. It's difficult to keep track of 'em and from the sounds of it, they've struck again."

"I know," Reese said. "Ford's gas station is about 10 miles out of town. Probably it's the sheriff department's jurisdiction, now that I think about it."

"That's fine, we work together with them on different cases," Jeremy explained. "Neither our police department nor the sheriff's office are territorial, and I hope we can keep it that way."

"That's good," Reese said.

"Tell me again what was stolen," Jeremy said. "I'm asking in case we get more break-ins around here that are of a similar nature. Might help us catch the culprit."

"Some junk food, cheap jewelry and a bejeweled rattlesnake diorama." The words rolling off of Reese's tongue seemed ludicrous in her own ears. Hopefully Jeremy wouldn't laugh, but she could not blame him if he did.

Jeremy, ever the professional, didn't even crack a grin as he jotted down the details. It's possible he'd heard crazier things in his time with the police department in Sage and wherever else he'd worked. If so, Reese would have loved to hear them.

"I'm making a note of this in our database of robbery investigations," Jeremy said, leaning forward to scroll through his large screen. "It might come in handy."

"I figure the kids were looking for easy money," Reese said.

"Yeah, I have to agree with you on that," Jeremy said. "With all the bling you say is pasted on the diorama, they probably thought they'd found buried treasure."

"No doubt," Reese agreed.

"We'll do what we can," Jeremy commented. "But since you're working on this, you'll probably find it before we get a chance to even begin looking."

"Hopefully," Reese said. "I thought you might have some ideas about where I could start my search."

Jeremy leaned back in his chair, then stretched out his long legs that ended with two nicely-polished black cowboy boots. "I'd start by hitting all the local pawn shops."

"Good idea," Reese said, then a funny feeling gripped her midsection.

She could have easily come up with the pawn shop idea herself. Nevertheless, the excuse to touch base with Jeremy was a good one, she decided. That way, he'd become accustomed to weighing in on her cases if she needed his assistance.

"If I was an ornery teenager looking for a quick buck, that's where I'd take my stolen goods," Jeremy added.

"Exactly," Reese said. "High school kids get bored and antsy in the summer when school's out."

"That, they do," Jeremy agreed. "Hopefully they didn't cart the diorama too far away. My bet is that they didn't."

"Probably not." Reese smoothed strands of dark hair away from her face. Her cheeks burned as she realized she'd taken Jeremy away from his work for her own selfish reasons. "I'll check out Rose's Antique Shop and the Goodwill, too."

"Have a look at Wilson Pawn down on Silver Avenue and Black Jack's Pawn on Main Street."

"Look at you," Reese exclaimed. "You haven't lived here long and already you're familiar with the lay of the land."

"I'm trying to get up to speed real fast on the area."

Reese lifted her brows.

"It's my goal to get familiar with the city and the surrounding area."

"I can tell you're going to be a real asset for the MVPD." Reese withdrew the notebook in her purse and wrote down the names of the pawn shops.

"If those don't pan out, there's always Medicine Bow Pawn off of Highway 287," Jeremy added.

"Hopefully, I'll hit paydirt."

"No stone unturned, right?"

"Right," Reese said.

"You can't have too many people in the community with the goal of maintaining law and order, as long as they don't become vigilantes," Jeremy said. "But I do have a couple of requests."

"What?" Reese asked.

"No. 1, stay out of trouble. Since we're understaffed here, and one of our detectives just up and left us with no warning, our resources are stretched as thin as a rubber band. I don't want to have to deploy the cavalry to scrape you out of a back alley."

"Got it," Reese said.

"No. 2, let us handle police matters and don't take unnecessary risks. Since you were a detective with the DPD, I know you're confident and capable. I also know you don't carry a gun. If you need help, call me."

"I'll mind my P's and Q's," Reese promised.

"And No. 3, since you're helping Ford Presley find his snake thingy, see if you can find a good time to ask him and the family questions about Bella's accident."

Reese leaned forward, propped her elbows on Jeremy's desk and cupped her chin in her hands. "What's going on?"

"When I heard the radio call about the accident, I drove right down to the river to get a handle on the situation. Things were topsy-turvy, so getting questions answered was difficult at best." Jeremy put his hands together, twiddled his thumbs, then continued. "From what I understand, she was with her church group. When she fell overboard, the river guide and a few other folks dove in the water to try and help her, but she floated out of their reach."

"Hmm, I could understand that happening if she'd hit her head or had been injured in some way," Reese commented.

"Witnesses said no, that she didn't appear to be hurt," Jeremy said. "I understand from the church group members I questioned that she was a good swimmer. It bugs me why she didn't try to get back in the raft."

"That's a good point," Reese said. "It is puzzling."

"I've investigated a few river drownings in my time, but this one seems suspicious."

"What do you think happened?"

Jeremy shook his head. "I can't exactly put my finger on it. It's just a—"

"Gut feeling," Reese finished for him.

"Yep."

"Instinct is a great tool to rely on," Reese said. "I'll do some digging, try to find out more."

"By the way, it's good to see you again," Jeremy said.

"You, too."

"Now that we've had a chance to talk, I've got a proposal to make."

Uh, oh, Reese thought. Her hands trembled slightly as she asked, "What kind?"

"I talked to Chief Barnes about keeping you on retainer," Jeremy said. "Instead of only paying you to help with random cases, we'd like to have you work with us on a regular basis. The department will benefit from having your expertise, since you're a former cop."

"What did he say?"

"He thinks it's well worth it. First up, we want you to investigate Bella's drowning and write the accident report."

"That will free your detectives and officers to work on more pressing problems," Reese said.

Jeremy nodded. "Exactly. Just keep track of your time so you can give us an accounting after each case."

They studied each other momentarily, then Reese stood. She felt wobbly, like a colt trying out its legs for the first time. Jeremy had just offered a fantastic opportunity.

"It's a deal," Reese said.

When Jeremy also rose, they shook hands. Her skin tingled as it pressed against his calloused fingers.

"How do you want me to follow up on Bella?" she asked.

"Question her family and friends, and check into whatever else you think might help. I'd also like you to visit with the rafting company owner."

"Got it," Reese said.

Turning around, she left Jeremy's office and cleared out of the building. She headed to her truck, pleased that so far, her PI business was doing well. At first, she'd been hesitant about hanging up a shingle in a town the size of Meadowlark Valley, which hovered around 40,000 residents. It seemed that she'd been worried for no reason.

Waves of heat hammered down on the street, shimmering with blinding white intensity. She felt as though she might melt into a puddle of goo right here on the sidewalk. The only thing marring the summer day was the wildfire haze that blotted out the blue sky.

Climbing into her truck, she determined that since she couldn't bring back Bella, and she couldn't put out the fires, she would do her damnedest to find Ford's snake diorama.

Chapter Five

Before taking off, Reese rolled down her window for air, then called the pawn shops, the antique store, and the Goodwill. She described the rattlesnake diorama to owners and managers, hoping they might recall acquiring it. None of them could verify for certain whether they had, and of course, they encouraged her to come in and have a look for herself.

Thus, Reese's day was filled with driving to several different secondhand joints, trying to track down the missing snake display. She spent hours pawing through stacks of junk.

The landmine of items she sifted through amazed her. She found cake decorating and candy making supplies for dirt cheap, and had she been so inclined, she could have set up shop making confections.

If she enjoyed fishing, camping, canoeing and hunting, she could have purchased everything she needed to enjoy the great outdoors. Power tools, along with hammers, hacksaws, wrenches, and screwdrivers were in plenty of supply. Had she wanted to learn carpentry, she could have purchased a full complement of building aids to help her repair her home or even perhaps construct a new one.

Having come up empty handed despite her search; she trekked along to yet another potential place where she might find Ford's diorama. Stopping along Highway 287, she parked in front of the Medicine Bow Pawn Shop. The day was waning and the sun hung low in the salmon-colored sky, courtesy of the toxic wildfire atmosphere.

Determined to keep looking for Ford's diorama, she walked

toward the shop. If nothing here matched his description, she felt duty-bound to scout out more pawn shops tomorrow. Even though she found the idea unpleasant, she intended to explore in a wider circle and check some of the surrounding communities.

She climbed wooden steps in front of the quaint old brick structure, opened the door, which set off a tinkling bell, and walked inside. No one stood in the register area, so she set to work scouring the shelves—a huge task since they brimmed with vintage stock.

Several items caught her eye, unfortunately, not what she was looking for. She found a shelf full of colorful 1930s-style ladies' hats. A filing cabinet held sewing patterns for infants, men, and women's clothing from several historical decades.

Examining old garments on a spinning rack, she couldn't resist picking out a black silk 1950s halter-style cocktail dress featuring a full skirt. Not that she had anywhere to wear it, but a girl just didn't know when she might be invited somewhere fancy, and this dress would be splendid.

She also selected an oversize flannel shirt from the 1970s that would look awesome with a white T-shirt and boyfriend-style, high-waisted jeans, which for some crazy reason, were making a fashion comeback.

A young girl had appeared behind the counter, so Reese took her items to the register. As the girl tallied up Reese's choices, she realized she'd wasted an entire afternoon looking for Ford's diorama, with nothing to show for it but clothes she didn't honestly have room for in her closet.

She wanted them because, after all they were fun. Did she need them? No—not any more than she needed a hole in her head.

Stewing about her impulse purchases, she paid her bill.

"Neat stuff here, huh?" The clerk, probably in her late teens, popped her gum.

She wore a button-down print dress, and long, curly red hair flowed over her shoulders. A magnetic name tag announced her name as, "Dana."

"You have a diverse selection," Reese agreed as she watched

Dana slide her purchases into a bag. "Lots of attention went into curating the items on your shelves. Did you set them up?"

"Yes, I did," she said, her smile wide.

"I enjoyed my search."

"Did you find what you were looking for?"

Dana gazed steadily at Reese with her bright, cornflower blue eyes, and Reese guessed her to be around 16 or 17.

"No."

"That's too bad," Dana said.

"I'm not surprised, really," Reese said. "I called ahead to talk to the store owner to see if he had anything like what I'm after, and he said he didn't. I still wanted to check for myself, just to be sure."

"Maybe I can help," Dana said.

"I doubt it," Reese said. "I looked all over for this particular item. Didn't see anything resembling it."

Dana frowned. "You probably talked to my dad, Scott Evans, when you called, right?"

"Yes, that sounds like it," Reese said. She wasn't entirely certain. All the names of the people she'd spoken to today had become a blur in her mind.

"He and my mom are going through a divorce. My mom ran off with this construction worker a couple of weeks ago..." Dana rolled her eyes. "I'm sure you don't want to hear all the gory details. Anyway, my dad's a mess. He's like the walking dead right now, and I don't blame him. Mom's being a real witch. The thing is, Dad probably didn't think to check his back room. That's where he cleans things up and makes repairs. He hasn't looked around in there for days."

Dana came out from behind the counter and motioned for Reese to follow her. "Come on. Let's go see."

"I appreciate it, Dana."

"No biggie. Dad says he's leaving this place to me as my inheritance, and I hate when he talks about that. Anyway, I figure I need to learn how to run the business. I don't want to miss a potential sale."

"You must be a big help to him," Reese said.

"I like to think I am." Dana opened a door and flipped a switch on the wall. They entered the back room, now illuminated by a couple of flickering fluorescent lights. "What exactly are you looking for?"

Reese described the diorama. While speaking, she glanced at the shelves along the walls, which held rusted farm implements, clocks, musical instruments, carved tables, and probably a million and one other items. Basically, Reese decided, anything your heart desired.

"Wow, that really is unique," Dana said. "Then again, we've run across some other odd items over the years. When you're in this business, nothing surprises you. Except the taxidermy items, like the piece you're looking for, always give me the creeps. It doesn't seem right to stuff animals and pose them like they're alive. It's cruel, if you ask me. And creepy."

"I'm not a big fan, either," Reese said. "I'm trying to find it for a friend."

"They'd really appreciate something like that? Honestly, that's weird."

A sharp one, this girl. Again, Reese didn't want to delve into the matter, so she said, "He likes unusual pieces."

"You're a good person to go to all this trouble."

"Hmm," Reese said noncommittally.

Dana walked over to a dark corner, and Reese followed, her nostrils twitching from the musty odor. A pronghorn antelope head hung on the wall next to a moose head. Several sets of bent and twisted antlers perched next to an assortment of bleached buffalo skulls.

Clustered on a large board were stuffed rabbits, a badger, an owl, and some rainbow trout. Red, yellow and blue butterflies contained in jars covered one spot. Next to them, a sleek red fox with a white-tipped tail and black legs held a stealthy pose on a huge rock, all supported on a wooden base.

Chunks of petrified wood intermingled with other oddities, for example, a stuffed chicken wearing a blue doll dress, a mummified bat viewed through a window in a small box, and a stuffed squirrel standing on a branch, dressed in an orange hunter's vest and holding a shotgun.

Reese ran her gaze over the lot, looking for her prize. There were so many offerings, she found it difficult to focus long on any one thing. Then a flash of bling caught her eye from beneath a colorful, southwest style blanket.

Moving aside the fringed turquoise, red and gold material, she got a better look. Rattlesnakes, posed just as Ford described, slithered across a desert-themed base. The rhinestones embedded in their eyes and on their tails sparkled brilliantly.

Her heart picked up its pace, and she ran her fingers along the base to try and locate a brass plate like the one Ford had mentioned. When she found it, she tilted the piece in order to make out the writing.

Bingo.

"Diamondback Revenge," she read aloud. It felt like she'd hit a jackpot in Las Vegas.

"That's what you were looking for?" Dana asked, her voice laced with excitement.

"Yep," she responded.

Dana laughed. "I told you we might have what you were looking for."

"Do you recall who brought it in?"

"Some teenagers dropped it off this morning. I thought it was hideous, but my dad told me he believed it might sell. The boys said their grandpa had moved into an assisted living home, and they were helping their parents clean out his basement."

"I see," Reese said, realizing it was just as she'd suspected. School ought to be in session year-round, like in Japan and Australia, to keep certain kids from looting and terrorizing their communities over the summer break.

"I think it's butt ugly, but if that's what you want, it's yours." Dana made a face as she studied the diorama. "My dad hasn't priced anything in this back room yet, but I'd sell it to you for, let's say, fifty bucks."

Although it had been stolen in the first place, Reese knew she shouldn't have to pay a dime. However, Dana's dad hadn't known the merchandise was hot. It wasn't worth getting technical at this point.

"You've got a deal," Reese said.

Chapter Six

Reese forked over the money to Dana, then hauled the diorama and her other purchases out to her truck and popped them into the back. She fished her cell phone from her purse and called Jeremy.

"Detective Savage," he answered.

"Hi Jeremy," Reese said. "I found Ford Presley's snake diorama."

"Where was it?"

"At the Medicine Bow Pawn Shop," Reese said. "Some teenage boys brought it in. I'm glad you suggested I check there."

"Yeah, well, I figured that might be a good spot."

"I'll type up the details for your incident report and shoot it over to you."

"Great." Jeremy called out to someone, then came back on the line. "I've got to go."

"Sure, I'll talk to you later," Reese said.

Next, Reese called Ford to let him know the good news, but he didn't answer. After leaving a message, she drove toward his place to deliver Diamondback Revenge to its rightful owner.

Miles flew past as her Bronco trekked down the two-lane highway, the air conditioning once again on full blast. The route was mostly deserted, except for the occasional vehicle whizzing by.

Today's temperature still soared, even though it was late afternoon. Smoke from surrounding wildfires created a dusty brown haze across the rolling landscape. Reese sniffed, noting the Bronco's interior even smelled like a campfire.

It wouldn't do to have the entire state of Wyoming go up in flames, although Reese realized the wildfire raged in only one forested area. Hopefully it wouldn't spread farther before firefighters or Mother Nature extinguished it.

When she came upon Ford's crumbling store building, she pulled into the parking lot and stopped. A couple of tumbleweeds blew across the dirt and gravel expanse, reminding her of a lonely outpost in the Old West.

She grabbed the snake diorama and got out of the truck, then walked inside the store. The lights were on, but nobody was home, so it seemed.

Last time she'd stopped by there were no other customers. The Barking Squirrel was definitely not a hopping business and she doubted Ford made a large income from his retirement venture.

"Is anybody here?" she called out as she placed the diorama on the counter.

No answer.

Overhead fixtures brightened the room, showering the shelves of rattlesnake oddities with a bright glare. Reese didn't spot Ford at his typical spot behind the cash register. That didn't mean anything in the grand scheme of things, but for some reason, she sensed something amiss.

The back of her neck prickled.

Reese clutched her keys between her fingers, just in case she needed to use them as a weapon. She feared someone might be skulking around, up to no good. Maybe those teenagers had come back to steal more stuff.

"Ford? Where are you?"

Slipping behind the counter, she walked through a door into a back room. She hated to snoop, but she doubted Ford would have left things open and unattended on purpose.

A knotty pine wall featured two rows of big game antlers. Beneath them, a dozen or more vintage license plates from all over the country displayed colorful designs. Boxes and barrels indicated this must be the stock room.

Several containers had been ripped open and contents spilled across the floor. Cans of barbecued rattlesnake bites, rattlesnake jewelry and other kitschy snaked-themed items lay abandoned like pirate booty.

Reese frowned. It looked like Ford had been frantically searching for something. Or had there been another break-in?

"Hey, Ford," she called out, concerned when there was no answer. "Are you all right, buddy? It's Reese. I found Diamondback Revenge."

She pulled aside a black curtain and stepped into another room. Humble living quarters filled the space, which boasted large movie posters along the walls. The films were mostly from the 40s and the 50s—black and white movies Reese's grandmother had enjoyed watching during the afternoon.

A couch, a recliner and a TV filled one corner. A kitchen area with an old metal table and chairs rested beside a short counter with a few upper and lower cupboards. A two-burner stove and a small refrigerator nestled next to it. A narrow single bed, a chest and a nightstand sat beneath a window covered with tattered brown curtains.

The place reeked of grease, dirt and cigarette smoke.

"Help…"

Recognizing Ford's voice, Reese moved further into the room where she found him curled up in a fetal position, his face bloody and twisted. It appeared that he'd been badly beaten.

Quickly, she knelt down and placed a hand on his shoulder. "Ford?"

"Oh-h-h," he moaned.

Reese whipped out her cell phone and dialed 911, then put it on speaker. She explained the emergency to the operator as she hustled over to grab a towel. She used it to gently dab Ford's wounds.

"Stay with me," she told him. "Help's on the way."

"Is the victim conscious?" the operator asked.

"Yes," Reese told her.

"Try to keep him that way," she prompted

"Who did this to you?" Reese asked Ford, alarmed that his breathing came in shallow gasps.

"H-he knows…" Ford's eyelids fluttered, and he passed out.

Reese leaned over to check his breathing, thankful she still felt it puffing from his bruised mouth. However, it bothered her that he'd lost consciousness. That wasn't a good sign.

It seemed like forever before she heard sirens wailing in the distance. They became louder until it seemed they were right outside. Someone entered the store and called out "Emergency Services!"

"Come through the open door behind the counter," Reese yelled back.

Several individuals entered the room. Once an EMT in a black uniform began working on Ford, Reese stood back, relieved to let him handle the situation. Her heart hammered with apprehension for Ford, and she wrung her hands, wishing she could do more.

She finally noticed the police officer standing nearby speaking into a radio strapped on her shoulder.

"I'm Officer Berry," she said to Reese a few seconds later. "I understand a Mr. Ford Presley owns this place. What happened to him?"

"I found him this way when I stopped by," Reese told her.

"How long ago?" Officer Berry asked.

Reese glanced at her watch. "Maybe twenty minutes or so. I can't say for sure, but as soon as I found him collapsed back here, I called 911."

She explained more about how she knew Ford, which wasn't a lot, since she'd only recently met him.

When the EMTs got Ford stabilized, four of them lifted him onto a stretcher. Reese followed them, stopping in the front of the store when they took him out of the building and loaded him into an ambulance.

Officer Berry, who'd eased up beside her, asked, "Do you have any idea of who might have hurt him?"

"There was a break-in here the other night," Reese said. "We figured a bunch of bored teens had done it, and that seems to be the case. Maybe one of them came back."

"Did he report it to the police?"

"Yes," Reese said.

"What was stolen?"

"Some snacks and cheap jewelry," Reese said. "And a snake diorama, which was a gift from his daughter. He'd hired me to find it, and that's what I came to return today."

"Why you?"

"I'm a private investigator," Reese explained.

"I see," Officer Berry said. "Where is this snake diorama now? I'd like to take a look at it."

"Over on the counter," Reese said, pointing toward the bejeweled snakes.

The sound of a vehicle engine rumbled out front and a large 4X4 truck pulled up to the curb. A few seconds later, a tall, elderly woman in dark blue scrubs got out and hurried toward the store. As she entered, Reese noted her neat, graying hair was secured in a bun, but her expression was agitated.

A tall man wearing a striped, long-sleeved shirt and jeans entered the store behind her. Probably in his mid- to late twenties, he sported a large gold belt buckle that displayed a bull, a rider and the letters PBR.

When he removed his Stetson and ran his hand through his brown wavy hair, Reese realized he must be Ford's son, Ian. He bore a nearly identical appearance to his father, only a younger version.

"What's happened?" The woman, obviously Naomi, continued speaking. "When I got the call that my husband had been hurt, I came as soon as I could."

"I'm Officer Berry and this is Reese Golden, who found your husband," she said, then nodded at Reese. "Ms. Golden called 911 and an ambulance is taking him to the hospital as we speak."

Ian draped an arm around his mother's quivering shoulders.

"What's going on? Is he, oh my Lord!" Naomi's expression clouded over.

"He's in good hands," Officer Berry added. "But someone assaulted him."

Naomi began to sob. "Oh my God!"

"Let's go be with him," Ian said, steering Naomi toward the door.

"I should have driven out and checked on your father when he didn't come home last night," Naomi insisted, then met Officer Berry's gaze. "My husband is a stubborn man and we've been having an ongoing argument about him keeping this place. Yesterday we'd fought about it again, so when he didn't show up for dinner, I figured he was avoiding me and had decided to spend the night here. He's also upset about our daughter, Bella, who recently drowned…"

Naomi cried pitifully.

"Mom, you couldn't have known he'd been hurt," Ian said. "Let's head to the hospital now."

"I m-might as well have stayed there," Naomi said.

"You're a nurse?" Officer Berry asked as she studied Naomi's scrubs.

"Yes."

"You'll know how to help your husband as he recovers," Officer Berry said.

"Like your son said, none of this is your fault, Naomi," Reese said.

"I can't help but feel guilty." Naomi dashed away a tear.

"How did you find my dad?" Ian asked, meeting Reese's gaze.

"I'd come out here to drop off his missing snake diorama," Reese said.

"That old thing?" Ian asked. "The one stolen during the break in?"

"Yes," Reese said. "He was desperate to get it back. I'm a private investigator and he hired me to find it."

"Where did you find it?" Ian asked.

"In the back room of a pawn shop," Reese said.

"That was a stroke of luck," Ian said. "I think it's creepy, but Dad will be happy you found it."

"I realize this might not be the best time to ask, but were you with your sister when she went on that rafting trip?" Reese asked him.

He nodded. "That was a hell of a day."

"I'm sorry to bring it up, but we're all trying to make sense of this," Reese said in an apologetic tone.

"We?" Ian asked.

"I'm working with the police."

Ian nodded. "I was riding in a different raft, but I saw it all go down."

"I understand she wasn't able to make it back to her watercraft," Reese said.

"From where I was, it didn't seem like she tried to save herself. Which isn't like Bella at all, considering she's a strong swimmer."

"I can hardly stand this," Naomi said. "I'm starting to feel like this family is cursed."

"That's nonsense, Mom. We've just had a run of bad luck." Ian kissed his mom's cheek, then looked up.

"Do you mind if I call you later?" Reese asked. "I'd like to talk to you some more about that day. I'd also like to check on how your dad's doing."

"That's fine," Ian said.

Ian gave Reese his number, which she typed into her cell phone.

"We'd better get going, Ian," Naomi said, her voice stronger and seemingly filled with purpose. "Your dad's going to need me."

"You won't be alone, Mom," Ian said. "He'll need us both. I don't have any rodeo events scheduled in the near future, so I'll be right beside you."

Naomi glanced up at her son and sighed. "How many times have we told your father that he needs to sell this godforsaken place?"

"Too many times, Mom." Ian met Officer Berry's gaze. "Do you know who attacked my dad?"

"Not yet," she said. "Detective Savage and our crime scene workers are on their way. We'll get to work on the case ASAP."

"Good," Ian said. "I want to know what SOB did this so I can go and deck him."

"Leave it to the courts to hand out justice," Officer Berry advised him. "Do you know if anyone would want to hurt your dad? Maybe someone he recently had an argument with?"

"Everyone gets along with my dad," Ian said. "He's a great guy. That's why it's weird someone attacked him."

Chapter Seven

"You don't need to hang around," Officer Berry told Reese. "I'll tell Detective Savage what you told me."

"I'll stay, if you don't mind," Reese said, remembering Ford's comment to her before he passed out. "I'd like to have a word with Detective Savage."

"Be my guest," Officer Berry said. "Don't touch anything in that back room, though."

"Of course not," Reese agreed.

Reese paced the floors, all the while wondering who had attacked Ford and why. Remembering that Jeremy had tasked her to write up Bella's accident report, she used her cell phone to see if she or Ian were on social media sites.

Both had Facebook and Twitter accounts, which she scoured through, looking for any indication of trouble, hurt feelings or grudges on the part of anyone they knew. Nothing seemed alarming—Bella's friends discussed various styles of painting and their preferred mediums. Her church friends weighed in now and then and gave updates on current events. Ian's buddies traded jokes about bull riding and shared success tips.

Reese checked to see if Naomi or Ford were active on any sites, but she didn't find anything. She even checked to see if Hunter Northwood had accounts, which he did. He communicated mostly with clients and promoted sales for his sign shop, Ad Pro.

Nothing there of any real interest, she thought. No smoking guns indicating anyone who had beefs with the family and no indications anyone would want to take out their frustrations on Ford.

Reese brewed a pot of coffee and poured a cup of the dark, steaming liquid, which she handed to Officer Berry.

Officer Berry sipped. "Just what I needed. Thanks."

"I thought it might help," Reese said.

"We cops do like our coffee. Most of us anyway."

A short time later, Jeremy and the crime scene investigators arrived, and the workers slipped into white protective suits. A couple of them cordoned off the area outside the building with yellow crime scene tape, then the team assembled in the back room where Ford had been assaulted. Wearing gloves, technicians walked around swabbing blood drops, dusting for fingerprints, taking notes, photographing items and sketching scenes.

Reese stood back, watching and remembering. The process of evidence collecting always fascinated her. It took solid skills to gather items that could be important to a case. CSI workers had to be careful not to miss anything that might be important or inadvertently contaminate pieces, which they would ship off to the Wyoming State Crime Laboratory to conduct forensics testing.

Unlike TV shows, perpetrators were rarely brought to justice in a swift manner. Linking an individual to a crime scene often entailed a lengthy wait.

Jeremy eventually walked over to Reese; his eyes crinkled at the edges. She could tell he had a lot on his mind.

"How's it going?" she asked him.

"Like always. There's plenty of evidence to process, and never enough time and manpower to do it as thoroughly as I'd like."

"All you can do is your best," Reese said, remembering back to her days on the DPD. "By the way, Ford's snake diorama is over on the counter."

Jeremy glanced at it. "You said teens took it?"

"Yep."

"That's another case off the books."

"You're welcome."

Jeremy chuckled and said, "Thanks."

Reese grinned.

"Officer Berry mentioned she already questioned you about finding Mr. Presley in his back room. Did you have something else to tell me?"

"Ford mumbled a few words after I found him."

Jeremy pulled out his notebook and a pen. "What?"

"He managed to say, 'He knows.'"

"Could be he referred to his attacker," Jeremy said as he jotted down the information.

"Made no sense to me," Reese said. "Did you notice all the ransacked items in the stock room? It's almost as if the intruder was looking for something."

"Yes, we noticed that," Jeremy said.

"Judging by the boxes that were torn apart, the item must be small," Reese suggested.

"Could be."

"I bet the intruder thought Ford knew where it was located, but the old guy refused to talk. So, the intruder beat him up, hoping he'd eventually crack." Reese tapped her chin, thinking.

"Something's going on behind the scenes that we'll have to figure out."

"I think you're right," Reese speculated. "I'll be talking more with Ford's son, Ian. He and his mother, Naomi, stopped by here before heading off to the hospital."

"Officer Berry mentioned that." Jeremy lifted his dark brows. "What did you think about them?"

"Naomi was upset, and rightfully so. Ian said everyone likes his dad and he doesn't know of any enemies. I asked about the day of Bella's rafting accident and Ian said he also found it strange she didn't try to swim back to the raft."

Jeremy stroked his chin. "I'm glad you're helping us—I know how thorough you are."

"No problem," Reese said. "You know I like things resolved."

"That's a fact."

"There's something else I've been mulling over," Reese said. "Naomi mentioned that with the recent incidents, she fears her family is cursed."

"People get fatalistic when trouble brews for their loved ones," Jeremy said.

"Right, I've encountered that too," Reese said. "An idea occurred to me after she said that."

"What's on your mind?"

"I'm wondering if Bella's drowning accident and Ford's assault are somehow connected."

"You have great instincts, Reese," Jeremy said. "That seems to be a real stretch, though."

"I don't know, but it's bugging me," Reese said.

"I'll follow up with the pawn shop to find out the names of the teenage boys who sold Ford's diorama to them," Jeremy said. "Could be they came back here to find more goods to rip off and Ford caught them."

"And they attacked him," Reese said with a nod.

"I'll see if they have an alibi for where they were today. Meanwhile, follow up on any other leads you might uncover."

"Sure," Reese agreed.

"Stick to my rules, though," he warned. "Don't try to be a hero."

"You know me," she said.

"Which is why I'm reminding you to stand down if things get too hot."

"Cross my heart," she promised.

Mainly, Jeremy didn't want her to get into trouble. Reese could take care of herself, even without a weapon. She was determined to find out who had assaulted Ford. Also, if there was something fishy about Bella's drowning, she wanted to get to the bottom of it.

Chapter Eight

As Reese drove home, ideas rattled around in her mind about Bella's death. No doubt the rescue team's helicopters, thermal drones, dogs, and boat teams had done a thorough search for her body. Strong instinct told Reese her friend's remains were probably caught in some obscure place in the river. Trapped underwater, her corpse may never be found.

She shivered.

Recovering bodies in waterways posed numerous difficulties for authorities. Half drowning and struggling victims were typically swept miles from the exact spot where they fell in. Arms and legs often became entangled in fallen trees, bridge pilings, or underwater rocks and other hazards. Too often, deadly outcomes were reported, and, as Jeremy had pointed out, people often disappeared and were never found.

The tragic circumstances haunted their friends and families for the rest of their lives.

It was such a damn shame. While she'd been acquainted with Bella in high school, they'd never been close. Nevertheless, they had been fellow Spartans, and she felt a certain sense of loyalty to the Meadowlark Valley High valedictorian.

With a flash of memory, Reese recalled promising to attend Kiki's meditation class this afternoon. "I almost forgot again!"

Kiki had been asking her for months, although in a friendly way, for her to try one. She believed the session would help Reese relax, since apparently, according to Kiki, she exuded tense vibes. Also, Kiki insisted Reese's aura projected black and gray. Whatever that meant. Nevertheless, she supposed those colors weren't good.

Glancing at her speedometer, she realized she was poking along, so she stepped on the gas. White bits of ash drifted across her windshield, and a campfire scent permeated the Bronco's interior. She frowned, uneasy about the devastation in Medicine Bow National Forest.

So far, except for a pall of muddy gray smoke spreading across the sky like a giant mushroom, this section of Wyoming remained unaffected. Shadowy deep green colored the prairie and a purple mountain range was silhouetted against the horizon.

She thought about the brave firefighters, along with people who lived in the threatened communities. Reports stated the wildfire had torched nearly 20,000 acres so far, and many towns had been evacuated. The dry, windy conditions weren't helping.

"Please, send us a downpour," Reese pleaded with the forces of nature.

Movement caught the corner of her eye. She slammed on her brakes, stopping in time to watch a pronghorn antelope sail past her front fender. Heart hammering, she shifted the Bronco into park.

It hadn't been that long ago that Betty had been in the mechanic's shop after taking a tumble down a mountain slope. She didn't want the old, restored vehicle to suffer any more trauma.

A herd of six, white-butted critters meandered across the road as though they hadn't a care in the world. They hoofed it down into the ravine and began munching on thick prairie grass, raising their heads now and then to glance around.

"Feeding time," Reese murmured, thinking that when she lived and worked in the big city, she never had to worry about wildlife. Now, it was a part of her world again. Deer and pronghorn preferred to do most of their grazing during the early morning and early evening—she needed to remember that.

When she deemed it safe to resume her journey, Reese shifted back into drive, rolled past the pronghorn and headed toward Meadowlark Valley. By the time she entered the city, replica Victorian gas lamps lining main street twinkled in the early evening shade.

Not much was happening, although a canoodling couple sat on a bench outside of the old brick Empress Hotel. A boy in a ballcap rode a bicycle on the sidewalk, with a shaggy dog trotting alongside. Most of the businesses were dark, but the Western Moon Café's sign still blared with neon intensity.

Reese's stomach growled; she could sure use one of their juicy hamburgers about right now, and she was sorely tempted to stop and indulge. She glanced at her watch. Nope, she didn't have time. Kiki's meditation class started in 10 minutes, and she couldn't disappoint her friend.

"I'll throw together something when I get home," she muttered to herself as she drove to the end of the block and parked in front of Kiki's shop.

Painted mint green with white, gingerbread trim, the Gothic-style cottage had housed a prominent railroad executive and his family in the late 1800s. Kiki had purchased the property and restored it. The downstairs contained her shop and her meditation studio, while the upstairs housed her small living quarters.

Grabbing her oversize handbag that held her exercise outfit, Reese jumped out of the truck, locked the driver's door and headed up the steps. She brushed past pots bursting with white petunia blossoms and lush hanging ferns. Amazing, Reese thought. Kiki could resurrect the deadest of plants, so it seemed, and she could work miracles on flowers and shrubs.

Reese's brown thumb regularly produced dead foliage and weeds. She felt certain plants withered the second they entered her home, regardless of whether she'd even touched them.

As she entered the shop, a soft glow illuminated the room. Shelves and displays overflowed with crystals, candles, herbs, windchimes and other assorted metaphysical paraphernalia.

Soft music featuring flutes, harps, chimes, and tweeting birds drifted through the shop. A pleasant scent of patchouli and other spices wafted into Reese's nostrils. She breathed deeply, already feeling relaxed. Even though she would rather have gone home after a day spent chasing down Ford's stolen diorama, and then finding him assaulted in his gas station, she had to admit Kiki knew how to set the mood.

"It's about time you got here, lady," Kiki said as she hurried toward Reese. Barefoot, she wore black yoga pants and a slouchy white top that slanted down one shoulder. "I thought you'd stood me up again."

"No way," Reese responded. "Not after I got an earful of guff when I missed your last class."

"You can change in the restroom," Kiki said, pointing down the hall.

Reese raised her brows. "Do I have time?"

"Barely, but I want you to be comfortable." She shot a glance at Reese's attire. "Cowboy boots and jeans don't seem to fit that bill."

"You're the boss," Reese said. "Just so you know, I found Ford's diorama at a pawn shop today, but when I stopped at his store to deliver it, I found him in his back room. He'd been assaulted."

"Holy cow!" Kiki placed her hands on either side of her face.

"I called 911, and now he's in the hospital," Reese assured her. "The cops are investigating what happened, and I'm also lending them a hand."

"Do you all have any idea who might have done it?"

"Not yet."

"I'm so sorry to hear about Ford, but I suppose now all we can do is send positive, healing wishes to him," Kiki said as she walked toward a doorway.

"I'm keeping tabs on him through his son, Ian," Reese said. "I'll share his health updates with you."

"I appreciate it," Kiki said. "By the way, we're all in the meditation studio when you're ready."

Reese took care of everything she needed to in the bathroom, changed into her yoga outfit and glanced at herself in the full-length mirror. Her preference for work outs consisted of wearing sweat pants and a big old T-shirt. Fortunately, Kiki had guilted her into purchasing an outfit from her store so she wouldn't look like a bum.

She'd finally found one to suit her style, a tie-dye, spaghetti strap tank top and leggings with a lattice detail near the ankle.

She only took a quick peek at her lavender and Navy-blue getup before she scooted out of the john and headed to class.

In the studio, five ladies sat on colorful floor cushions placed on the surface of a giant white fur rug. In various states of repose, and wearing a variety of yoga outfits, the women talked and laughed along with Kiki.

The white walls were decorated with jute macrame hangings and a large mandala wall decal. An objet d'art featured a black background with a lily pad at the bottom. Words in large white print said, BE HERE NOW.

A tall rubber plant, a jade plant and an Elephant Ear shrub filled one corner. In front of the greenery, a low table held a pagoda-shaped incense burner, a thin trail of fragrant blue smoke curling above it. A fountain featuring copper butterflies emitted the soothing sounds of a stream bubbling over stones.

Reese felt the everyday tension and pressure fade. The tight pinch between her brows began to diminish.

Kiki patted a cushion beside her and met Reese's gaze. "Come, sit. It's time to get started."

Everyone crossed their legs in a typical yoga pose. Reese took her place on the large pillow and did her best to concentrate on the here and now, just like the sign recommended.

"Welcome, everyone, to our meditation session," Kiki said. "As your wellness coach, I hope I can encourage you to find your personal power which will allow you to journey to your inner bliss."

Kiki closed her eyes, and everyone cheerfully obeyed by doing the same.

Reese maintained a secret vigil by peering through her lowered eyelashes. She didn't feel she could surrender herself to complete darkness. Not just yet, anyway.

"Remain comfortable in your seated position, back and spine straight," Kiki said in a soft tone. "Allow your thoughts to drift to a calming place, like an ocean beach or a still forest. Remind yourself that even though the world is full of unknowns, you will meet all challenges with a willingness to handle anything."

Reese couldn't help but think of Bella. Sensitive and intelligent, she was the girl classmates had predicted would go places, i.e., become the first female president of the United States or the CEO of a huge company. Or perhaps become an Olympic gold medalist in the swimming competition.

Listening to Kiki's instructions, Reese focused on breathing slowly, deeply, doing her best to bring fresh air into her lungs. Despite her attempts to rein in her thoughts and to be present in the moment, her mind drifted.

Recalling her high school years, she walked the halls of Meadowlark Valley High, seeing the students talking, laughing and slamming their locker doors. Quiet Bella headed to her space, not far from Reese's, where she'd place her violin for safekeeping until music class.

"Allow yourself to release negativity, which will heal all psychic wounds," Kiki said. "Hear your heart sing, see the truth in you—that you can sail through all difficulties."

Reese could hear her heart, all right. It wasn't singing, though. It thumped with the rhythm of her past. She remembered how Bella had loved art and the imaginative pencil drawings and paintings she'd created, which had frequently been displayed around the high school. She'd won numerous competitions, which garnered her blue ribbons and mentions of her accomplishments in the school newspaper and the local newspaper.

"You are beautiful, strong and competent," Kiki continued. "Your power to overcome is within you."

The newspaper stories written about Bella's accomplishments had been glowing. People admired and respected her. Girls in their class wanted to be like her, although there must have been a few harboring jealous thoughts.

"Understand the world is a place of growing and knowledge in your human experience," Kiki said. "Envision fear, regret and anger washing from your skin in a warm, gentle rain."

Reese filled her lungs with air, released it and felt her breathing from the top of her head to the tip of her toes. Her body flooded with sweet relaxation and she appreciated the opportunity to take it easy.

Yet, her mind returned to Bella's death and Ford's assault. She envisioned Bella at the river with her church choir group, enjoying the camaraderie. No doubt she'd been laughing along with her friends at the thrill of being carried down the river on the rushing waves.

When Bella had been swept away, people had attempted to rescue her, to no avail. She'd disappeared under the waves at a certain point.

As if that hadn't been tragic enough, someone had attacked Ford and put him in the hospital, fighting for his life. Who would have hurt the elderly gent, and why?

"Namaste," Kiki said as the room's serene silence wrapped around Reese.

A phone jangled, destroying the perfect moment.

Reese recognized the buoyant tone—an old-style office phone ring. It belonged to her. She dove for her purse and fished around in the depths to locate her cell. It seemed to take forever until her fingers clamped around the device.

Ian Presley's number appeared on the readout as she flipped a button to silence the sound. She'd call him back as soon as she finished up here.

Everyone in the room, including Kiki, turned to glare at her.

"Reese, we turn off our ringers in the meditation space," Kiki said, her voice sounding like that of a teacher scolding a disobedient student.

"I know you told me," Reese said. "I'm so sorry. I have no excuse for forgetting."

The ladies nodded in agreement, muttering to each other as they pushed onto their feet and stood. A few tossed her accusatory glances.

"Remember to take some of the free tea samples by the door," Kiki called out to the group. "It's a calming chamomile I blended earlier."

"Thank you," several of them replied, smiling and waving as

they shuffled past a butler's tray on metal legs, which held the small white packets.

"This was your first class, Reese," Kiki said as she rose and stretched her arms above her head. "I'm certain next time you'll remember to silence your phone ringer."

"I'm not sure it's a good idea for me to this again." Reese stood up, placed her hands on her hips. In order to loosen up more, she gently twisted right and left a few times.

"Why not?"

"I couldn't find a happy place when I meditated," Reese admitted. "I thought about Bella and Ford."

"You didn't clear your mind properly," Kiki suggested. "I'll help you learn to do that. It's not always easy to let your inner self be free."

"Don't I know it," Reese agreed.

"I'm sad about Bella, too, and I can't imagine who would want to hurt her father," Kiki admitted.

"That's what I plan to find out."

"Watch out, don't get in a kerfuffle with the police about snooping around," Kiki warned.

"Good thing I'm working with them. Along with trying to find who Ford's attacker was, they want me to write up Bella's accident report."

"That's a decent gig, but I can't blame you for being a tad emotional."

"I've got to remain professional," Reese said. "Jeremy warned me to stay out of trouble, though."

"He should know that trouble finds you," Kiki said with a chuckle. "How's he doing, by the way?"

"He's settled into his new digs and he's getting acquainted with the community."

"What do you think about having him in town?"

"Meaning what?" Reese asked.

"It seemed like there was a spark between you two when I saw you together. I just wondered, well, you know."

"I have no idea what you're talking about," Reese insisted.

"Come on, don't tell me you didn't feel it. You'd have to be made of stone, otherwise."

"Yeah, well, we have a lot in common. We both want to see justice served, so it stands to reason we would. Get along fine, I mean."

"Blah, blah, blah," Kiki mocked. "Remember, at the end of the day, you do have a personal life."

"Right now, Jeremy and I are both busy solving crimes. That's all."

"Sure. And I'm a monkey's uncle."

"My focus is on work," Reese insisted.

"Well, if anybody can get to the truth, it would be you, my friend." Kiki patted Reese's shoulder. "You're the best."

Chapter Nine

Reese changed out of her yoga gear and into her regular clothing before she left Kiki's. Climbing into her truck, she remembered she needed to return Ian's call. Grabbing her cell, she punched in his number, and felt relieved when he answered. There was nothing worse than the frustration of playing phone tag.

"Ian, glad I got a hold of you," she said.

"Sorry we couldn't talk much the other day."

"It was a rough time. By the way, how's your dad doing?"

"Not good, I'm afraid. He's still in intensive care."

"Darn! I'm so sorry to hear that."

"It's bad. The docs say he suffered a TBI and his brain started swelling, so they put him in a medically-induced coma to reduce the inflammation. It might be weeks before he wakes up. And hopefully when he does, he'll be okay."

"I trust our local medical professionals to know what they're doing."

"Mom and I are hoping for the best," Ian said, his voice unsteady. At this point, it's all we can do."

"Is it okay if I get Bella and Hunter's address from you?" Reese asked. "I want to swing by and visit him, offer my condolences and all that."

"It's 101 Haywood Avenue."

"Do you think he's home right now?"

"I'm almost positive he is. He's keeping a low profile. I don't even think he's eaten since she died."

"Maybe I can tempt him with dinner."

"I doubt it."

A beep sounded on the connection and Reese frowned. "Is that your phone or mine?" she asked.

"It's mine," Ian said. "It's my mom calling. She's staying at the hospital with my dad, so I've got to take this. I'll catch up with you later."

"Sure," Reese said as she hung up.

She started up Betty and headed to the Western Moon Café where she picked up a quart of chicken soup—the famous cure-all, and then headed to Hunter's place.

As Reese parked by the curb and cut the engine, she saw him standing next his large silver SUV in the driveway. She loved the sign she'd hired him to make for her PI business; a carved wooden one with white letters. It had just the right western flair to attract the locals' attention, yet it wasn't too flashy.

Gripping the chicken soup container, she got out and walked toward him, noting the dark circles under his eyes.

Poor guy, pining for his wife, she thought. Chicken soup wasn't really going to cut through his grief.

"Hunter?" she quietly asked.

He glanced over at her and blinked, as if he'd just noticed her for the first time. "Who are you?"

"I'm a friend of Bella's, and I also recently purchased a sign from you."

He didn't comment.

"I'm so sorry about what happened to her." She held up the container. "I brought you dinner. Maybe if you put something in your stomach—"

"I can't eat right now," he managed in a broken voice. "I've got to find it."

He opened the truck door, leaned inside, then swept his hand under the seat and around on the floor. He peered into the back cargo area and then walked around to the other side of the vehicle, opened another door, and began searching again.

Reese noticed the make and model, a Cadillac XT, a vehicle that was definitely way out of her price range. Speaking of expensive, the Northwood's stately brick home, located in an exclusive downtown neighborhood with manicured lawns and mature trees, must have cost a pretty penny. All the real estate around here did.

She didn't imagine the income Bella had brought in from the sale of her paintings and the revenue from Hunter's sign shop, housed in a modest-sized outbuilding on their large corner lot, provided a huge yearly salary.

Did the Northwoods have a champagne taste on a beer income?

None of my business, she thought. Still, her interest had been piqued.

Meanwhile, as she watched Hunter staring at his SUV, she realized the charitable thing to do would be to offer assistance.

"What are you looking for?" she asked him again. "Maybe I can help."

A tall man, probably around six feet, he ran his hands through his salt and pepper hair, making it messier than it already was.

"No, I'll handle it," he said.

"What's missing?"

He was silent a moment, as if gathering his thoughts. "Bella's wedding band. She took it off in the car a while ago and we couldn't ever find it."

"I see," she said. "Maybe if you take a break and have something to eat, you'll feel better."

Hunter glowered at her.

"It might perk you up, give you fresh energy."

"I doubt it."

Despite his grumpy attitude, she smiled and handed him the soup container. ""Your father-in-law isn't in very good shape, either."

"I'm surprised he survived the attack. Other men his age might not have."

"How did you know about it?" Reese raised her brows.

Hunter was quiet for a few seconds, then said, "Ian called and told me."

"I see," Reese said. "It'll be a while before Ford is out of the woods."

"No doubt."

"Does he have any enemies that you know of?" Reese asked. "Someone who would want to hurt him?"

"Ford? No. He's an all-around good guy."

"Do you think someone tried to rob him again?"

"Maybe they wanted the money in his register. They could have beat him up, trying to get him to open his cash drawer."

"That's plausible," she said.

"People these days will do about anything to make a quick buck."

"From what I've seen in my line of work, I'd have to agree," Reese said.

"You shouldn't have bothered," Hunter said, holding up the soup container.

"That's the best chicken noodle in town, and I promise, I did not make it."

He frowned and said, "Whatever."

"I hate to bring this up," she said. "But can I ask you a couple of questions about Bella?"

He sighed, then asked, "What do you want to know?"

"Did she seem sad lately?"

"Sad?"

"As in depressed."

"No."

"If something was bothering her, she might have felt hopeless. That could be why she didn't try swimming back to the raft after she fell out."

"Who mentioned that?"

"Witnesses."

"They're off their rockers," Hunter responded. "Bella had a wonderful life. Everything was going great."

"Okay, I just wondered. Um, are you sure the two of you weren't arguing about anything?"

"Of course not," he snapped. "What do you care, anyway?"

"I'm helping the local police."

"Why are they investigating her death? It was an accident."

"It's standard procedure. Just to rule out any irregularities."

"Do they suspect me of having anything to do with it?"

"I'm only trying to clarify some things."

"Well, I'm tired of the inquisition, and I don't appreciate innuendos that I had anything to do with Bella's drowning."

Hunter walked around the SUV, closing doors. Clutching the soup, he hustled inside.

Reese couldn't blame Hunter for being moody, considering his wife had just passed away. She beelined back to her truck, feeling as though she stood on home plate with a bat in her hand and had struck out again.

When she was five, her mother had put her on a T-Ball team and she'd spent more time making circles in the dirt with her sneakers than learning the rules of the game and honing her skills. Needless to say, she never played again after that torturous season.

So far, everyone she'd questioned had claimed that Ford didn't have any enemies and they couldn't imagine anyone wanting to hurt him. Maybe it had been a random intruder that attacked him or those teenage boys.

Too bad Ford didn't have a web cam mounted in his store for security. Earlier, she and Officer Berry had noticed the lack of one, otherwise, the police might have had a chance of identifying the culprit.

Reese drove home and parked, then walked inside her house, dropping her purse and packages on the kitchen table. Since she lived alone, she liked noise because it seemed welcoming. As was her typical habit, she switched on the TV in the front room and listened to the local news channel.

Taryn Jones, a newer anchor with pale, smooth hair and a stern expression, reported updates about the southern fire, which firefighters were still having trouble getting under control.

"The Rockrimmon Peak Fire has now grown by nearly 1,000 acres. As of today, it is at a total of 125,006 acres with 21 percent containment."

Last time Reese had heard, the fire had destroyed much less property. She chewed her lower lip, disturbed by the loss.

"Helicopters and air tankers have been deployed in order to evaluate the damage and several building protection plans are being put into place. It is tireless work for fire crews who are working relentlessly around the clock to contain the blaze." Taryn shuffled some papers. "In other news..."

At one point, investigators had announced that they believed a lightning striking on dry timber had sparked the inferno. Firefighters must be under intense physical drain from constantly battling those flames, Reese's thought.

Mr. Bojangles padded into the room, meowing his head off while jumping onto the couch beside her. He head-butted her hand, making it known he wanted her to scratch his ears.

"I hear you loud and clear, buddy," she said as she rubbed his favorite spot. "You know I'm here to serve."

When her cell rang, she hustled back to the kitchen and walked over to the table where earlier she'd dropped her packages from Medicine Bow Pawn, along with her purse.

"Yeah, yeah, yeah," she said impatiently as she dug through her handbag contents, searching for the jangling phone. Picking it up, she answered, "Reese Golden."

The line went dead, and the phone number was a strange conglomeration of numbers.

"Of course, the jerk hung up on me," Reese growled. "There's nothing like a good prank call to make your day."

• • •

When Reese's cell phone rang the next morning, she feared it might be another random sales call, so she refused to answer. She glanced at her clock on the nightstand. In glowing neon red, the digits said: 7 a.m., and the room radiated with soft violet light.

Rolling over, she stretched her arm across forehead, waiting for the jangling to stop. When it went silent, she managed to fall asleep again, snug and content beneath her bed covers. A short time later the ringing started up again, so she grabbed her cell.

"Golden Investigations," she answered groggily as she got up and padded into her office.

"Reese, hi! It's Heath Steele."

"Mmm," she murmured.

When she didn't acknowledge Heath, he added. "From Steele and Oatman Law Firm here in Meadowlark Valley. Remember that case I'm working on about insurance fraud?"

After a few seconds, Reese recalled that that Heath represented a man who, about a year ago, had a fender bender with a young lady named Janet Mayweather. Afterward, Mayweather claimed she had suffered severe whiplash and other spine injuries.

Since then, Mayweather had incurred sizable medical debt from chiropractors and other medical professionals. The man's insurance company had paid the bills. At a certain point, however, they refused to pay further, believing they'd met their contracted financial responsibility for reasonable injuries.

Mayweather had sued to continue receiving disability coverage, despite the insurance company's objections.

Heath had hired Reese to follow the young lady, who she'd photographed dancing and horseback riding. He believed those photos would help him convince the judge to dismiss the lawsuit.

"I remember the case, Heath," she assured him as the cobwebs in her brain cleared.

"I've discovered through my sources that Ms. Mayweather is also taking tennis lessons. Can you swing by the Windflower Recreation Center and snap some shots of her practicing with her coach? I go to court next week and I believe that evidence should help make my case."

Stifling a yawn, Reese said, "Do you know when these lessons are?"

"I found out Ms. Jones has one at 8:30 this morning."

So much for going back to bed, Reese thought.

"I'm on it," Reese promised.

"Thanks," Heath said. "The check's in the mail, as they say."

After hanging up, Reese walked into the kitchen and made coffee. The aroma of fresh brew inspired her as she headed into the bathroom and started the shower. She stepped in, revived by the warm, pulsating water. After she'd soaped up, shampooed and rinsed, she thought she heard her doorbell ring.

Pulling aside the plastic curtain covered in pink flamingos, she listened closer, and heard someone knocking on her front door.

"Cheese and rice," she growled, stepping out of the tub and reaching for a towel.

Uttering that euphemism reminded her of when her mother used to say it around her and Jesse. It had been her mom's style of swearing, but in a PG rated way, so that she wasn't using bad words with her kids.

The doorbell rang again as she donned her robe and walked into the front room. Opening up, she discovered Ian Presley standing on the porch. He removed his Stetson and pressed it against his chest.

"Sorry, Reese," he drawled. "I know I should have called first."

"No worries, what is it?" she asked, noting he wore his gigantic gold PBR belt buckle again. Ian looked troubled, and she could tell he was anxious by the way he shuffled his booted feet.

"I wanted to show you where Bella's accident happened. I'm going out to assist the search and rescue folks again. We're determined to find my sister's..."

"I get it," Reese said sympathetically. "What about Hunter, is he helping, too?"

"He's got some sign installation appointments this morning, but he said he'd be along later to help."

"Did you call and tell him about your dad yesterday?"

Ian blinked. "I can't recall exactly," he said.

"When I stopped by some dinner to Hunter last evening, he said you had."

"Then I obviously did," Ian said. "It was a confusing day."

Reese tucked away that tidbit, not exactly certain what it meant.

"I'd like to go out to the river and have a look since I'll be writing up her accident report," she said. "But I need to be somewhere in about an hour."

"Sorry for showing up out of the blue," Hunter said. "We can do this another time."

"No, I want to work this out. Come in and let's talk for a bit."

Reese stood aside so he could enter. She led him into the kitchen, invited him to sit at the table, and poured him a cup of coffee.

"I'll go get dressed and when I come back out, we can make plans to meet later," Reese said.

"Sure," Ian said.

"I won't be long."

In her room, Reese quickly slid on jeans, a top and her boots. At her make-up table, she ran a brush through her hair, applied mascara and lip gloss, then went back out to the kitchen. She grabbed a cup of coffee for herself and sat down across from Ian.

"Every day, I'm hell-bent on finding my sister," Ian said. "It's like a fever. Life goes on around me, but I'm numb to it."

"It's got to be difficult," she said. "I realize how devastating Bella's death has been for you and your family. And now having your dad in the hospital, it's tough."

"I don't even care about the PBR season anymore," Ian explained. "Everything in my world has come to a grinding halt."

"I know it's hard to imagine right now, but it'll get better." Reese sipped her coffee, then glanced at her watch. "I can meet you at the river after my appointment."

"Great. Call me when you're ready to head out and let's meet at the Grizzly Rafting Company."

"Are you thinking about filing a wrongful death suit against them?"

Ian shook his head. "Mom and I hadn't even considered that. As far as we can tell, they didn't do anything wrong. The company even refunded the church group's booking fee and they seem as upset as we are. The incident goes on their safety record, you know."

"That's exactly what should happen," she said. "Whether or not they were at fault."

"I also wanted you to know that we're holding a candlelight

vigil at 7 p.m. on Thursday at the Fellowship Church. It's for both Bella and my dad."

"Are you and your mom really up for that? And Hunter? When I stopped by to visit him yesterday evening, he seemed distracted."

"People keep asking what happened to Bella, and everyone's worried about Dad. We figured the vigil would help."

"Maybe it will."

"You'll be there, right?"

"I'd feel like I was intruding. Bella and I weren't close."

"Honestly, we want you there."

"All right, I'll come."

"Who knows?" Ian gave a shaky smile. "Maybe there'll be some good news about my dad by then."

Reese noted the time. She needed to get over to the recreation center and take those photographs for Heath. Pushing to her feet, she met Ian's gaze.

"See you in a bit."

"Later, then." Ian stood and strode out of the door.

Chapter Ten

After firing up her Bronco, Reese drove over to the police department, deciding she'd better check in with Jeremy before starting her day. When she approached Steve Daniels' desk, he waved her down the hall. "Detective Savage is in, and he wants to see you."

"Thanks," she said.

"How's it going?" Reese asked Jeremy as she entered his office cubicle.

He looked up from his computer and stood. "Glad you stopped by. How's the investigation into Bella Northwood's drowning coming along?"

"I'm going out to the river today to have a look around."

"Good," he said, his hands resting on the back of his black leather chair.

"I'm meeting with Ian Presley and Alex Huckman, the owner of Grizzly Rafting Company."

He nodded. "You can find out first-hand what happened."

"That's the plan. When I'm finished with my investigation, I'll type up my findings and send them to you."

"I'll let you get to it, then."

Reese started to leave.

"Hey," Jeremy said.

She stopped and spun around. "Is there anything else?"

"Nah," he said after a couple of seconds, even though an unspoken comment seemed to be hanging in the air.

"Later, then."

Reese exited the police department, then drove over to the

Windflower Recreation Center, a two-story gray brick building surrounded by evergreen bushes, that had been in existence for the last several years. It offered a full gym with showers, an indoor track and exercise rooms where various classes like yoga for the more mature members and gymnastics for the little ones were offered.

Reese parked in the lot, put on her cowboy hat and went inside, showing her membership card at the front counter.

"Hi Karen," she said to the attendant, a young lady whose short, dark hair had blue highlights today. She dyed the colors frequently, but it always looked cute. Karen was about five years younger than Reese, and Reese knew her because she'd taken skiing lessons with Karen's older sister Darla, when they were in high school

As the kid sister, Karen frequently caused havoc during her and Darla's hang out sessions where they'd discussed boys or fashion or school gossip. Karen didn't like being left out of their conversations, so she made herself annoying, which drove Reese and Darla crazy. With Karen being younger and less experienced in the love department, Darla and Reese weren't interested in her opinions.

It appeared their history still rubbed Karen the wrong way, considering the way she peered at Reese. Sometimes, people had a hard time letting go of the past.

"Morning Reese," Karen said, frowning as she studied her attire. "You're not working out in those clothes, are you?"

"No, I'm meeting someone," Reese said as she scanned her membership card and signed the check in register. "I won't be long."

"Well then," Karen said, her gaze still disapproving.

Reese walked through the turnstile and headed down the hall past a fitness center where people exercised on stationary bicycles, treadmills and elliptical trainers. In the large gym, people played basketball or jogged around the track.

After passing by the pool and sauna, Reese exited a door and made her way outside to the tennis courts. Surrounded by walls, two rectangular, artificial turf tennis courts sat with nets stretched across the center.

One court was occupied with a man wearing black athletic shorts and a red polo shirt. He stood beside Janet Mayweather, who wore a short pink skirt and a white racerback tank top.

By the way the man, obviously Janet's instructor, was helping her hold the tennis racquet, it appeared he was teaching her the forehand shot—one of the first players learned. Learning the forehand shot was essential for game success.

Mayweather did not look disabled by any means. Reese bit her lower lip in disapproval of the woman's deceitful tactics to try and squeeze more from Heath's client's insurance company.

Noting several spectators clustered on the bleachers, Reese walked toward them. She lifted her hand and waved in their direction, as if she knew them. She went over and sat down, then pulled out her cell phone. Holding up the camera, she snapped shots of Janet bouncing around without a care in the world, her long red pony tail lifting in the breeze.

"Hi," a little boy in a T-shirt and shorts, who looked around 10, said to Reese. He sat down on the bench in front of her and turned around to stare. His freckled expression radiated boredom.

"Hi," she said.

"Do you like tennis?"

"I've tried it a time or two. It's not really my cup of tea."

"What does that mean?" He gave her a puzzled look.

"I don't like it."

"Me neither. But my mom wants me to learn."

"Where is your mom?"

He pointed to the seats right next to the court's edge where a middle-aged woman and a younger version of her sat talking.

"That's her beside my sister Cammie," the boy said. "They love tennis and we're supposed to start lessons today. I think it's dopey."

"It's good to learn new things."

"I suppose," he said. "My name is Kenny. What's yours?"

"Reese," she said.

"What are you taking pictures of?"

Busted. And, by a kid, no less.

"I'm a freelance journalist," Reese said, using her favorite cover story again. "I'm writing a story about tennis."

"Do you like that job? Writing, I mean. I think it would be boring."

"It pays the bills."

Reese took a few more shots, then sent them to Craig. After texting Ian to tell him she was heading out to the Grizzly Rafting Company, she rose and turned to her new friend.

"Enjoy your tennis lesson, Kenny."

"I won't," he responded, his expression grim.

Reese climbed down from the bleachers and headed to her Bronco. Switching the gears in her mind away from Craig's fraud case and toward Bella's rafting accident, she exited onto the highway and headed toward the canyon.

About 15 minutes later, Reese parked in front of the rafting company's log cabin-style structure. A large awning over the porch displayed a yellow raft that held eight grizzly bear sculptures wearing orange lifejackets and clutching paddles. All the critters smiled and appeared to be having the time of their lives.

"Cute," Reese muttered as she got out of her truck, walked past a black company van with white lettering, and stepped onto the wooden porch where Ian and another man stood talking.

"Reese," Ian said as she approached him. "This is Alex Huckman, the owner. He was the guide on Bella's raft."

Alex reached out and they shook hands. Sturdily built with broad, muscled shoulders, around 6 feet tall and probably in his late twenties, he wore water shoes, camouflage shorts, and a red windbreaker. Tufts of dark hair stuck out from beneath his matching ball cap.

"Ian mentioned you're helping the police investigate," he said, a slight drawl accenting his deep voice.

"Yes," Reese said. "How long have you owned the rafting company, Alex?"

"Closing in on three years, now."

"What are your background qualifications for this type of work?"

He gave her an odd look and Ian gave her a pointed stare.

"Standard questions," Reese said. "I'm just getting all my facts straight, you know?"

"I practically grew up on the Guadalupe River near Austin, Texas," Alex explained. "I became a fanatic about water sports—fishing, swimming, rafting, you name it. Eventually I went to guide school, became certified in CPR, swift-water rescue and the like, then got hired by a rafting company."

"I see," Reese said.

"It's the typical background for a river guide," Alex continued. "After a while, I decided I wanted to strike out on my own."

"Why did you come here to set up shop?"

"I moved to Wyoming because I love the mountains. I worked up in the Jackson area for a while at a rafting company, then set up my own place here on the Trout River. I've loved practically every minute of it." His expression clouded over. "Except when Bella fell off the raft."

"That was an awful day for all of us, buddy," Ian said, placing a hand on Alex's shoulder.

"Are you two friends?" Reese asked.

"We hang out on occasion," Ian said. "When I'm in town, we'll maybe go grab a beer or two."

Alex shook his head. "I'm still upset that with all my rescue training, I couldn't help your sister. The current wasn't even running very fast that day."

"It's just weird," Ian said with a sniff.

"Let's take a ride over to where we last saw your sister," Alex said to Ian. "I don't know if that will help with your report to the police, but you can at least see where it happened."

He began walking toward the company van Reese had seen earlier.

Ian followed Alex and commented, "Reese, you can get a good feel for the lay of the land."

Reese kept pace beside the men, ready to absorb even the smallest details about what had happened and to observe the river scenery with sharp eyes. Alex led them to the black company van, and they all got in.

After starting up the engine, Alex pulled out of the parking lot and drove down a road alongside the wide, blue-green river. Buff-colored buttes covered in dusty green shrubs rose on all sides.

Reese rolled down her window and listened to the roaring rapids. She shivered, thinking of Bella struggling beneath the rapids, unable to breathe, dying.

Chapter Eleven

Alex pulled into a sandy area where brightly colored inflatable rafts were lined up, waiting for people to climb aboard. He parked and they all got out, then walked down toward the cove where a man dressed in a red windbreaker and a matching ballcap like Alex wore was busy working on a raft.

"Hey, Joe," Alex said, waving at the man. "Rigging up for a trip?"

"Hey, Alex," the guy said, studying Ian and Reese closely. "Got some guests coming in about an hour. A group of Japanese business people who scheduled a team-building activity."

Alex nodded, and Joe returned to his duties.

Coffee brown canyon walls rose on each side of the water, the rocky banks covered in scruffy green sagebrush. A grade held old railroad tracks that trailed along the riverside into the distance. Overhead, the sky arched like a blue silk canopy, dotted with white tufted clouds. A warm breeze brushed Reese's cheeks, and she pushed strands of hair out of her eyes

Only the atmosphere's smoky haze marred the beauty, along with random fire ashes drifting like random snowflakes.

"It was a perfect day when Bella fell out of the raft," Ian said in a tight voice.

"The three rafts carrying the church group members were in good shape," Alex added. "We'd been paddling along, enjoying the gentle rapids."

"Who all was on the trip that day?" Reese asked, just to be certain she had her information straight.

"The Fellowship Church choir, 13 people, which included

Carla Washington, the choir director," Ian said. "Earlier, we'd had lunch at the Grizzly Bar and Grill."

"That's right," Alex said.

"All of us are so busy, it's hard for us choir members to get together for an outing," Ian said. "But we all managed to make it on the rafting trip that day."

"I see," Reese said.

"Bella's raft was in front of me," Ian said, then caught his breath. "I could hardly believe it when she fell out."

"No one could have expected that," Reese said.

"I can't help but feel responsible," Ian said.

"You couldn't feel more responsible than me, since I was the guide in her raft," Alex said.

"It doesn't sound like it's anyone's fault," Reese pointed out.

"This damn river took my sister." Ian looked away; his shoulders slumped.

Reese folded her arms across her chest. "Describe to me exactly what happened and when."

"We started right from this beach," Alex said. "We were floating along and my passengers were in high spirits as we paddled. About a mile down the canyon, we hit a patch of white water—but nothing terrible, nothing we couldn't navigate."

"Show me where," Reese said. "Let's go further downriver."

They all went back to the van and crawled in. Alex drove for a short time, then pulled over alongside the road. Everyone got out and they all trotted over to the riverbank.

"See that outcropping of dark rock that juts out slightly into the water?" Ian pointed into distance. "There's also a small sandbar in the middle of the river."

"Yes," Reese said as she spotted it.

"It was right there that she fell out," Ian said. "People started shouting and everyone panicked, but the current took her. Alex and I all jumped in the waves and swam after her, but she disappeared around that chunk of rock."

"She was just...just gone," Alex said. "I swam back to the raft and got everyone safely to the landing spot. Then I got on my radio to call search and rescue."

"I searched along the river and the banks where she'd disappeared." Ian shook his head. "Before long, teams of people were combing the area. And still, we've found nothing."

No wonder Jeremy felt like something wasn't right. She peered downriver again, scanning the horizon.

"I agree, I'm surprised Bella didn't come back the raft or make her way over to the river bank," Reese commented.

"I'll always feel guilty," Alex commented. "I keep going over what I could have done differently. Bella was my responsibility, along with all of my passengers."

They were all silent for a minute.

"One of the things we're trained to tell guests is if they fall overboard, that they shouldn't fight it, but that they should let their life jackets keep them afloat." Alex met Reese's gaze. "Maybe that's why Bella didn't try swimming to the raft."

"She was wearing a helmet, right?" Reese asked, wondering if Bella had hit her head and been stunned senseless.

"Yes, it's required," Alex said.

"If she hit her head on those rocks hard enough, it could have cracked her headgear," Ian said. "The bottom of the river has tangled undergrowth. She could have easily gotten caught up in that."

Reese studied the men, judging their reactions. Both looked extremely troubled.

"Search and rescue helicopters have even flown over the area," Alex said. "They've been thorough."

"I'm glad they were on the scene right away," Reese said.

Alex looked down at his feet, then back up again. "I'm strict about our safety standards and practices. Unfortunately, there's always a risk that goes along with rafting."

"Have you ever written up any of your staff members for violating rules or guidelines?" Reese asked.

"A minor infraction here and there, but nothing that would cause me to fire an employee," Alex said.

"And I'm assuming there's never been any accident of this sort before?"

"No, none."

Reese envisioned Bella floating down the river and disappearing beneath the rapids. What a tragedy for everyone, especially her family, to have her die at such a young age.

A niggling sensation teased Reese's brain, but she didn't comment because she wasn't sure what was bothering her. The strange feeling remained however, teasing the edges of her thought process, but she pushed it away.

"Are we in trouble?" Alex said. "Something like this could ruin my company."

"You're worried about your company? I lost my sister," Ian commented, scowling at Alex.

"Sorry, dude. I didn't mean to be disrespectful, but I've worked a long time to build this outfit."

"Hey, you two, settle down," Reese told them. "Splitting hairs over minor details won't solve anything and it definitely won't bring back Bella."

The men relaxed some, but an electric current simmered around them both.

"What will you tell the police?" Alex finally ventured to ask.

"I don't see any foul play or spot any irregularities," Reese said. "I'd rule this as a tragic accident."

No one spoke as the three of them walked back to the van. Like a wisp of a ghost, a shadow on the riverbank moved and took a woman's shape. Reese could have sworn Bella stood there, reaching out to her.

"Find me, Reese. I need help."

Reese shook her head, and the apparition disappeared.

• • •

Back in her office, Reese placed want ads in two local newspapers, requesting people who were at the river the day of Bella's accident to contact her if they'd seen or heard anything that might help with the report she was writing for Jeremy.

Next, she looked up communities along the Trout River where Bella could have turned up if she'd made it out of the water. It was a long shot, but she didn't want to rule anything out. If she'd hit her head and injured herself, she might have been dazed and confused.

Maybe she'd wandered for a while before someone had picked her up and taken her to a hospital. If she was dead, or unconscious, she could still be out there somewhere in the forest.

Although afraid she was wasting her time, she began looking up hospital numbers on her computer and making calls to see if any females around 30 years old had recently been admitted who lacked identification. Or if any unidentified females around that age were in the morgue.

By her reckoning, there were only three medical facilities she should check out. By the time she dialed the last hospital located in Big Gap, she was ready to say Bella had died in the river.

"Big Gap Memorial Hospital," a female voice answered. "Autumn Lopez speaking."

"Hi Autumn, my name is Reese Golden, a private investigator from Meadowlark Valley. I'm looking for a young woman who may have been admitted to your hospital with no identification."

Autumn was silent for a moment, then said, "I'm new here, so I'm going to transfer you to my supervisor Ms. Davenport, so she can visit with you."

"Sure, I'll hold," Reese said.

"This is Astrid Davenport," a woman announced when she came on the line. "I'm the Patient Affairs Coordinator."

Reese gave Ms. Davenport her name, explained she was a private investigator and that she was working for the Meadowlark Valley Police Department.

"I'm searching for someone who would have been admitted within the last few days," she explained. "It's possible she hit her head after a rafting accident and doesn't remember who she is."

"I see," Ms. Davenport said. "Can you describe her?"

A thread of hope lifted within Reese. The other hospitals had told her straightaway that they couldn't give out patient information. Summoning an image of Bella, Reese described her features.

"She's in her early thirties and tall, probably around 5'8" or 5'9". She's got dark hair and dark brown eyes and is athletically built."

"Caucasian?"

"Yes."

"Any tattoos, scars or birthmarks?"

"None that I'm aware of," Reese said.

"All right, Ms. Golden, please hold for a moment while I confer with Dr. Bradford with the hospital Board of Directors. He'll be able to tell me whether someone fitting your description is here or not and what we are authorized to share with you."

"Thank you," Reese said as the hold music began playing. It seemed like an eternity before a voice came on the line again.

"Ms. Golden, this is Dr. Chester Bradford. I'm afraid we're unable to reveal anything to you. It's against hospital policy."

"I understand."

"However, if there is someone from local law enforcement working on this case, we'll be able to share more. They can contact me directly."

Dr. Bradford offered his phone number and Reese scribbled it on a notepad.

"You've been a great help," Reese said.

After she hung up with Dr. Bradford, she dialed Jeremy, anxious to share her ideas with him. He'd probably think it was a crazy idea to consider Bella might have made it out of the river and someone had taken her to a nearby hospital. Yet, she didn't want to rule it out, even if the possibility was slim.

"I've got a lead on a Jane Doe," she told Jeremy when he answered his phone.

"You don't believe it's Bella, do you?"

"I can't honestly say one way or the other," she said. "But if it's a possibility, I think we should investigate."

"You're right," he said.

Chapter Twelve

The next day, the two of them rode in Jeremy's unmarked police vehicle, a dark blue Chevrolet Trailblazer, to Big Gap. It had a lightbar at the top of the windshield that Reese knew Jeremy could activate if needed. The dashboard contained a good-sized computer screen and a police radio. On the outside, the Trailblazer looked innocuous, however, she imagined it could rocket into action whenever needed.

As the miles passed, they discussed the idea Bella of surviving her accident. Neither of them held out much hope, but for the family's sake, they didn't want to dismiss the possibility.

When Jeremy contacted Dr. Bradford, the doctor had given a basic physical description of a recently admitted patient. She matched Bella's build and hair color, but her head injury was so severe she couldn't speak.

Dr. Bradford explained that hikers had discovered the woman near a forest service road located along the Trout River and had called 911. Administrators were currently in the process of notifying local law enforcement agencies, hoping they could locate relatives.

Reese watched the passing landscape outside of her window. Brown prairie swells dipped and rose, stretching across the land. Distant mountain ridges jutted into the blue sky, again marred by the wildfire haze.

Jeremy drove past a small reservoir nestled at the base of two peaks, edged by tall pine, spruce, groves of birch, aspen and thick shrubs. A couple of homes perched on nearby bluffs, overlooking the valley.

Tall trees began to appear on either side of the highway, and the vehicle climbed up a hill, then the road dropped into a flat plain shoring up the buildings of Big Gap. The city stretched into the distance, edged by housing developments and more established neighborhoods.

"I didn't realize Big Gap had grown so large," Jeremy commented.

"I didn't either," Reese said.

Jeremy turned off the highway and followed an exit into town.

"It would be a miracle if this patient is actually Bella," he said, echoing Reese's inner thoughts.

"I know," Reese agreed.

A niggling sensation made Reese feel that they were tilting at windmills. Yet, she knew she'd never be able to live with herself if they didn't have a look.

After navigating through the city streets, Jeremy pulled up in front of Big Gap Memorial Hospital's one-level facility. It sprawled like a pale sand crab across a grassy campus landscaped with boulders, gravel and tall, swaying tufts of ornamental grass.

"Thanks for helping me with this," Reese said, meeting Jeremy's gaze.

"Of course," Jeremy said, his detective's badge glinting in the dim sunlight. "It's in the MPD's best interest, too."

They exited Jeremy's Trailblazer and entered the hospital through large glass sliding doors. Upon entering the plant-filled main corridor, the two approached the information desk, above which hung a painting of the Laramie Mountains.

"I'm Detective Jeremy Savage from the Meadowlark Valley Police Department," he said, pulling aside his dark suit jacket so the receptionist could see his badge. "I'm here to talk to Dr. Bradford."

"Is he expecting you?" the dark-haired young lady said.

"Yes, I've got an appointment," Jeremy said.

The receptionist placed a call, then pointed at the couches in the reception area. "Have a seat," she told Reese. "Detective, please come with me."

Jeremy gave Reese a silent glance, then followed the receptionist down the hall. Soft music played in the background as Reese eased toward several plump turquoise chairs clustered beside a round coffee table.

Every piece looked comfortable, but she plopped down on the end of a brown leather couch near a gas fireplace inset into a buff-colored slate brick wall. A shiny green peace lily sat opposite her in a tall wrought iron planter.

Anxious, Reese pulled out her phone and scrolled mindlessly through her feed, not really registering the newsy updates. The Small Business Council had posted a reminder about a meeting being held tonight. She belonged to the organization, but hadn't attended any of their events in a while.

Wondering whether Ford was a member, she decided she might show up and ask a few questions. Maybe the council members had theories about who had attacked him.

A short time later, the young lady returned to the reception area and took a seat at her desk. She scooted behind her computer and began typing.

When Jeremy returned to the waiting area, a tall man in a white coat accompanied him. Reese assumed he must be Dr. Bradford. The man's graying hair and dark-rimmed glasses lent him an air of authority and his creased forehead hinted at his years of experience. He held a clipboard that held a stack of white paper.

"It's unfortunate you came all this way only to be disappointed," he said to Jeremy.

"We needed to see for ourselves," Jeremy said. "Meanwhile, my office will post a news release about your Jane Doe in case anyone in Meadowlark Valley knows her."

"We appreciate it," Dr. Bradford said. He nodded at Reese, acknowledging her, then turned and walked back down the hallway.

Reese stood as Jeremy approached her, shaking his head.

"Not her," he said.

"I knew it," Reese said, disappointed. She'd hoped against all odds they'd found Bella, but wasn't surprised by the outcome.

"We both realized it probably wasn't going to work out," Jeremy said.

"I know."

Reese walked with Jeremy outside into the smoky air, her mind full of new ideas about how to track down Ford's attacker.

"Have you come with any leads on who might have beat up Bella's dad?" Reese asked Jeremy.

"Nope," he said. "Have you?"

"Not yet. But I plan to attend a Small Business Council meeting this evening. Maybe I'll overhear something that'll help me zero in on a suspect or two."

"That'd be great."

"The local business owners get pretty vocal about the current gossip," Reese added. "I'm certain the topic of Ford's attack will come up."

"Let's hope they point some fingers," Jeremy said.

"Definitely," Reese said.

They got in Jeremy's truck, belted up, and he drove away from the hospital, back toward Meadowlark Valley. Reese's mind began churning as she wondered if Ford had ticked off any local business owners. If so, it must have really set someone off, if they'd become upset enough to attack him.

The last time she'd talked to Ian, Ford was still unconscious and remained in critical condition. The prognosis didn't look good, and Reese wondered if he'd ever wake up.

• • •

That afternoon, she was watching local news on her kitchen TV, eating a low-calorie frozen meal she'd nuked in the microwave. She was only paying half attention to it, figuring when she finished, she'd head into her office and sit down at her computer to finish some work on her background investigations.

"The SBC meeting," she muttered, remembering it was tonight.

Glancing at the clock, she noted the time, realizing she had two hours before it started. Good, she could still make it.

"School is back in session for the local district, and educating our children is an ever-evolving process," the news reporter on the television was saying.

Between bites, Reese looked up to see Kendra Etheridge, a local reporter standing in a brightly decorated classroom clutching a microphone. With her butter-colored hair styled into a short pageboy style, she wore a plum-colored dress. Next to her stood a lady with dark curly hair and glasses dressed in a plaid top, a jeans skirt, and sandals. A microphone dangled from her collar.

Surprised to hear school had started, Reese continued listening to the segment.

"Mrs. O'Day, a fifth-grade teacher at Meadowlark Valley Elementary, is teaching her students how science and technology can enhance their minds," Kendra said. "Mrs. O'Day, will you please give us a description of what your class is doing right now?"

Smiling eagerly, the teacher began talking, using her hands to emphasize her points.

"We are utilizing the online resource of World Traveler, which the kids are working with to research the earth's natural sciences. World Traveler is a great site that offers lesson plans for teachers as well as maps, podcasts, online instructors, educational videos, and other things to help students."

"How did you hear about it?" Kendra asked.

"Mr. Osbourne, another fifth-grade teacher here at Meadowlark Valley Elementary, told me about it. We're both working on the same unit."

"What are your students learning?"

"I want them to understand topographic maps, which can help with land management. For example, historical maps are snapshots of an area's physical and cultural features in the past. Current maps of the same area can show how that same area looks after development, and it provides a view of how land masses change and evolve over time.

"Who can use World Traveler?"

"This resource is available to everyone," Mrs. O'Day said. "For business professionals, the topographic maps are great tools for everyday use in government, science, industry, land management planning, and recreation. I understand this is also useful for law enforcement agencies."

Mrs. O'Day's comment cleared some of the cobwebs in Reese's mind. She recalled one drug bust where the DPD's vice squad had obtained a warrant and put a vehicle tracker on a suspect's car, which subsequently led them to a marijuana field.

Instead of physically following him, they had pulled up an online GPS map to follow his movements in order to locate the place. With that information, they went on to conduct a drug bust and subsequently arrested several suspects.

Reese stopped eating and headed to her office. She had work to do, namely sign into World Traveler and have a look at the Trout River on a GPS map the day Bella drowned. She could also pull up Ford's gas station and see what vehicles had been there the day he was assaulted.

Chapter Thirteen

The second Reese stepped into her office, the doorbell rang.

"Figures," she muttered as she turned around and headed through the front room to answer it.

When she opened up, Kiki stood there, hands on her hips, a small bag gripped in her hand. A yellow headband held back her dark curly hair and she wore a wide legged jumpsuit in a watermelon color.

"You missed my meditation class today," she said, her brows raised.

Reese invited Kiki inside, closed the door and said, "Follow me."

"Nice to see you, Kiki," Reese's friend said in a friendly mocking tone. "How's your day been, Kiki? Anything new happening in your life, Kiki?"

"Sorry," Reese said as she entered her office. "I know I'm distracted. It's been a busy day."

"Spill."

"Jeremy and I located an unidentified patient in a coma at the Big Gap Memorial Hospital. A Jane Doe. We hoped maybe Bella had hit her head, but managed to crawl out of the river and someone got her help."

"So?" Kiki's eyebrows arched

"When we drove over this morning to check it out, it wasn't her."

"Shoot," Kiki said.

"We knew it was a long shot to hope she'd survived, but still disappointing to find out the young woman wasn't Bella," Reese said.

Kiki held out the bag toward Reese, the silver bracelets on her wrist clinking. "I brought by the peppermint essential oil you ordered. You sure must like this stuff since you get it a lot. Do you bathe in it, or what?"

Reese chuckled. "I soak cotton balls with the oil and place them on my window sills."

Reese took the bag and placed it on her desk.

"Does that protect you from Bigfoot or maybe the Bogeyman?

"Spiders supposedly hate the stuff, and I hate spiders, so it's a win-win."

"Does it really work?"

"I still find them occasionally, but I think the peppermint oil wards off most of the beasties. It's a natural pesticide and I love the fragrance."

"What about your bad dreams? Does it help with those?"

"No, I still have those. And I'm having the weirdest daytime imaginings."

"Like what?"

"I was at the Trout River looking around the area where Bella fell in." Reese plopped in her desk chair and met Kiki's gaze. "I swear I saw Bella on the riverbank, waving to me. She even called out to me."

"Well, that's not creepy or anything," Kiki said sardonically. She scooted over a ladderback chair and made herself comfortable. "What's up?"

As Reese turned on her computer, she told Kiki about the segment she'd heard on the news regarding Mrs. O'Day's class at the local elementary school. She explained they were studying topographical maps using the World Traveler website.

"I was really stuck, trying to figure out what to do next." Reese brought up the internet and navigated to the site. "Hearing that story, it occurred to me I could use World Traveler to check out GPS maps of the river the day Bella had her accident. Also, I realized I could navigate to Ford's service station on the day he was attacked."

"You might be able to see who was there that day," Kiki said enthusiastically. "Maybe you can find out who Ford's attacker was."

"I'd hoped the same," Reese said.

Tongue tucked in the corner of her mouth, an old habit of hers when she tried to concentrate, Reese brought up the map of Wyoming and enlarged it in order to locate the Trout River.

Kiki leaned toward the computer, watching the monitor.

"How will you know exactly where Bella's raft overturned?"

Reese increased the magnification until it reached the highest level. "There are some specific landmarks along the riverbank that I remember. Alex, the river guide, and Ian pointed them out."

Kiki peered closer. "You can see all the mountains, along with nooks and crannies of the land. Creeks, rivers, towns, and landmarks—it's incredible."

"It really is," Reese agreed. "This technology has been around for a while, and we used something similar when I was with the DPD, but I've never thought to look into online resources."

"There's the Trout River," Kiki said, pointing to the screen.

In the date range chart, Reese typed in the day of the accident. When the site refreshed, she located the Moose Rafting Company on the map, then followed along the snaking waterway to the cove area where Alex said all rafts start their journey.

"What exactly are we looking for?"

"I'm not sure, but take note of anything that might seem out of place," Reese said.

"Got it." Kiki continued peering at the landmarks.

"There's the road that follows along beside the river," Reese said as she slowly moved south in the direction the raft traveled. "You can see the old narrow gauge railroad tracks along the other side, high up on the bank."

"This is so detailed," Kiki commented. "I would never have expected the site to have such good visuals."

"Ah, ha, there's the sandbar Alex said he navigated around, and the rock outcropping near where Bella fell off of the raft." Reese's blood tingled. "Alex said Bella floated away from them so fast, they couldn't fish her out of the water."

"Was it choppy?" Bella asked.

"Alex and Ian claim it wasn't."

Reese continued moving the curser south, closely studying tiny human images on watercraft moving downriver. The area was mostly surrounded by wilderness, a real backwoods region.

"What is that?" Kiki said, pointing toward a dull orange square nearly hidden by shrubs.

Hovering over the object, Reese pressed the right button of the mouse, which enabled her to increase the size again. She squinted at it, tilting her head this way and that.

"Looks like the front of a pickup," Reese commented.

"How strange, it's parked out in the middle of nowhere," Kiki said. "Do you think somebody abandoned an old junker out there?"

"Could be," Reese said. "Let's see if it they dumped it recently or if it's been there a while."

She typed in the date before the accident, and the truck was still there. Then she typed in the date before that, and it didn't appear on the map. That spot had remained vacant until the day before the accident, when the orange truck appeared. Reese next typed in the date after Bella's accident, and the truck had disappeared.

"What do you suppose that means?" Kiki asked.

"Not sure," Reese said, curiosity prickling in her brain.

"Could be coincidence," Kiki suggested.

"Right," Reese added, ruminating about the various possibilities.

Kiki leaned back. "I suppose we shouldn't read too much into it. That truck could have been parked there by anyone for any reason."

"Either way, it's a good detail to keep in mind," Reese said. "This is how investigations go—you gather up all the clues, like puzzle pieces even if they don't make sense at first. Later on, hopefully, you can fit them all together into a big picture."

Reese located Ford's service station on the map the day he was assaulted. There wasn't much movement around his place, solidifying her theory that he didn't have too many visitors. A few vehicles came and went, along with several people.

"The figures are too tiny to identify," Reese said.

"It didn't hurt to have a look," Kiki said.

"Thanks for the peppermint oil," Reese said.

She reached into her back pocket, pulled out enough money for the oil and paid Kiki, then walked with her friend to the front door.

Once Kiki drove away in her Honda CRV, Reese returned to her office.

Holding her chin, Reese studied her evidence board, which had begun to come alive with yellow sticky notes bearing different ideas and theories about how Bella had died, and who might have attacked Ford.

Was it someone he knew? Had a customer become angry with him?

Reese wrote her thoughts on a sticky note and put them on her board. Her head began to pound with all of her wild ideas and assumptions. Massaging her temples, she shut down her computer, switched off the lights to her office and headed into the kitchen.

Bo wound his way around her feet, meowing loudly, switching his tail back and forth. Lord have mercy, Reese was guilty of not feeding him his wet food on time.

"I know, I'm a bad cat mama," she said. "Shoot me at sunrise."

Pulling out a can of seafood delight, she scooped some of the glop into his dish, effectively squelching his hissy fit. He hunkered down and began consuming his fishy supper.

The local news on TV finished and now some detective show was on the air. Amazing, Reese thought, how much time she could kill when she went off on a tangent and began a bout of online surfing. She put a plastic lid on the rest of the cat food and slid it into the refrigerator. Then she cleaned up her half-eaten dinner and dampened a dish cloth which she used to wipe off her counters.

By now, Bo was meticulously washing his paws.

"You're happy as a clam, aren't you?" she told him as she switched off the lights and headed into her bedroom.

Bo trotted past her and jumped on the bed's colorful patchwork quilt her grandmother had stitched. He curled up, then stared at her, waiting for her to join him.

"Not yet, buddy," she said. "I've got to get ready for the SBC meeting. Maybe somebody will mention Ford and they'll all start talking about him. I wonder if one of the members has a gripe with him. What do you think?"

Bo yawned, put his head down on her pillow and closed his eyes.

Reese chuckled. "You're a lot of help."

Chapter Fourteen

Dressed in a cream-colored blazer, a black top, black jeans and of course, her cowboy boots and hat, Reese drove over to the Chamber of Commerce. In front of the renovated stone train depot, where the Chamber and a couple other businesses were housed, she parked.

Grabbing her purse, she headed inside and took the elevator to the third floor. Once she got to the large meeting room, which by now was filled with other small business members seated in metal folding chairs, she glanced around.

A buzz of conversation filled the air as people spoke animatedly with each other. The air conditioner must have been on the fritz because it was warm and sticky. Some of the ladies fanned themselves and most of the men had removed their ties.

At the front of the room, Kelly Waters, the president of the Small Business Council, shuffled papers on a lectern. She owned a nail salon, the best in town as far as Reese was concerned, and her perfectly polished red nails flashed in the fluorescent lighting.

With the intention of mingling, Reese found a place to sit by several other folks, including bespectacled Henrietta Fletcher, who owned a local flower shop. Ben Crockett, a strapping fellow, who owned a lumber and hardware store that had been in business more than 50 years, sat next to her. Nearby, tall, slim and gray-haired Sarah Jane Owens dominated the conversation by talking about the new cotton fabric she'd just received for her quilting store.

"Hi," Reese said as she lowered down in a chair next to Sarah Jane.

All three turned to stare at her with questioning gazes.

"I'm a newer member," she quickly explained, shaking everyone's hands. "Reese Golden, private investigator. I started my business a little over six months ago."

"Ah, yes," Ben said. "Welcome."

"It's good you could attend," Sarah Jane added.

"How nice you managed to make it tonight," Henrietta added. "Let's see, when did we see you last?"

"A few months ago," Reese said, definitely feeling a twinge of guilt. "I've had a lot going on."

"I suppose that's what we all want, dear," Sarah Jane said, patting Reese's hand. "Plenty of customers coming through our doors."

"If I could have everyone's attention, please," Kelly spoke in a loud voice. "I'd like to get this meeting started so we can take care of the matters at hand and get home to our families."

Murmurs of agreement floated throughout the room and people settled in their chairs.

"Tonight, we're finalizing the preparations for our small business showcase slated to be held September 20th in the rec center gym."

"That's a Saturday, isn't it?" someone asked.

"Yes," Kelly confirmed.

"I've got a question," a man said as he stood.

Reese recognized him—Derek Washington, who was married to Clara Washington, the Fellowship Church choir director. Clara had been a close friend of Bella's.

"Yes, Derek, what is it?" Kelly asked.

"Ford Presley had signed up for a table with me," Derek said. "I'm paying my half tonight, but since Ford's in the hospital, can I just go ahead and pay for the entire table and use it to advertise my convenience store?"

Kelly hesitated for a moment, then said, "Ford will probably be better by September. If not, let me check with Naomi to see what she'd like us to do."

"But why can't I just—"

"That's my decision, Derek," Kelly said in a curt tone. "If Naomi's not interested, I'll offer the other half of your table to another council member."

Derek's face clouded over and he knitted his brow.

"Did you have any other questions?"

"No," he growled.

Throughout the rest of the meeting, Reese darted glances toward Derek, noting his foul mood. She sensed his dissatisfaction about Kelly's decision, and she wanted to visit with him after the meeting. Hopefully, it wouldn't go on and on, since the room temperature soared like an oven and she felt like a chocolate bar melting over a fire.

To Reese's relief, the session ended before long. Everyone, including Kelly, seemed ready to get out of this hot box and they hustled toward the door. Reese walked out with the crowd, looking for Derek. She saw him standing beside a sidewalk bench, smoking.

"Hi Derek," she said as she made her way toward him.

"Reese," he said with a nod. "Long time, no see."

"I manage to keep myself busy," she said.

Derek took another drag on his cigarette.

"You sounded upset about Kelly's decision," she commented.

"Stubborn woman," he said. "I should have that table to myself. I deserve it."

"Why do you say that?"

"I've had my gas station and convenience store much longer than Ford, almost 15 years. Ford's place has only been around for a few years. I warned him we were too close to maintain good cash flow. I don't like having to share customers, you know?"

"Is it really that big of a problem?"

"Yeah, it is," Derek said. He took a long drag on his cigarette, then exhaled a cloud of smoke. "Once the old guy started up, my gas sales fell along with my other revenue."

"I'm sorry to hear that," Reese said, her suspicions about Derek increasing.

"It really sucks. I wish he'd retire or..." Derek fell silent.

Reese studied Derek in a different light. Had he been so jealous of Ford that he'd beat him up? She realized business competitors often went to battle, but she'd never considered Derek to be a vindictive person. Nevertheless, the possibility existed.

"Derek, you didn't take out your frustrations on Ford, did you?"

He dropped his cigarette butt and smashed it beneath his heel. "What the hell? Are you accusing me of beating up Ford and putting him in the hospital?"

"What were you doing the afternoon he was attacked?"

He scowled at her. "What's it to you?"

"I'm working with the police on Ford's case."

"I can't believe you'd suspect me," he said, and gave a dramatic sigh. "The kids had a play that afternoon at their vacation Bible school. Clara insisted that I attend. So, you can get that filthy idea out of your head."

"I need to talk to Clara to verify your alibi."

"Be my guest. She's at the church running a choir practice. You'll be able to catch up with her there."

"Why are they practicing this late?"

"They're holding a dress rehearsal for their performance at the Presley's candlelight vigil tonight."

"I see, thanks Derek."

"You're not welcome." Derek spun around and headed toward an older model car. He got in, slammed the door and sped away.

"I probably won't win too many friends and influence many people in town," Reese said as she walked to her truck. In her line of work, she had to be nosy.

At least Betty never judged her.

• • •

Reese stopped at the Fill-and-Go gas station. She didn't need fuel, but she needed something to snack on and a drink. Inside, she searched the aisles stuffed with sugary and salty items, selecting a small bag of peanuts. She grabbed a diet soft drink from the refrigerator section and paid for everything at the counter.

After a sip of the beverage to wet her parched throat, she drove over a couple of streets to the church and parked in front of the white clapboard building with green trim around the stained glass arched windows.

Hopping out of the truck and walking toward the green double doors, Reese recalled attending services here as a child. She'd always felt safe and protected within the church's sheltering walls—especially positioned beside her family.

Brimming with nostalgia, she entered the vestibule and basked in the sound of the choir drifting through the air. Trained from a young age to be reverent and respectful inside the house of worship, she stepped softly across the tile floor.

A wall decal above a matching blue couch and chairs declared, "Welcome friends, enter with praise and joyous thanksgiving." Beneath it sat a small table holding a lovely floral arrangement and a candle on a mirror.

Pushing through another set of double doors, Reese entered the chapel, which held wooden pews on either side of the aisle. Since it wasn't quite dark yet, dusky light poured through a large round, stained glass window on the back wall that depicted saints and angels. Six large antique pendant lights on chains suspended from the ceiling, giving off a soft glow.

Constructed in the late 1800s, the church projected a comfortable, worshipful feeling and it had a rich history. Local lore claimed that a famous gunslinger had been married here, then had gone up to Deadwood, South Dakota, to gamble. Unfortunately, he'd run into trouble when he'd stolen a horse. Back then, justice was swift, and he'd met his maker after swinging from the gallows.

Church members in black slacks and white tops stood on a dais in the sanctuary, their voices harmonized in a worshipful tune. Dressed in identical attire, her brown hair pulled up in a bun, Clara stood in front of them, hands raised as she directed the music. Another choir member sat at a piano providing an accompanying melody.

Reese had done plenty of growing up within these walls, and she decided it was high time that she attend Sunday services more often, at least to honor her mother and grandmothers' wishes. Sliding into one of the pews, she sat down. After the crazy happenings of daily life, this was a place to come and relax, and to embrace the knowledge that a greater power presided over the world.

"Okay everyone," Clara said, let's take a 15-minute break."

The choir stopped singing and Reese watched as people stepped off the dais, talking to each other. Just then, Clara turned around and noticed Reese. With a smile and a little wave, she approached her.

"How are you doing, Reese?"

Reese stood and smiled. "Since the roof of the church didn't cave in, I suppose I'm safe and sound. But I managed to piss off your husband earlier."

"How?"

"At the SBC meeting, I asked him what he was doing the day Ford Presley was assaulted. Derek isn't too happy with the competition Ford's store is giving his place."

"Derek was with me at the kids' vacation Bible school performance." Clara gave her a puzzled look.

"That's what he said."

Reese wondered if there would ever come a day that she would settle down and have kids. Considering her current status, it seemed like a farfetched idea. But who knew what the future may hold?

Clara raised her brows. "Why in the world would you think my Derek would have anything to do with assaulting Ford Presley?"

"I'm working with the police to try and track down Ford's assailant. Since Derek and Ford have bad blood between them, I had to ask."

"What did Derek say that made you question his integrity?"

"He mentioned being irritated that Ford set up shop so close to his store. Says his income's dropped."

"That's true," Clara said. "But we're making out fine. There's a little less wiggle room in our budget."

"Sorry to hear that."

"Like I said, we're making out fine. Derek might be a hot head at times, but he'd never do something terrible like beating up an old man."

"Give him my apologies," Reese said.

"By the way, how did you know I was here?" Clara arched her brows.

Reese took a seat on the bench. "Derek mentioned it. Along with verifying Derek's whereabouts the day Ford was attacked, I wanted to ask you a couple of questions about Bella Northwood."

Clara sank down beside Reese, her expression grim. "I'm just sick about what happened. It's so unfair. She was taken too young."

"I'm sad, too," Reese said.

"Why are you asking about Bella?"

"I'm helping the local PD with Bella's accident report," Reese responded.

"What do you need from me?"

"When I talked with Alex Huckman, the owner of the Grizzly Rafting Company, he mentioned that Bella had taken other rafting trips," Reese said. "He said your choir group went on one last summer and two this summer."

"That's true," Clara said. "Bella loved rafting and she was always willing to help anyone who seemed anxious. She'd take the extra time to go over the rules and explain safety features."

"Why did you choose to bond over rafting adventures?"

"They're fun trips and they build camaraderie. We're asked to do a lot of performances around town, including for our church, and it gets intense sometimes. This helps us blow off steam."

"Why did you choose Huckman's rafting company? There are others around here."

"All of them offer the same type of experiences," Clara said. "I love those cute bears on the building. I suppose that's what attracted me."

"So, except for the bears, Alex's company was a random choice."

"Yes."

"What was your first thought when you saw Bella go overboard?"

"I was in a different raft, so it was a second or two before I realized she'd fallen in. I could hardly believe it, but I felt certain she'd be all right. At first." Clara sighed, and her eyes glimmered with tears. "It turned into a nightmare."

"You two were good friends, weren't you?"

"Yes." She brushed a piece of lint from her dark slacks. "We've been besties since we were kids. I'm having a hard time with this. I miss her."

"Do you know if Bella was having any problems in her life before her accident?"

"If she was, she didn't confide in me," Clara said. "Although a part of her always seemed sad. When she came to my house for dinner and hung out with Derek and me and the kids, she was, well, I guess you could call it wistful. I always figured she was trying to decide about having kids herself."

"Did she visit you at home frequently?"

"No. We mostly went to lunch after choir practice. We did charity work together and she was devoted to her painting."

"Who do you think would want to hurt Bella's dad?" Reese asked.

"Gosh, I have no clue, but I pray for him every night." Clara clasped her knees as she glanced toward the ceiling. "I remember a couple of weeks ago Bella mentioned she and her dad were hanging one of her paintings in the downtown gallery. This guy came by and said he wanted to buy it right then and there."

"That was good, right?"

"Not really. When Bella gave him a price, he started shouting that it was highway robbery. She wouldn't go lower, so he made a scene. Willow, the gallery owner, threatened to call the police, but Bella's dad said he'd handle it. When Ford tried to get him to leave, the guy decked him. Gave him a black eye. It was awful."

Reese pulled out her notebook. "Did Bella mention the guy's name?"

"No. Willow might know. You could ask her."

"I'll do that," Reese said as she stuffed the notebook back in her purse.

Clara sighed heavily. "Do you think Bell...well, do you think she let herself drown?"

"I can't say."

"Lord rest her soul," Clara murmured. "You know, last time Bella came to dinner, she gave me a small journal. Hold on and let me go get it, it's in my bag."

Clara walked up to the lectern and grabbed a black leather purse, which she carried back to the pew and then sat down. She reached inside and fished out a small notebook with a red leather cover and handed it to Reese.

"It's full of doodles and poetry," Clara said as she rifled through the pages. "Bella felt things deeply. I'm not really into poetry, so I have no idea what any of it means. It's beautiful, though."

"Lots of people keep journals," Reese said as Clara handed the book to her. "Maybe it helped her see life clearer."

"I've been so busy I haven't studied it much. Maybe you'll find a passage that foreshadows her accident. If she was in a dark place, it's possible she hinted why."

Reese flipped through several pages, briefly glancing at the random drawings and poems before she dropped the journal into her purse. She noticed some intriguing passages, but needed to get going.

"Thanks for letting me look at this," Reese said. "I'll go through it as soon as I have the chance."

Clara stood. "Everyone in the choir should be returning soon—we're only on a break. If you find anything buried in those poems, let me know."

"I'll see you at the candlelight vigil. I can tell your performance will be awesome."

Clara smiled at the compliment, then returned to the sanctuary. Reese left the church, eager for the chance to look through the journal. It might allow her a glimpse of Bella's world.

For some reason, she realized that her interest in Bella's death wasn't only meant for the police accident report. It had become personal, especially since she continued having strange dreams and hearing Bella's pleas for help.

Why was she so fixated on her friend's drowning?

Chapter Fifteen

The next morning, Reese crawled out of bed, put on her running gear and jogged toward the park. The warmth of the day began to soar as the sun rose higher in the pink and orange clouds of the eastern, wildfire-hazed horizon.

As her feet pounded the pavement, her mind began to churn. Although the emerald green lawn, shrubs, and late summer flowers filled her vision with beauty, she was preoccupied. Her mind cluttered with potential motives as to why someone would attack Ford.

Finishing her run, Reese returned home, showered, then dressed in jeans, her boots, and a black and white bandana halter top. It wasn't the typical attire she preferred for work, but considering the heat, she wanted to dress light.

In the kitchen, she slipped her cell phone from her purse and called Jeremy, but he didn't answer, so she left him a message telling him that today, she planned on looking into leads on suspects in Ford's assault. She poured herself a glass of orange juice and drank it, instead of her typical coffee. The idea of consuming something steaming hot didn't appeal to her, even though she'd miss the caffeine.

Withdrawing the journal from her purse, she read several of Bella's rhyming verses. Page after page, she delved into her friend's deepest thoughts and desires. Appreciation for Bella's artistic talent also expanded as she studied the intricate doodles and swirls.

Bo slunk out of the bedroom, yawned and meowed for his breakfast. Reese fed him, watching in amusement as he gobbled up the food in his dish. Finished, the furball jumped up onto the window ledge to observe the outdoor kingdom brimming with birds, dogs, people, and passing cars.

Reese glanced at her watch, realizing she needed to get going. In her office, she dropped Bella's journal on her desk, intending to delve into it as soon as she got the chance. She headed out to the kitchen where she grabbed her oversize handbag and keys.

When her cell phone rang, she stopped to answer it. "Hello?"

"Hi, it's Ian."

"Hi, there. By the way, how's your dad doing?"

"Not so good. The doctors put him in an induced coma," he said.

"Wow, I'm so sorry this is happening."

"He's got brain swelling from his injuries and supposedly this treatment will reduce the risk of brain damage."

"What does your mom think?" Reese said.

"She believes it'll help. With her medical background, she'd know."

"I'm sure she does," Reese said.

"You'll be at the candlelight vigil tonight, won't you?"

"Of course," she said. "At 7 p.m., right?"

"In the Meadowlark Valley Park. We're gathering near the new stone water fountain the Faye family donated."

"I thought it was going to be at the Fellowship Church," Reese said.

"It was, but we decided the park would be better. Bella and Dad," Ian choked up, then cleared his throat. "They both enjoyed being outside. As a family, we all loved hunting, fishing, hiking..."

"And when your dad is better, I'm sure he'll be back slugging away in the great outdoors once again," Reese said.

"I hope you're right," he said. "Detective Savage mentioned that you're helping the police look for suspects in his attack."

"That's right," she said.

"I sure hope you find the S.O.B."

"I'm doing my best," Reese said.

"We'll see you later, then," Ian said. "We plan to keep the vigil short and sweet."

"Good idea," Reese said. "That'll be easier for you all."

Reese clicked off her cell and dropped it in her purse. She glanced one more time at Bo perched by the window. "No wild adventures in toilet paper unrolling again, okay, buddy?"

He studied her with his steady green eyes, his ears twitching.

Shaking her head as she left the house, Reese figured the little brat had devious plans on his mind. She'd probably come home to a toilet paper-palooza.

• • •

Reese wanted to talk to Willow about the man who had attacked Ford. She drove over to the Clay Art Gallery; an old red brick building decorated with white gingerbread details. It had been built around 1880 for a railroad executive and his family. A couple of other families owned it after that, then it became a boarding house and finally a four-plex apartment where a budding movie actress had been murdered in the 1990s.

Just a kid when it happened, the story had haunted Reese for a long time. It still chilled her to the bone thinking about it.

Years passed and eventually the home fell into disrepair. Willow Fisher, an artist from northern Wyoming, moved to Meadowlark Valley, purchased and renovated the property, and turned it into an art gallery. Currently it housed artwork from local and regional artists—paintings, sculptures, wooden carvings, and ceramic pottery.

After climbing out of her truck, Reese walked onto the large, old-fashioned porch and stepped inside the gallery. Polished wooden floors sparkled beneath the bright lights that showcased walls covered with paintings. Shelves displayed ceramic bowls and jugs, along with bronze sculptures. Soft music danced on the air, offering a relaxed atmosphere.

Reese recognized Willow standing in a corner of the room, talking to a short, stocky man in a dark suit. She didn't want to interrupt, so she browsed, admiring the artwork until she found one of Bella's newer paintings.

Dated from a week ago, right before Bella drowned, it depicted a cabin surrounded by lush woodland. It was spectacular, but off to the right, a raging fire moved through the forest, turning the trees into blackened stubs and ravaging anything in its path.

"Hmm," Reese muttered, noting a recent change in Bella's art. She'd seemed troubled of late. What had happened recently to alter her mood?

Reese remembered attending Bella's wedding to Hunter last month. Had she changed her mind about that decision? Was there trouble in paradise?

"I'm probably grasping at straws," Reese whispered. Bella was most likely trying a different style of painting in order to spread her wings artistically.

Bella, I hope you're at peace, she thought.

Each painting price ranged from around $500 to $1,000, depending on their size. Other artwork within the gallery had similar prices. Why had that man that had punched Ford been so upset? Why had he insisted that Bella discount a painting just for him?

"Hello, may I help you?"

Reese turned to see Willow, a tall, slender woman in billowing gray slacks and a bohemian floral print top. With her slender hands, long red nails, and shoulder-length black hair streaked with gray, she looked like a striking piece of art.

From newspaper articles and photographs of the gallery, Reese had become familiar with Willow. She didn't know the woman personally, though.

"I'm admiring Bella Northwood's paintings."

"She is a talented gal, isn't she?"

"Definitely," Reese said.

"It's such a shame she's no longer with us," Willow commented. "You've heard about her rafting misfortune, haven't you?"

Reese nodded. "I'm working with the police on her accident report."

"A gruesome task." Willow gave Reese a puzzled look. "One hates to be so crass about the situation, but why you?"

"I'm a private investigator."

"I wasn't aware we had anyone in town who did that sort of work."

"I'm actually a native of Meadowlark Valley," Reese said. "I moved back home from Denver to start my business."

"And you're interested in Bella's work?"

"We went to high school together."

"My, my. We've lost a great talent full of imagination and creative ability." Pointing at Bella's collection of paintings, Willow added, "She'd only recently begun to express in her work both the light and the dark side of life—the yin and yang of how the world revolves."

"Do you think she depicted what was reflected in her personal life or simply life in general?"

Willow held her chin as she studied the paintings. "It may be both. Only Bella would have been able to tell you that."

"Was Bella's work popular?"

"Very. People came from miles around to buy her paintings." Willow chuckled. "Bella made a small killing with her sales. I used to tease her that my percentage would help fund my retirement."

They both smiled.

"Do you recall one customer who recently came in here and made a scene? He wanted to purchase one of Bella's paintings and objected to the price. Her father tried to escort him outside and the guy decked him."

"I remember that! It was frightening and I feared the man would pull out a gun. Why he became so violent, I'll never comprehend."

"Did you know him?

Willow shook her head. "I believe he mentioned he was from back east."

"He didn't give his name?"

"Not a syllable. He mentioned he was just browsing."

Well, darn, Reese thought. She'd hoped to get a lead on a possible suspect in Ford's recent assault. So much for her visit to the gallery. It had, however, given her an idea of Bella's mindset at the time of her death.

It didn't matter for the accident report, but it mattered to her. By all accounts, it seemed Bella had been deeply disturbed by something happening in her life.

"I appreciate your time," Reese told Willow.

"Of course, dear. I've got some paperwork to do, but please, enjoy yourself among all of this creative energy." Willow swept her hand around the room, then headed toward a counter.

Reese wandered through the gallery a while longer, then left and headed home. Her stomach growled. She felt starved for some annoying reason. Maybe it was because sometimes she got so preoccupied with work that she forgot to eat.

The Western Moon Café offered the best food in town, as far as Reese's appetite was concerned, so she decided to stop and grab a bite.

She parked in front of the building and strode inside the establishment, decorated with antique kerosene lamps, wagon wheels, and numerous Wyoming-themed items like stuffed jackalopes and mounted pronghorn antelope heads.

A hostess wearing jeans, a white blouse and a tan apron bearing the café logo greeted her and led her to one of the booths.

"I already know what I want," Reese told her. "Your Jackrabbit Special."

The girl nodded. "I'll let the kitchen know you'll have the cheeseburger and onion rings."

"Perfect," Reese said, her stomach giving another growl.

Since the café didn't have many customers, it wasn't long before the waitress, also wearing a tan apron and similar attire as the hostess, brought her food on a thick crockery plate. As Reese began eating her meal, she felt guilty for consuming so many calories, yet the tasty satisfaction seemed worth it. After all, it wasn't that often she came here and indulged.

Country music filled the air as she studied the tidy surroundings dotted with potted ivy plants and ferns. Eventually, her gaze landed on the painting hanging by her table. It featured a caramel-colored prairie with patches of green around a red barn in the distance.

Low hills provided a backdrop, with purple mountains behind them. Fluffy white clouds floated through a blue sky. Reese appreciated the serene setting and how it captured a typical lazy summer day. The artist's signature caught her eye—Bella. An older painting, she realized, spotting the date from a couple of years ago.

Reese finished her dinner, and signaled the waitress for her ticket.

"Here you go, hon," the waitress said as she stopped by Reese's table and plopped down a piece of paper.

Glancing at the tag on her blouse, Reese noticed her name was Lois.

"Thanks, Lois," Reese said, handing her enough money to cover the bill and then some. "Please keep the change."

"Thank you, that's very generous."

Reese nodded toward the painting. "This is nice."

"I love Bella's paintings, too," Lois said. "She's a local artist, you know. When the café owner redecorated this place a few years ago, she purchased that painting from the Clay Gallery here in town. And you just watch, Bella's paintings will skyrocket in price. That's always what happens when artists die."

"It really does," Reese said.

"I'm so sad about her accident. How awful for her family."

"No doubt," Reese agreed.

"I can't believe someone beat up Bella's father the day after she died," Lois commented. "So badly the poor old guy's in the hospital."

"Do you have any idea who'd do such a thing?"

Lois glanced around, probably to make certain her co-workers or the owner didn't notice her lingering. Obviously, she didn't want to get in trouble.

"Ford Presley likes to go out drinking Saturday nights," Lois said in a conspiratorial tone. "I heard that he'd get to talking about Vietnam and how all wars are started by bureaucrats who know nothing about military strategy. His ramblings irritated lots of people and he got into it with some of the customers."

"Bar fights?"

She nodded. "Always at the VFW Post. Then he'd come home sloppy drunk and poor Naomi, his wife, would have to put up with him."

"Do you know Naomi?"

"She's a friend of mine. Comes in here sometimes after her hospital shifts for coffee and pie. Once in a while Ford meets her here, too."

"Did Naomi ever mention who Ford fought with?"

Lois scratched her cheek. "Let's see, right off the top of my head I can't recall. I'd have to think on that a bit."

Reese reached into her purse, fished out a business card and handed it to Lois. "If you remember, let me know."

"Sure, sure," Lois agreed.

As Reese left the café, she decided she had a great opportunity to talk to Naomi about Ford's bar fights at the candlelight vigil. How interesting, she thought. Ford's family had made him sound like a guy who wouldn't irritate anyone or make enemies.

Apparently, that wasn't the case.

Meanwhile, she headed over to the VFW post. Hopefully someone over there would remember Ford's altercations and who he had rumbled with.

Chapter Sixteen

The VFW post was located on the southern side of town, actually in the county, so the city's no smoking regulation didn't apply. As she walked into the darkened bar, smoke swirled around her and her nostrils filled with tobacco aroma.

It was still early in the evening, so there were only a few customers at the tables. One guy played on a pinball machine, a cigarette hanging out of his mouth. A woman and a man stood on either end of a Foosball Table, flipping the handles and making tons of racket.

The bartender, a tall, heavyset fellow with a balding head, stood polishing the counter with a white towel. No one was seated there except for one guy on a corner stool nursing a mixed drink and reading the paper. Reese headed over and ordered a beer.

When he returned with a cold can, she handed him a twenty and told him to keep the change.

"That's mighty generous," he said.

"Would you mind answering a few questions for me?" Reese asked.

"Depends," he said.

"What do you know about Ford Presley?"

"Comes here every Saturday night. I suppose since he's in the hospital, it might be a while before he stops by again."

Reese sipped her beer, then asked, "Can you think of anyone who might have put him there?"

"He had a few brawls in here." He flipped the towel over his shoulder. "Nothing serious."

"Who did he fight with?"

"A few different guys over the years, but they shook hands and made up afterward. Why are you askin' all these questions?"

"I'm helping the police try and find his assailant. We can't have people like that running loose in the streets, beating people up within an inch of their lives."

"Yeah, I get it. But here, we take care of each other here. We're all brothers."

"If one of your brothers is having an anger issue, wouldn't you want to help him?"

The bartender began polishing the counter again.

"What's your name, sir?" Reese asked.

"Frank."

"Frank, I understand what PTS can do to a person."

"That so?"

Reese nodded.

"Are you a vet?" He narrowed his gaze at her.

"No. I'm a former police officer. Shot on duty. That stuff can mess with your mind."

"That's a damn fact."

"Please help me, can you think of anyone that might have taken an argument too far with Ford? Maybe lost control and couldn't stop punching?"

The bartender shook his head. "Not anymore."

"Why's that?"

"Buck Kirkbride was a hothead and both him 'n Ford got into it a lot. Both served in 'Nam and they didn't always see eye to eye." The bartender wiped his nose on the back of his hand. "Buck's dead now. Probably been a month since we put him in the ground."

"My condolences," Reese said.

"We all gotta go sometime," he said.

"Nobody since Buck died has had a fight with Ford?"

"Nope. It's pretty tame in here since old Buck went to glory. God rest his soul."

When a guy came in and sat down at the bar, Frank met her gaze. "I gotta get back to work now. Do ya mind?"

"I really appreciate you talking to me," she said.

He winked at her, then turned and walked toward his new customer.

Reese left the VFW, her suspect list still empty.

• • •

After driving home, Reese showered quickly and put on a sundress and sandals, wanting to appear in fresher condition for the candlelight vigil. She hurried out the door and hustled toward the park. It was a short walk from her house to the Faye family's stone water fountain, which they had donated to the park in memory of an elderly pet that had died.

Picking up her pace, she walked down the sidewalk past groves of trees, flower beds, and swing sets until she reached her destination. A haze of smoke obscured the sky, and she frowned as tiny flakes of ash drifted onto her eyelashes. The sun's brilliance was obscured, like someone had draped a curtain across it.

Although the wildfires were burning hundreds of miles to the south, communities far away from the danger were still being plagued by the fallout. Unsettled by the ashes floating around, Reese continued toward her destination.

A large group had already gathered around three large upright stones with circulating water bubbling from the top. The fountain design reminded Reese of the United Kingdom's Stonehenge, albeit on a much smaller scale.

Tall ornamental grass and plants surrounded the feature, with a collection of rocks mounded at the base. The bubbling sound provided a comforting lull, although it brought to mind the Trout River where Bella had drowned.

Dismissing that unpleasant thought, Reese edged toward the people, who were speaking in hushed tones to one another, some sobbing, as they held small, battery-operated candles. The church choir had gathered and the members sang a soft, touching religious melody, very appropriate for the event.

A folding table covered with a white tablecloth held a large portrait of Bella, along with several small, framed snapshots—high school graduation, her wedding, and one with her singing in the church choir. Clustered around the table legs were colorful stuffed animals and flower bouquets that people had offered in remembrance.

Kiki hustled toward her. "I almost thought you weren't coming," she said.

"I got held up," Reese said.

"Thanks for being here," Ian said as he came up beside them and handed them each a candle.

Reese clicked on the light.

Kiki flipped on hers as well.

"With the dry, fire conditions, we didn't want to use real ones," he explained in a sober tone.

"These are perfect," Reese said.

"Yes, a great idea," Kiki added.

He smiled sadly, then continued working his way through the family's collection of friends, acquaintances and loved ones, to hand out the flickering lights. He stopped briefly now and then to converse with them. Reese noticed Naomi mingling with the attendees, along with Hunter.

Before long, the group covered a large portion of the lawn. When Ian ran out of flameless candles, people produced their cell phones and flipped on the flashlight feature. It wouldn't be dark for a while yet, but the glow illuminated the smoky surroundings.

Naomi, Ian, and Hunter moved to the front of the crowd and stood beside the fountain. Ian hugged Naomi, who had red-rimmed eyes. Hunter disappeared for a moment, then returned carrying a sapling and a shovel.

When the choir stopped singing, Hunter spoke.

"We received permission from the park to plant this tree in Bella's honor," he said as he began digging a hole. The crowd murmured with agreement and several folks clapped.

Ian came forward and cleared his throat. "Thank you everyone for coming and we appreciate those of you who have helped us during this ordeal. It's overwhelming to see so many of you out here showing your support. And just so you know, search and rescue has…has called off their efforts to find Bella."

Disappointed sighs erupted from the crowd.

"How's your dad?" a man asked.

"He's still in a coma," Ian returned in a tired voice.

"I know your dad, and he's an ornery old coot," another man called out. "He'll be on his feet real soon, just wait and see."

Polite laughter drifted through the crowd. Naomi and Ian smiled, watching as Hunter shoveled in the last dirt on the tree, then tamped it down with one foot.

"It's comforting to know my sister had an impact on so many..." Ian's voice faltered and he studied the ground, appearing to take a moment to gather his thoughts. "Bella had such enthusiasm for life. I can still hear her joyful laughter and I'll always remember her spirit and kind heart. And my dad, I pray he'll recover and come back to us."

"Amen," the crowd uttered.

Kiki looped her elbow through Reese's arm, and they leaned against each other.

"May Bella rest in peace," Kiki whispered.

"Rest in peace," Reese repeated.

"None of this feels real," Ian continued. "Let's focus on how passionate Bella was about art and about the people in this community. She offered so much to the world, even though her life was cut short. We'll miss her, but please, let's honor her memory by loving one another and by spreading kindness."

Naomi opened her mouth, but it seemed difficult for her to form words. Finally, she said, "I believe there are many of you who would like to share a favorite memory of Bella, and offer hopes for Ford's recovery. When you're ready, please speak up."

The crowd murmured with agreement.

"I'll go first." Naomi cleared her throat and resumed speaking. "It goes without saying that Ford is the love of my life and I want him to come back to me. Ford and I met when Bella was 4, and I remember her as this quiet little girl. She was so shy and timid, but once she realized I wasn't going to bite..." the crowd chuckled, "she warmed up to me and we had the best times together. Besides the day Ford and I were married, the happiest day in my life was when Bella finally called me Mama."

Naomi broke down crying, and others began to sniffle as well. Ian wrapped her in his arms, and she rested her head on his shoulder.

A lady from the crowd came up to the front, sniffed, and began to speak. "I remember when Bella and I met at church a few years ago..."

After she spoke, numerous community members came up to the front to share their memories about Bella and offer their prayers for Ford's recovery. Reese felt touched, but she also had questions for Naomi.

"I'm going to mingle," Reese told Kiki after folks had finished sharing their thoughts.

"Good idea," Kiki said.

Reese strolled over to the shrine people had assembled in Bella's honor, admiring the flowers and stuffed animals.

A fair-haired little boy came up beside her, clutching a teddy bear and staring tearfully at Bella's portrait. "I'm so sad about Miss Bella. She's the best swimming teacher. I don't think I can learn now."

"You were lucky to have her, but I'm certain you'll get a new teacher who can help you."

He offered a toothless grin. "I'm in the tadpole group."

"You are quite the swimmer," Reese said.

"There you are, Craig," a petite redhead said as she came up and took his hand. "You shouldn't wander off from mommy."

"I wanted to leave this for Miss Bella." He carefully added his fluffy brown teddy bear to those piled in front of the table.

"Come along now," his mother said. She smiled at Reese and walked away with her little boy in tow.

From the corner of her eye, Reese caught sight of a guy in jeans bearing a TV camera on his shoulder. Beside him, clutching a microphone, reporter Taryn Jones stood. She wore a black suit jacket, a white skirt, and low heels.

"We're here in Meadowlark Valley Park along with local citizens who have gathered at a candlelight vigil to honor Bella

Presley Northwood, a local artist who drowned in the Trout River during a church rafting trip."

Taryn wandered among the crowd members, interviewing Bella's friends and family. Her cameraman panned around, filming the memorial shrine and other sites.

Making certain to steer clear of the local media, Reese walked up to Naomi and hugged her. "How are you holding up?"

"I'm surviving," Naomi said, patting Reese's hand.

"I talked to Lois at the Western Moon Café today," Reese said. "I hate to bring it up at a time like this, but she mentioned Ford's drinking problem."

"That Lois, she's such a gossip," Naomi said with a sigh. "Ford drinks too much, I know."

"And gets into fights at the VFW?"

"Yes, God bless him." Naomi bowed her head for a moment. "I've done my best to help him curb his anger issues, but he's so hard headed."

"I was under the impression he didn't have any enemies," Reese said. "But maybe there are some you might know of."

"When old Buck died, the guy he fought the most with at the VFW, there's no one he really has a beef with." Naomi's brows shot up. "You know, our neighbor, Drew Sutherland, might wish him ill."

"Why?"

"It's an argument between them about a stupid tree, if you can believe it," Naomi said. "It straddles the property line between both of our places, but it's getting old and Drew thinks it ought to be cut down. Says it's a hazard when the wind blows, which is practically all the time. He's afraid it's going to fall and damage his roof. Ford refuses to listen, so every time they see each other, they argue."

"That's not good," Reese said.

"Drew doesn't seem to be the type to attack someone," Naomi said.

"You never know," Reese said. "Are there any other incidents you'd like to share with me about Ford and his possible enemies?"

"What's this about Dad and his enemies?" Ian asked as he came over to stand by Naomi.

"Reese is investigating who might have hurt your dad. I mentioned the ongoing argument with him and our next-door neighbor, Drew."

"That damn tree nonsense," Ian said, hooking his thumbs in his belt loops. "I'd like to chop it down in the middle of the night and be done with it. They're both behaving like a couple of kids."

"That would make Drew happy, but your dad would be livid."

"Yeah, I know." Ian resettled his Stetson.

"If you think of anyone else who has an axe to grind with Ford, let me know," Reese told both Naomi and her son. "Don't rule out a single person."

"Sure, Reese," Ian said.

Reese visited with a few more people, then walked over to where Hunter stood. "The tree you planted is a lovely touch," she told him.

"Uh, huh," he said.

"You and Bella were still honeymooners," Reese said. "Had you two even celebrated your one-month anniversary?"

"Last week," Hunter said.

"It's such a shame."

"Life isn't fair sometimes," Hunter said. "But we'll all get over it."

Get over it?

Taken aback by his comment, Reese studied him closer, noting he didn't seem terribly upset about losing his wife of only one month. Remembering how distracted and distant he'd been the last time she'd talked to him, she decided he must be type of person who managed to quell painful emotions.

Men, typically raised to hide their sadness, were often prone to such behavior.

"What are you going to tell the police about Bella's drowning?" Hunter's eyes narrowed.

"As far as I can tell, it was an accident."

"What about suspects in Ford's beating? Find any?"

"The investigation is ongoing."

"Humph," he said. "S'cuse me."

Hunter meandered through the crowd, occasionally stopping to talk with people.

Reese shook her head. No one could ever accuse Hunter Northwood of being a personable guy. What had Bella seen in him?

Chapter Seventeen

Reese mingled some more, then she noticed Hunter walk toward the center of the crowd where a tall gray-haired woman in a dark blue dress stood, along with a snowy haired gentleman wearing jeans and a western-cut shirt. A younger man stood nearby wearing similar attire. Both wore Stetsons.

It had been a long time since Reese had seen Hunter's parents. She'd forgotten what a striking couple they were. Hugh, Hunter's younger brother, had also come along to pay his respects. He resembled Hunter, but seemed a tad taller.

Pearl, Hunter's mother, pecked Hunter on the cheek and his father, Walt, patted his shoulder reassuringly. It seemed they'd been affected by the sudden death of their daughter-in-law. Reese had only considered the Presley's loss—she hadn't thought about how the Northwood family would handle the loss.

Pearl and Walt Northwood owned the Flying W Ranch in the northern part of the county, a spread that had been in their family for at least 100 years. A working ranch, they bred and raised their own cattle and large herds roamed freely over the grassy hills.

"I see Hunter's folks showed up," Kiki said as she eased toward Reese.

Reese nodded. "I imagine they are as upset about Bella as Hunter is."

"It seems that way," Kiki commented. "Since they are talking with each other, it seems he's gotten over being disinherited."

"What happened?" Reese met Kiki's gaze.

"It all went down when you were living in Denver," Kiki said. "It fed the rumor mills for months about how Pearl and Walt disinherited Hunter because he wasn't behaving the way they expected."

"What exactly did he do?"

"He went out drinking nearly every night and got into drugs. He refused to finish college or work on the ranch and basically sat around waiting for his parents to hand him everything he wanted. Eventually, they kicked him out and told him to make his own way."

"Wow, for a guy that's been given everything on a silver platter, that must have been rough."

"From what I understand, it was. But Pearl and Walt finally relented and gave him a small inheritance. That's when he got his life together and bought his sign company. When his first wife died, I heard he got some cash from her life insurance settlement, too."

"I didn't realize Hunter had been married before."

"Uh, huh, he was."

Wait, wasn't he supposed to inherit the ranch?"

"Rumor is that in their family trust, Pearl and Walt are leaving it to Hugh."

"Really?"

"Supposedly, they think Hunter's little bro, Hugh, is still more capable of running operations."

"This is all news to me," Reese said.

"Well, now you know the rest of the story, for what it's worth."

"How awful for Hunter to have lost his first wife, too."

"And his second wife ran off not long after they were married."

Reese gave a low whistle. "Bella was Hunter's third wife?"

"Yeah, if I got that tidbit of gossip right."

"He's definitely unlucky in love," Reese said. "The Northwood family is very prominent around here, aren't they?"

"They have tons of influence over the way things go. Money talks, as they say."

"That's not right," Reese said.

"Yet, it's the truth," Kiki reminded her. "I'm sure you saw how the Denver muckety mucks and top bananas forced their ideas onto everyone about running the city."

"Unfortunately, I did."

"Gotta run," Kiki said with a wave. "Talk to you later."

Reese lifted a hand in farewell, and turned to face the crowd again. She noticed Hunter standing with a tall, beautiful brunette beneath a gnarled cottonwood tree. They were located quite a way from the gathering, near thick bushes, and she sensed they didn't want to be seen. But she had a keen eye.

Hunter talked to the woman briefly, then kissed her on the cheek. Slowly, the woman turned and walked away, glancing over her shoulder at Hunter before she headed toward the parking lot. It was a longing look, one that said—*come hither*.

That didn't seem right. Hunter had just lost his wife.

Could the woman be one of his relatives? She didn't think so; the look the woman had given Hunter seemed intimate. Curious, Reese decided to follow her. She dropped the electronic candle into her purse, where it mingled with her makeup, mints and wallet, then headed to where Betty awaited her.

She jumped into her truck, drove away from the park and remained careful to stay far behind the woman's little red sports car. As she trekked north, up to Elk Haven Estates, Reese followed behind her at a reasonable distance.

This was an exclusive part of town where affluent, white-collar professionals in Meadowlark Valley typically purchased their large, stylish homes. Only in her dreams could Reese ever live here.

Located on a bluff overlooking the city, it boasted large parcels of rolling land covered with extravagant structures. The majority of properties were in the multimillion-dollar range, although occasionally some went for less, especially if they weren't in the best condition.

From this vantage point, residents could enjoy the distant, yet breathtaking mountain views from their lodgings. Reese tried not to let her jaw drop as she drove past ski-chalet inspired houses, spacious Tuscan polished stone bastions, and mansions reminiscent of rustic French chateaus.

She rarely drove up here, but her grandparents had talked about how construction on the neighborhood had begun back in the 1980s. That meant the trees, bushes, and other shrubs were well-established and had grown to lush proportions throughout the hills. The entire neighborhood reflected good taste and gracious living.

Reese thought of her humble old house downtown, and felt a tad unworthy, which she realized was foolish. It was her family estate, although tiny, and she loved every board and nail. The memories she'd made there could never be replaced.

The sports car turned into a wide lane surrounded by emerald green, manicured lawns. It zipped toward a Georgian style country house constructed of pale white stone, its squarish architecture sitting atop a knoll peppered by cottonwood trees with tall shrubbery hedges on either side. In the foreground, an expansive rock garden with flowering bushes surrounded a pool adorned with a fountain, which reflected the setting sun's fiery rays.

A fenced pasture on the property held two horses munching contentedly on grass. They lifted their graceful necks and switched their tails as they watched the sports car, but continued to chew nonchalantly as it passed by.

Reese stopped at the end of the drive, her Bronco tucked behind large a stone wall surrounded by blooming yucca plants which bore the address, 5632 Mustang Lane. Written on a mailbox posted nearby were the names, Dr. Henry and Mrs. Ivy Drake. About six months ago, in the newspaper's obituaries, she'd read that Henry Drake, a well-known local surgeon, had passed away from a sudden heart attack.

The sports car pulled into a paved circular driveway, and parked beneath a covered carport. A door on an oversize five-car garage opened, revealing a boat. Reese had no doubt that behind the other doors sat a motorhome, several ATVs, and probably a large, luxury vehicle.

After getting out of the sports car, the brunette, who Reese assumed must be Ivy, walked inside her home, closing the garage door behind her. Reese decided to watch the house for a while, just to see what might happen. She needed to find a better place to park though, because anyone coming down the main road would spot her.

She noticed a barn not far from where she was currently parked. That looked secure enough, so she drove onto a field and parked behind the structure.

In front of her, a rusted old truck rested beneath a laden apple tree, along with an old jalopy that looked like it had seen better days in the 1940's. A large stack of firewood topped by a roll of chicken wire mesh provided more cover. Fortunately, she still had a clear view of Ivy's house.

Reese played a game on her cell phone to pass the time. The setting sun painted the fire-hazed sky with flaming orange and purple clouds as tiny bits of ash drifted across her windshield. As lavender twilight swept across the land, Reese noticed a vehicle turning off of Mustang Lane and into the driveway.

The silver Cadillac SUV immediately jogged her memory. She'd seen it when she visited Hunter and he'd been rabidly digging through it. Reese clicked off her phone and set it aside, watching as the SUV pulled under the carport.

Hunter stepped out of the SUV and glanced around as he straightened his tie and suit jacket. Then he walked up to the door and knocked. A few minutes later, Ivy opened up and scooted two large Doberman Pinchers out past her legs. Hunter gathered her in his arms and passionately kissed her. They held each other for a while longer, then she pulled him inside and closed the door.

Reese had unconsciously been chewing on a fingernail, but when the two disappeared inside, she pulled it from her mouth.

"Hunter and Ivy Drake are having an affair," she muttered, shocked by her discovery. "Holy mama, he's not letting any grass grow under his feet."

Reese's mind began clicking with ideas, mainly why Hunter was already romancing another woman when his wife was barely cold in the grave. Had he and Ivy been having an affair before Bella's accident? Maybe that's why he'd been preoccupied and even rude at the candlelight ceremony.

The Dobermans trotted out from behind the bushes and stood spread-legged in front of the old truck. Lifting their heads in the air, they stared at Reese's truck. Teeth bared, they began pacing and barking.

"Time to go," she muttered. After starting up Betty's engine, she drove away from her hiding spot. Navigating onto the main road, she headed into town.

• • •

Back at her house, Bo greeted her with a long meow. She leaned over to scratch his head, then went into her office, flipped on a lamp and signed onto her computer. She pulled up the internet, then decided she ought to check her email first. As she scrolled through messages, Bo jumped on her desk, sat down and began methodically licking his paws.

"Hey, fish breath," she told him.

She barely paid attention to the subject matter she looked through, since her mind was still on Hunter. She'd known about his family before she headed off to college, but she'd never met them. Since Hunter was older than she, he ran in different circles. After her talk with Kiki, however, she decided she wanted to see what she'd missed during her absence.

Why it was important, she couldn't say. As it often happened with cases, gut feeling urged her on.

She logged onto her favorite background search engine and plugged in Hunter's name. Information about his sign business, Ad Pro, appeared. She discovered he was 40, although she thought he looked much younger. Her cell rang, and she sighed with frustration. Noting it was Kiki, she picked up.

"Hey lady, I'm standing out on your porch. Let me in."

"What are you up to?" Reese asked.

"I'm talking to you," Kiki said.

"Ha, ha." Reese clicked off her phone and headed out of her office to open the front door.

As she entered the living room, Kiki flipped the overhead light switch. "What are you doing in the dark? Trying to save on your light bill?"

"I'm not sitting in the living room," Reese explained. "I'm doing some online research."

"Ah, you're buried in your bat cave. That explains it."

Reese chuckled as she walked back to her desk, sat down in her office chair and began scrolling through lines of information.

"It's late," Kiki said as she pulled up a chair and sat beside her. "Seriously, can't you give it a rest?"

"No, not yet. I found out that Ivy Drake and Hunter are having an affair."

"Huh?"

"It was strange," Reese said. "I saw Hunter talking to this gorgeous brunette woman, and after he kissed her—"

"He what? Kissed her, you said?" Kiki's brows arched.

"They were away from the crowd and I'm sure they figured no one could see the two of them."

"But you did."

"I was curious," Reese said. "It's in my nature, I suppose. Anyway, when Ivy left the candlelight vigil, I followed her."

"Of course, you did," Kiki said.

Ignoring Kiki's smart aleck response, Reese continued. "She drove this sweet little red sports car up to Elk Haven Estates and parked in front of a gigantic home. The mailbox had Dr. Henry and Ivy Drake's names on it."

"Dr. Drake died about six months ago," Kiki said. "I saw his obituary in the newspaper. It claimed he died of a heart attack."

"I saw that too," Reese said.

Kiki leaned forward and rested her elbows on her knees. "What happened next?"

"Hunter arrived a short time later, driving his fancy silver SUV. Ivy opened the door and they started canoodling like there was no tomorrow. She pulled him inside and, well, we can both imagine the rest of the story."

"Geez, that really surprises me, Kiki said. "Hunter's always acted like he deserved to have it all, but wow. Bella's barely been dead a few days."

"He was cheating on Bella before the accident, I bet." Reese massaged her forehead. "Here's an idea—what if Ford found out about Hunter's affair and confronted him? He would have been livid that his son-in-law was cheating on his daughter. He probably tried to deck Hunter, but wound up instead getting his butt handed to him."

Kiki snapped her fingers. "I think you're definitely on to something. But do you believe Ford would try to take on a man half his age?"

"I do," Reese said. "I've been asking around about him and I discovered he often gets into bar fights at the VFW. Apparently, he's pretty opinionated about politics and that irritates a lot of the folks."

"Ford and Hunter in a fight would be like a lit match tossed into gasoline," Kiki said. "They're both hot heads, it seems."

"Let's see what else we can find out about Hunter," Reese said, glancing at the computer screen again. "Let's see…his first wife was a woman named Lisa Tremblay. They lived up in Buffalo before she died about eight years ago."

"Does it say how she died?"

"Her newspaper obituary mentions that she passed away unexpectedly, causes unknown," Reese said. "That's somewhat suspicious."

"I'll say," Kiki agreed.

Reese noted how much the photograph of Lisa, a pretty, long-haired brunette, resembled Bella.

"She looks a lot like Bella," Kiki said as she studied the photo.

"I was thinking the exact same thing," Reese said.

Reese scrolled down the screen and brought up another newspaper article about Hunter. Her eyes went wide as she read it.

"Listen to this; when Hunter was still living in Buffalo, after Lisa died, a young woman named Kay Maxwell filed a stalking complaint against him and requested a restraining order from the police."

Kiki pointed at the bottom paragraph. "The complaint was dismissed because she failed to appear in court."

"No wonder Hunter moved back home," Reese said. "Even with the complaint dismissed, the idea that it had been lodged surely gave him a bad reputation.

"Why do you suppose the woman didn't show up for court?" Kiki asked.

"Could be she forgot about the hearing," Reese said. "That happens more than you would think."

"Or she was intimidated," Kiki said.

"Maybe," Reese added.

"But by who?" Kiki rubbed her cheek and looked into the distance. "Do you think Hunter's family put pressure on her to back off?"

"I wouldn't put it past them. They couldn't allow something their prodigal son had done to blemish their stellar family pedigree."

"True."

"They also could have paid her to back off," Reese said. "They definitely have the money."

"Millions, in fact," Kiki said.

"After all that hullabaloo, Hunter moved home to Meadowlark Valley and opened his sign shop," Reese said.

"Speaking of the Northwood family and their money, that must be when Pearl and Walt decided to hand over that small inheritance to Hunter," Kiki said.

"The one you mentioned at the candlelight vigil?" Reese asked.

"Exactly. They probably paid him after the all the hullabaloo he caused in Buffalo, then warned him to stay out of trouble."

Reese studied more information on her computer screen. "A few years after moving back here, Hunter married a woman named Jayla Weeks."

"Another pretty brunette," Kiki said. "I remember her coming into my shop a time or two. I heard the marriage didn't last more than a few weeks."

"Jayla must have decided they weren't right for each other."

"Maybe the way Hunter squeezed the toothpaste tube drove her crazy," Kiki said, then snorted with laughter.

Chapter Eighteen

"I'd love to hear Jayla's side of the story," Reese said.

"I wonder where she is now," Kiki said. "I heard she left town after she broke it off with Hunter."

Reese plugged Jayla Northwood into her people finder app, but found nothing. She tried Jayla Weeks, but that name also came up a dead end.

"There's a guy named Herbert Weeks who runs a hobby and craft store near my place," Kiki said. "Maybe he's a relative."

"I'll check him out," Reese said, then yawned and stretched. "Wow, I'm pooped. I'll have to pick this up tomorrow."

Kiki yawned, too. "Now look what you made me do! Oh, well, I'd better get home. Are you going to church tomorrow? Pastor Weathers is holding a special service to commemorate Bella at 10 o'clock."

"I think I will," Reese said, thinking that perhaps Ford's attacker might attend. Not that she'd be able to pick him out of the crowd, but she might get some clues as to his identity.

"I'll save you a place," Kiki said. "Hopefully the roof won't cave in with the two of us there at the same time."

They both chuckled as Reese followed Kiki to the front door and locked it after she left. Then she headed back to her office. She printed a few items including the police blotter brief information about Hunter and his first wife's obituary. On yellow sticky notes, she wrote potential leads to follow up on for Ford's attacker, including keeping a watch on Hunter and following up with Herbert Weeks at his hobby shop.

"He knows," she remembered Ford saying before he passed out. That still stymied her. Who had Ford been talking about?

Yawning again, she shut down the computer and turned out the lights. Her bed was calling, and by the time she'd gotten ready to crawl between the sheets, her eyelids felt like lead weights. Bo jumped up on the covers and curled up beside her.

After Reese switched on her fan, the humming sound helped her fall asleep. Later, the dreams began and she found herself on a river raft that pitched through rough waves. She screamed when it soared over a colossal waterfall. Down she fell, straight into the crashing onslaught.

At the base, she shot into the freezing depths and her clothes caught on rocks, holding her captive. Panic sank sharp claws into her and she twisted from side to side, trying to break free. Bella came to her rescue in the form of a mermaid. She touched Reese, which transformed her into one of the mythical sea creatures, complete with long flowing hair and a shimmering tail.

Bella took her arm and they swam away in a flash of silver. Joy surged through Reese's fishy-fashioned body as they meandered through the blue depths.

"Help me," Bella said, bubbles coming from her mouth as she spoke. "I'm still waiting."

Reese opened her eyes, took a deep breath, and realized the dream hadn't been real. Her digital watch noted in glowing red that it was only four o'clock in the morning. Sweaty and sticky, she rose and padded into the bathroom to get a cool drink of water from the sink, then splashed it over her face and arms.

"Maybe I'm losing it," she muttered, crawling back into bed.

Rolling over, she punched her pillow a couple of times, threw aside the covers and closed her eyes. Sleep refused to come as she considered why her unconscious continued fashioning dreams about Bella.

The police had hired her to write a report about Bella's drowning accident—that's all.

Of course, she decided that since Bella had been a fellow classmate, she couldn't help but be affected by the loss. As ideas swirled in her mind for the next hour, she tossed and turned.

"I'm sorry about what happened to you, Bella," she murmured

in the darkness. "But your dad is still with us, and my focus needs to be on finding who attacked him."

Reese felt somewhat better, yet it seemed a heaviness still rested on chest. Maybe, she decided, in time it would fade. Finally, she settled into a fitful sleep.

• • •

The next day, despite feeling drained, Reese managed to drag herself out of bed. She showered and dressed in a black sundress with white polka dots, then slipped into her black lace up sandals.

In the kitchen, she grabbed her purse and headed out the door. Digging her keys from the jumbled items in her bag, she jumped into her Bronco, started it up, and headed toward the Fellowship Church. The parking lot was nearly full, so it took several minutes to find a space.

The service had already begun as she entered the chapel. The choir and the congregation were singing and a hushed reverence gripped the atmosphere. People turned to stare at her, no doubt wondering who had interrupted their worship.

Smiling apologetically, she noticed Kiki seated in a pew toward the back in the center aisle. Reese hustled over and slid into the seat next to her.

"Wow," Kiki whispered playfully. "Just had to make an entrance, didn't you?"

Reese frowned, but remained silent, aware her friend liked to give her guff about being late. She could excuse herself today by saying it was all Bo's fault, but she decided it would be ridiculous to blame it on her canned cat food-addicted feline.

When the song ended, Pastor Weathers, an elderly, white-haired gentleman in a black clergy robe, probably in his late sixties, stepped up to the lectern. He smiled at the audience, then began speaking.

"Good morning everyone," he said. "I fear we all have heavy thoughts weighing on our minds this morning. For example, the terrible wildfires, along with the death of our fellow parishioner, Bella Northwood, and the attack on her father, Ford Presley.

I have no doubt that we are all bothered by these unfortunate developments."

Murmurs of agreement rose from the audience.

"Some fear that natural disasters are God's judgements against humankind's transgressions and sins. However, natural disasters strike with no warning and no indication of what is to come. In the Bible, God warned wicked individuals about what would happen to them if they did not repent."

Weariness crept over Reese, and she tried her hardest not to drift off.

"He loved them, as he loves us all," the pastor continued. "and he wanted to give them a chance to repent and declare him as the one and only God before he exacted his judgment on them. When they refused to repent of their sins, then, and only then, did he bring on a natural disaster. He summoned things like mighty earthquakes to crack open the earth and swallow unrepentant souls. Because of Jesus Christ's sacrifice on the cross, these days, we can repent of our sins. That is why we are misguided to believe tornadoes, tidal waves, deadly car accidents, or other unexpected occurrences can be attributed to God. They are caused by nature, raw and simple. In Job, 20:34, it says…"

Reese's gaze drifted toward the large vase of red and yellow gladiolas sitting in front of the lectern. Viewing the blossoms gave her a warm, tingling sensation as she recalled those her grandmother used to grow in the backyard.

"I don't know how many of you were able to attend the candlelight vigil honoring Bella Northwood and Ford Presley yesterday," Pastor Weathers continued. "It was touching to see so many friends and family members in attendance. Bella is gone from us, but may our prayers lift up brother Ford and strengthen him so he may leave the hospital healed and whole. Amen."

"Amen," many in the congregation echoed. Some of the members sniffed and sobbed, and a couple of the ladies produced handkerchiefs to dab at their red noses.

"At this time, let us show our love to everyone, including our dear family members. Don't wait until they are gone. Our loved ones are the ties that bind, the salve that heals our wounds, and they create our connection to the world."

Even Reese sniffed a little, hearing the pastor's guidance.

"In John 13: 31–38, Jesus shares with us his thoughts about us caring for one another. He tells us many things in these scriptures, but to me, this is the main thought he wished to impart. He said, 'As I have loved you, so you must love one another.' "

Reese thought about her own family members. Had she declared her love for them enough? Before they died, did they know how much they meant to her?

She noticed Naomi and Ian sitting in the center section, a few pews in front of her and Kiki. Hunter sat near them, along with his mother, his father, and his brother. Reese studied Hunter's broad shoulders, wondering about his troubled life. Could he have honestly beat up Ford if the old guy had accused him of cheating on his daughter?

In her line of work, she'd seen people do worse.

As if Reese's steady gaze burned holes in his suit jacket, Hunter turned and stared directly at her.

She smiled.

"Ask yourself, have you put things right with people?" Pastor Weathers asked. "Have you asked for God's forgiveness for your transgressions against him?"

A strange expression crossed Hunter's face—guilt, Reese swore. He studied her a moment longer, then turned back around.

Chapter Nineteen

Reese slept in the next day, Saturday, because she had a fever and a stomach ache. Since she'd been running around so much, she figured she'd probably picked up a bug somewhere. She only got up to feed Bo, drink some juice and take some medicine.

Back in bed, her fan on full blast, she managed to sleep more, but nearly suffocated from the heat. Her dreams were wild and riddled with visions of Bella at the river. In the early evening, she got up and took more medicine, showered, then went back to collapse on her mattress. With her skin cooled down, she was finally able to get some decent sleep.

The next morning, she felt better. By the time she dragged herself out of bed, she realized that it was too late to attend regular Sunday church services.

"Next week, I promise to go," she muttered to Bo. He stared at her with his steady green gaze, then laid his head back down on her bed. He seemed unimpressed.

Reese showered and dressed. Having put off house cleaning forever, she dove into a frenzy of vacuums, mops and dusters. Afterward, she straightened up her office, which looked like it had been hit with a tornado.

Before she knew it, the day had ended. She went to bed early, glad for the peaceful, fever-free rest, which she really needed. For once, nightmares didn't plague her, and she awoke, ready to get busy.

Dressed in workout gear, she headed outside for her morning routine, enthusiastic about starting the day. The feeling faded as she watched the sun rise amidst the smokey haze, very much resembling a bright red cherry tomato. Jogging around the lake, she decided the smoke and tiny bits of ash fluttering through the air weren't healthy for her lungs.

It crossed her mind to temporarily cancel her jogs. She wouldn't do it though, fearing it would be all too easy to never resume the exercise. After deciding against that imprudent thought, she felt better.

Back home, she showered and dressed in her favorite jeans and boots, along with a short sleeve cotton top, tie-dyed with an ocean blue color. She called Jeremy, composing a message in her mind in case he didn't answer.

"Good morning, Reese," he said when he finally picked up.

"Same to you," she said.

"How goes the suspect search for Ford's attacker? I haven't heard from you in a bit."

"I had the flu or something over the weekend, but I'm better now," Reese said.

"Sorry to hear that," he responded.

"As far as Ford's case goes, I have plenty of potential leads on his possible attacker, but nothing's come up solid," Reese said. "So, my investigation continues. I have one theory, though."

"What's that?"

"It appears Hunter is having an affair with Ivy Drake," Reese told him. "I'm wondering if Ford confronted him about it, and they fought."

"Do you really think Hunter and Ivy are romantically involved?"

"I saw them kissing at Bella's candlelight vigil. I followed Ivy home, then pretty soon Hunter showed up and they were all kissy-kissy. What do you think?"

"Well, go with your gut," Jeremy said.

"You got it, boss. Today, I'm going to try to find the whereabouts of one of Hunter's ex-wives, Jayla Weeks."

"He was married before he and Bella got together?"

"Hunter's first wife died, and Jayla was his second wife. I'd like to ask her why she left him."

"Maybe the Northwood's firstborn son isn't so easy going—could be he's got a bad temper," Jeremy suggested.

"That's the angle I'm following up on," Reese said.

"I'll let you go then so you can start your day," Jeremy said. "I've got a ton of work to plow through myself."

"I'll stay in touch," Reese said.

Grabbing her purse, she left the house and headed downtown, which was only a few blocks away. She passed by The Celestial Eye, and continued down the sidewalk until she spotted the craft shop Kiki had mentioned.

Herbert's was spelled out in large white letters on the front of the small brick building. Beneath the name, it also said: Since 1963. What a long time to be in business, Reese thought.

Strolling inside, she examined various displays featuring model trains, hot rod and custom car building kits, model airplane and ship building kits, tools, paint, and other craft supplies.

A wooden rack along one wall held modeling magazines. A nearby shelf displayed collectable coins and stamps. Next to it were boxes of puzzles, board games, and role-playing games.

No one was at the counter, so Reese waited patiently, hoping someone would appear. She hated wasting precious time, thinking of all the files clogging her in basket. She'd put off her background investigations for the time being as she worked police cases.

While puttering around, she spotted macrame pattern books and different styles of cord. Clear drawers full of colorful beads caught her eye and she sorted through them, admiring the colors and textures.

She stroked a jute plant hanger decorated with wooden beads, admiring the workmanship. Suspended from the ceiling, it held a fake fern with broad plastic leaves.

"Hello, can I help you with anything?"

Reese looked up at the tall, stocky man wearing a short sleeve turquoise-colored shirt. He also wore a camouflage apron tied beneath his belly. His gray hair, cropped gray beard, and round metal-framed glasses made her feel like she was visiting Santa's workshop, especially since he held a small hammer.

"Yes," Reese said as she eased toward the counter. "Are you Herbert?"

"In the flesh," he said.

"I hope you can help me," Reese said. "I'm looking for Jayla Weeks."

He blinked and placed the hammer beside his cash register. "Uh, Jayla Weeks? Never heard of anyone by that name."

Reese noted hesitation in his voice, and she sensed he wasn't being forthcoming. "I thought perhaps you may be related. I'd like to talk to her."

He pushed an envelope on the counter beneath a large calendar and casually smoothed the surface. "Sorry I can't help you."

"That's disappointing," Reese said.

"Are you a fan of macrame?" he asked nodding toward the display. "That's the latest craze, so I understand. It was popular back in the seventies, when my dad ran the shop. He was the original Herbert."

"I've never tried macrame before," Reese admitted.

"Since folks are interested in that craft again, I started stocking some of the supplies and they're selling like hotcakes." He stroked his beard, his gaze taking on a glint. "My mom and my sister took classes back in the day. They demonstrated a couple of knots for me—which are simple. I even learned some of them back when I was in Boy Scouts."

"Boy Scouts you say, that's interesting," she commented.

"If you can't find the macrame items you want, I can always order them for you. It's not a problem."

"Thanks, but I need to..." She stopped herself from saying she needed to leave. In a flash of memory, she recalled Herbert shoving that envelope beneath the calendar. She sensed it contained something she needed to see, so she decided to do exactly that.

"On second thought," Reese stepped back over by the macrame display and picked up a roll of bright green cord. "Do you carry this in white?"

"Let me take a closer look at the brand," he said.

She set the cord on the counter.

Herbert examined it, then said, "You're in luck. I have more of that cord stocked in my back room. Excuse me a minute and I'll go look."

When he walked through a beaded curtain and disappeared, Reese hurried up to the counter, lifted the calendar and studied the envelope. The return address said J. Meredith in Cheyenne. Reese pulled out her cell and snapped a photo of it. Herbert remained in the back room stirring around, so she dared to slide out the correspondence.

The salutation said, "Dear Uncle Herbert, it was great to see everyone during Frontier Days in July, and I hope you can all come for another visit soon. My therapy practice is going well and I continue to add new clients…"

Did the J stand for Jayla? Meredith could be a married name. Reese imagined Jayla didn't want her uncle sharing information that she was living in Cheyenne, just in case she wanted to keep the knowledge from Hunter.

Reese wanted to visit J. Meredith. It she really was Jayla, Reese wanted to ask her why she'd left Hunter so soon after they were married. If Jayla mentioned that Hunter had tended to fly into a rage during arguments, perhaps he'd done the same with Ford. Hunter might have lost his temper and gone too far.

"Finally found it," Herbert called out from his back room. "I'll be right out."

Quickly, Reese stuffed the letter back inside the envelope and replaced it. Barely a second later, Herbert appeared with the merchandise in hand.

"This is a good choice," he said as he rang it up on his register. "Your project should work out nicely."

"This ought to keep me busy," she said.

"Don't you need a pattern book to get started?" He raised his bushy brows.

"Right," Reese said. She went back to the macrame display, pulled out a pamphlet for beginners, and brought it over to Herbert.

She paid for everything, watching as Herbert dropped the receipt and the items in a sack. "Thank you for your help."

"Come back anytime," he said.

As Reese walked out the door, she wondered what in the heck she was going to do with the cord. Maybe she could let Bo play with it. He'd have a blast. She really didn't intend to learn how to macrame. However, she'd managed to get some worthwhile information, and that made it worth every red cent she'd paid for it.

• • •

Back home in her office, Reese signed onto her computer and looked up J. Meredith in Cheyenne with a therapy practice. Just as Reese had suspected, she owned one called Spirit Amore, which offered counseling.

"What do you think, Bo, should I make an appointment for a therapy session?"

The cat sat on an empty shelf, amusing himself by using his paws to push around a red ribbon bookmark. He'd probably pilfered it from one of the dusty volumes.

Reese rested her hand on her chin as she watched him. "Don't you think that would be a better way to talk to her, than just barging in and asking questions?"

Bo glanced at her, then resumed batting around his new toy.

"Well, I think it is, even if you're not going to weigh in," Reese said. She picked up her cell phone and dialed the therapy office.

"Spirit Amore therapy," a man answered after a couple of rings. "May I help you?"

"I'd like to set up an appointment with Dr. Meredith," Reese said. "Do you have any openings this week?"

"I think she's all booked up, but let me put you on hold while I check."

Reese listened to the recorded elevator music until the operator came back onto the line.

"Thank you for waiting, ma'am," he said. "You're in luck. Dr. Meredith had a cancellation for tomorrow, so can you come in at 3:30 p.m.?"

"That's perfect," Reese said. It took approximately two hours to drive from here to Cheyenne, so she could definitely make the appointment on time.

"Your name?"

"Reese Golden," she said.

"And the nature of your visit?"

"I have a personal issue I'd like to discuss with her."

"All right, you're all set. Please arrive about 15 to 20 minutes early to fill out paperwork since this is your first visit."

"Of course," Reese said, then hung up.

Reese read some more pages in Bella's journal, stirring up more sad feelings about a life lost too soon. After setting it aside, she typed up a document with her findings on the rafting accident, then saved it to a work folder on her hard drive. Later, she'd do a spell check on it and review it for accuracy.

Next, she dove into the stack of papers before her and picked out a person to research for the Uniformed Services University of Health Sciences. That federal agency prepared graduates for service in the U.S. Medical Corps as doctors, nurses, etc.

"Okay, Mr. Brenner, let's see if you have any arrests, warrants, court summons or dismissed cases," Reese said as she began her online research. "If you were a good boy and have behaved yourself, you'll pass your background investigation."

Chapter Twenty

Reese had caught up on her background investigations by the time she started her drive to Cheyenne the next day. As she sailed down the highway, singing along to a cassette tape featuring 90s country music, she studied the passing scenery.

Smoky haze filled the sky, dimming the sun's rays. Nevertheless, the plains blossomed with late summer wildflowers and breezes swept across the tall buff-colored grass, giving it movement similar to the dips and swells of ocean waves.

She headed toward Laramie, a city of approximately 30,000 plus people and the home of her college alma mater, the University of Wyoming. The city, named for a French trapper, was originally founded in the mid-1860s along the Union Pacific Railroad tracks.

While in college, Reese had spent a good amount of time skiing with friends in the Snowy Range, about 40 miles away. They'd also taken trips to Yellowstone National Park during breaks to camp in the summer and snowmobile in the winter. There were so many recreational opportunities around here that a person could spend every waking minute enjoying the outdoors.

After passing through Laramie, she drove up through Pole Mountain Pass. Rocky mountainsides full of trees surrounded the highway. Driving through here always took Reese's breath away because of the pristine beauty.

Before long, the elevation evened out and strange, rust-colored rock formations scattered across the prairie, as if a child had randomly tossed their building blocks. As a kid, her family had taken her to the typical tourist stops along the way.

She'd chosen Ames Monument, Wyoming's very own pyramid, as

one of her favorite spots. Hewn with square stones, it approximately marked the highest spot on the First Transcontinental Railroad at 8,247 feet. Constructed in 1882 of light-colored native granite, it stood 60 feet high and 60 feet square at the base.

Another spot, fascinating to her fourth-grade self, was the famous Tree in Rock located in the median between the lanes of Interstate 80. In 1860, Union Pacific Railroad workers laying track found a skinny pine tree leaning out of a boulder, clinging tenuously to life.

Fourth-grade Reese been in awe of the Lincoln Highway Monument, a two-ton bronze head of Honest Abe perched on a 30-foot granite spire that peered down on visitors. She'd felt tiny standing beneath the monolithic statue of the United States' 16th president.

"Someday maybe I'll stop and visit all those places again," she said as a touch of nostalgia rippled through her.

Signs bearing the distance to Cheyenne soon appeared and it wasn't long before she sailed through Buford, a town of one person—the individual who owned the gas station. Next, she entered Wyoming's capital city of around 64,000 residents.

Famous for Cheyenne Frontier Days, the community hosted rodeos and other western-themed activities each July. That was another event she hadn't participated in for ages, and she decided she ought to pay another visit to it next summer. It was a rowdy, beer-soaked event packed with cowboys, livestock and tourists from all over the world.

She drove downtown to the original part in the city, which had been established as a Union Pacific Railroad camp back in 1867. Cheyenne had been nicknamed "Hell on Wheels" because of the violence surrounding railroad construction as it expanded westward.

After turning onto 17th Avenue, she studied the lovely Victorian homes. Some had been refurbished and were painted bright hues, their manicured landscaping and beautiful shrubbery enhancing the structures. Other homes remained in more humble condition.

Reese found the address for the therapy office and parked in front of the building. It was a smaller Victorian home painted pale yellow with white, gingerbread trim. The surrounding lot displayed lush green grass and flowering shrubs.

Upon entering the building, she found a reception area where a young man with sandy-colored hair sat behind a desk pecking away at a computer keyboard. Dressed in a white dress shirt and dark slacks, he looked up at Reese and smiled.

"Welcome to Spirit Amore. Do you have an appointment?"

"Yes, I'm here to see Dr. Meredith," she said.

"Excellent." He glanced at his appointment book. "Reese Golden?"

"Yes."

He handed her a clipboard with several sheets of paper attached. "Everything you need to fill out is highlighted in yellow. Have a seat and when you're ready, bring it back to me."

Reese sat in a wicker rocking chair and began filling out the paperwork. When she'd finished, she took it up to the young man.

"Thank you," he said. "Dr. Meredith will be with you shortly."

Reese returned to her seat, admiring the polished wooden floors, the nubby wool wall hangings and the palm plants bursting with green foliage. An old stone fireplace with a seashore painting hanging over it gave off calm vibes. Soft blue walls added to the relaxing ambiance.

She nibbled at a hangnail, then stopped herself. Admittedly, her nerves were drawn taut, considering she'd scheduled this appointment under false pretenses. She hadn't honestly come here for therapy, but hopefully she'd discover J. Meredith was indeed Jayla Weeks.

A tall brunette woman approached her, wearing a black top, a long black skirt and flat, black shoes. She wore her dark hair in a pageboy style with silver highlights and around her neck was a small diamond on a slim chain.

The brunette radiated an elegant, businesslike attitude, however, she also appeared caring and kind.

"You're Reese?" she asked, holding out her hand and smiling.

Reese shook it as she stood. "Yes."

"I'm Dr. Meredith. Please, come with me."

Reese followed her down a hall into a small office that also had been painted the same soft blue as the reception area. Sun streamed through a large window with lace curtains. More plants decorated the room along with comfortable chairs, a loveseat and plenty of bright pillows.

"Make yourself comfortable," Dr. Meredith said.

Reese sat on the loveseat and crossed her legs. She prepared to explain her true reason for being here.

Meanwhile, Dr. Meredith settled into a recliner and balanced a legal pad on her lap. "I understand from Dennis, my office assistant, that you have a personal issue you'd like to discuss."

"Actually, it's more of a work thing," Reese said.

Dr. Meredith leaned forward and met Reese's gaze. "I looked over your information and I see you're a private investigator. I actually specialize in working with professionals in high stress jobs. I've had great success in treating patients who are exhausted and overwhelmed. What symptoms are you exhibiting so I know how to tailor your treatment plan?"

"I'm not experiencing any symptoms, I—"

"They may not seem like actual symptoms, Reese. They come on slowly. You may not be sleeping well, your productivity levels may be decreasing, you may have lost interest in things that used to make you happy. Your relationships may suffer. For example, are you arguing more with your friends or your significant other?"

"Dr. Meredith, I didn't come here for therapy."

"I'm confused." With a frown, she leaned back. "What did you come here for?"

Reese reached into her purse and handed Dr. Meredith one of her business cards.

"I am a private investigator, that much is true. And I'm working on a case for the Meadowlark Valley Police Department."

Dr. Meredith's face turned an ashy shade.

"I'm investigating suspects in a local man's assault. I had some questions for you about Hunter Northwood. Was he your former husband?"

"How did you find me?" A vein throbbed in Dr. Meredith's neck.

"I visited with Herbert Weeks at his hobby store."

"My uncle disclosed my location?"

"Please don't blame him. I happened to see a letter on his counter. When I noticed the return address, J. Meredith, I took a chance that it might be you."

"I don't see how I factor into this," Dr. Meredith said, her voice icy.

"First off, I follow the same rules of client privacy that other professionals do. Including yourself."

Dr. Meredith continued to glare at Reese, but remained silent.

"Are you Hunter's ex-wife, Jayla Weeks?"

She closed her eyes and made a soft moan. "It's been years since Hunter and I were married. I thought certain I'd covered my tracks."

"You are Jayla, then?" Reese asked.

She nodded. "I don't want to talk about Hunter. I'd like you to go, please."

"I need your help. I believe Hunter assaulted someone, and the victim is still in the hospital, fighting for their life."

"What can I do?" Dr. Meredith's voice was hard and cutting. "My relationship with Hunter is something I've kept buried for a long time."

"Tell me what happened, Jayla. May I call you by your first name?"

"That's fine." With shaking hands, she placed her notebook on a table. She stood and began to pace. "I still don't see how I can help you."

"I did some research on Hunter and he's got some concerning things in his past," Reese said. "I'd like verification of my suspicions, and I hoped you could give it to me."

"I didn't know what he was capable of when I married him," Jayla said, her gaze wide.

"I understand your marriage to him only lasted weeks. Do you mind telling me why?"

"I feared for my life," Jayla said, her expression filled with alarm.

"Why?"

"He charmed me, but once he got the wedding ring on my finger, he changed. He started demanding things right and left—namely that I drink this special health smoothie that he mixed for me every morning. I started getting sicker and sicker, and I could barely drag myself to work."

"What happened?"

"I was always nauseated and I developed migraines. I was weak and couldn't think straight. By then, we'd only been married a few weeks."

"What did you do?" Reese asked.

"I got to the point where I couldn't handle working anymore, and the company fired me. Hunter's special smoothie was the only thing I was consuming and I'd lost a lot of weight."

"I bet you were frightened."

"I honestly believed I was dying. The doctors I went to couldn't find anything wrong with me. They said it was stress and exhaustion, so I thought getting fired might have been a good thing."

"You went through a lot, I can tell," Reese sympathized.

"One day I wandered into the kitchen when Hunter was making my smoothie. He sprinkled something from a package into the blender, but when he saw me, he quickly shoved it in a cupboard. He didn't think I saw him, I guess, because when I checked the cupboard later after he left the room, I discovered it was rat poison. Little green pellets of death."

"Oh my God!" Reese covered her mouth with her hands, shocked. "Did you tell the police?"

"No."

"Why not?"

"You know who Hunter's parents are, don't you?"

"Yes, but—"

"Everyone would have thought I was nuts to accuse him of poisoning me. His parents would have hired the best legal defense team money can buy. Or they'd have probably sent a hit man to kill me and make it look like an accident. People with that kind of money don't play around."

"I can't believe they'd do that too their daughter-in-law," Reese said.

"Pearl and Walt didn't like me," Jayla said. "Thought I wasn't good enough for Hunter since I came from a lower-class family."

"Seriously?"

"Those are the exact words they used when they found out we were engaged. I'll never forget the night we told them, and how they reacted."

"They sound pretty judgmental," Reese said.

"And downright nasty," Jayla insisted. "I've heard rumors of about some of the Northwoods' business dealings, and let's just say I wouldn't put it past them to get rid of me to shut me up. They've had their frustrations with Hunter, believe me, but he's still their son. They wouldn't let him go down for trying to poison me. And they wouldn't want word to get around that they'd raised a damaged person."

"Why would Hunter want to kill you, though?"

"I don't know, but I sure didn't stick around to ask. I pretended to drink the smoothie for a couple of days, but secretly dumped it into the sink drain. When Hunter finally left the house to go grocery shopping, I threw together a suitcase and went back home to live with my parents."

"I don't blame you."

"Hunter wouldn't leave me alone, though. He followed me everywhere and kept hounding me to come back to him. My parents, who have since passed away, gave me the money to move to Cheyenne and hire an attorney, change my name, and file for divorce. I haven't seen Hunter since then, thank goodness. That's why I was worried when you showed up asking questions."

"I only want to find out if you believe Hunter is capable of violently attacking someone."

"I think you know my answer to that," Jayla said. "What's he up to these days?"

"His current wife died a few days ago in a rafting accident, and I discovered he's already involved with another woman. He seems to have developed a deadly pattern with the ladies and he has a type—beautiful brunettes."

"His second wife is dead?"

"Actually, Bella was his third wife. His first wife died several years ago, before he married you. Under what I would call, suspicious circumstances. Now I'm wondering if he used rat poison on her, too."

"I had no idea I was his second wife," Jayla said. "That man is a dangerous liar."

"I think so, too," Reese agreed.

Jayla studied a spot on the wall, obviously deep in thought. "I hope I helped you with your case."

"You did. Hunter's definitely a suspect I'll be watching. Hopefully, the victim will wake up and tell us who attacked him, which will make the assault case easier to prosecute."

"I hope the victim makes a full recovery," Jayla said. "And that they are able to identify the person who hurt them."

"Tell me," Reese said. "Would you be willing to testify about what Hunter did to you? It would help a jury to understand what kind of a person he is if this goes to trial."

"I d-don't think I can," Jayla said. "His family would find out and would probably send someone to silence me. Or Hunter would find me."

"The police can protect you," Reese said.

Jayla gave a bitter laugh. "Sure, they will. Meanwhile, if I help your case, it would most likely destroy everything I've built. The Northwoods are vindictive."

"The police aren't going to tell them where you are. Besides, if it came to you giving a public testimony at Hunter's trial, I'm certain the prosecution would have enough evidence to put him away for a long time."

Jayla rested her head in her hands. "There would still be

repercussions for me, I'm certain. His family would never let up."

"You can help Hunter's victim get justice," Reese said. "He nearly destroyed your life, but you can see that he gets locked up."

Jayla took a seat in her recliner again. "After I left Hunter, I earned psychology and therapy degrees so that I could dedicate my life to helping others heal from trauma. One of those people included me. So, no, I won't agree to testifying against him."

"Jayla—"

"That part of my life is over. I was a survivor years ago, and I want to survive now."

"I know this isn't easy," Reese said.

"Slaying monsters never is," Jayla said.

Chapter Twenty-One

Reese drove back home to Meadowlark Valley after visiting with Jayla, mulling over her refusal to testify against Hunter. She couldn't blame her for not wanting to involve herself with the case, yet Reese knew she'd be a valuable witness if Hunter went on trial.

Downtown, she headed to the police department, parked and strode inside. "Is Detective Savage still here?" she asked Steve Daniels at the counter.

"He is, but he's on the phone," Steve said, glancing at his switchboard.

"I just need a word with him," Reese said.

"I suppose it's okay for you to head back there," Steve said as she breezed past him. "Detective Savage mentioned you're helping on some cases."

"Thanks," she said as she headed down the hall. Jeremy was indeed on the phone, so when she walked into his office, she waved at him, then plopped on a chair. She took out her cell and began to scroll through updates.

Reese darted glances at Jeremy as he discussed a new gang that had moved north from Colorado and now had begun operations in Meadowlark Valley. They'd been tagging property and dealing drugs—something the city definitely didn't need. Jeremy offered ideas about how their officers should approach the members and ways to prosecute them if they were arrested.

When Jeremy hung up, he scowled at her. "That was a confidential phone conversation," he said.

Reese, who had been practicing poor posture, sat up straight.

"Hey, you know me," she told Jeremy. "I'm a confidential type of person."

"Yeah, yeah, yeah," he said. "What's up?"

"What did you find out about those teenagers who ripped off Ford's diorama?"

Jeremy sat back in his office chair and rubbed his forehead. "I got their names from the pawn shop. They all have alibis the day Ford was assaulted."

"Crap," she said. "Of course, it couldn't be that simple to find out who hurt him."

"All three were at sophomore orientation," Jeremy added. "The high school principal verified it and several teachers said they saw them."

"So much for that theory," Reese said. "Hunter's a good suspect in Ford's assault, though."

"You found Jayla Weeks?"

She nodded.

"What did she say about her ex?"

"While they were married, she caught him lacing her breakfast smoothie with rat poison, and she's afraid of him."

"Why didn't she tell the police about the poison?"

"She was afraid of his family's influence and decided it would be better to leave town and start over."

"You believe Hunter went to see Ford the day he was assaulted, and they got into it about his affair with Ivy Drake?" Jeremy asked.

"If Bella had been your daughter, and you found out after she died that her husband had been cheating on her, wouldn't you want to punch out his lights?"

"I would, but didn't you check to see if Hunter had an alibi for that day?"

"I never even considered him a suspect. My bad. But I do now."

"Can't ever rule out family members," Jeremy reminded her.

"I know. And it's not like me to be bamboozled by a grieving spouse."

"I imagine that's a first for you," Jeremy said.

"Maybe it worked out for us, though. Hunter let down his guard when I saw him with Ivy."

"You and your X-ray vision," Jeremy said.

"No one escapes it," Reese agreed.

"I think it's time we pay him another visit.

"I agree," Reese agreed.

"So, Bella is Hunter's third wife?" Jeremy asked.

Reese nodded. "Seems the man's addicted to marriage, but things don't hang together very well afterward. He married his first wife, Lisa Tremblay, when he was living up in Buffalo. She died from an unspecified illness shortly after they were married. He moved back home to Meadowlark Valley where he married his second wife, Jayla Weeks, who left him after a brief time. Bella and Hunter were only married for a month."

"It's too bad Jayla didn't report what Hunter did to her."

"I can't really blame her," Reese said. "She was afraid his family would retaliate. You know how powerful the Northwoods are. If their name got some dirt on it, they'd be furious."

"Yeah, that's a good point," Jeremy said.

"Jayla said Hunter wouldn't leave her alone after she moved home with her parents. That's why her mom and dad helped her leave town and get a new life."

"Did you try talking with Jayla's parents?"

"She told me they're both dead now."

"We're not going to have an easy time trying to accuse Hunter of anything," Jeremy predicted. "When the Northwoods wave their magic wand, it makes all their troubles go away."

"We'll have to make sure we have a very strong case before we go after him."

"You're right." Jeremy thumped the desk with one of his hands and stood. He paced for a bit, then said, "What Jayla said about the rat poison has got me thinking. Do you suppose Hunter poisoned his first wife?"

"I'm wondering the same thing," Reese said. "Especially since her obituary mentioned she'd died from an unspecified illness."

Jeremy stopped at his desk to write something down on a

sticky note, which he attached to his desk. "We can always have her body disinterred for testing."

"True," Reese said.

"Would Jayla be willing to testify against him if the case goes that far?"

"Nope," Reese said. "I asked, and she's too afraid of the Northwood family to come forward. She figures they'd send a hit man after her and she'd wind up in a ditch."

"We'll see how this goes and if needed, we can subpoena her."

"I would hate to have to do that," Reese said.

"Me, too, but the law is the law. If Hunter's guilty of murder, he needs to be in jail. Just like if he's the one who assaulted Ford."

"Absolutely. And I have a theory about why Bella didn't try to save herself when she fell in the river. If Hunter had been poisoning her, she was weak and her mind was clouded. She wasn't herself."

Jeremy nodded "Considering his family's wealth, why would he want to off his wives? Surely he's gotten a big piece of the pie."

"Actually, he hasn't," Reese said. "I heard he's been cut out of the family will."

"The oldest son of our county's prominent ranching family has been disinherited? Hard to believe."

"According to rumors, Hunter got into drugs and turned into a bum. His parents kicked him out years ago and decided his younger brother Hugh would inherit their ranch."

Jeremy whistled. "That sure must have pissed off Hunter."

"No doubt. He likes fancy things, like his shiny Cadillac SUV, for example. Since he was raised with a silver spoon in his mouth, but can't count on his family to support him any longer, maybe he's been running a scheme to collect life insurance from deceased wives."

"What makes you think that?"

"I understand he received a nice settlement when his first wife died."

"Then when Jayla Weeks left him, she foiled his plan," Jeremy said.

"He got lucky when Bella drowned," Reese said. "It saved him the trouble of continuing to poison her."

"But he indirectly caused her death," Jeremy said.

"I think so, too," Reese said.

"This is a lot to process, but I believe you're on to something," Jeremy said.

"People do terrible things for money," Reese said. "It disgusts me."

"I'm going to call Hunter to see if he's home," Jeremy said as he reached for his phone. He dialed, but must have gotten voice mail because he hung up. "Maybe he'll be home later and we can swing by for a visit."

"Sounds like a plan," Reese said.

"Until we can catch up with him, I need a damn beer," Jeremy said. "I've been working late every night this week. Want to get one with me?"

Reese stood. "Let's go to The Vulture's Nest for a quick one."

Chapter Twenty-Two

Since Reese knew where the bar was located, she offered to drive, so they climbed into her Bronco. She started Betty's engine and directed the old girl to the west side of town where a few shabby motels lined the street. Then she turned onto Townsend Road, drove beneath a railroad bridge and went down a narrow street.

Sitting next to a streetlight was The Vulture's Nest, a teepee-shaped building covered in a stucco finish. When she'd been a kid, it had been an auction place that she'd visited with her grandfather. They'd found unique treasures, including furniture he'd shown her how to refinish and flip for a profit.

Reese pulled in and parked next to a small black sedan. It was only seven o'clock in the evening, however, several trucks and an assortment of other vehicles nearly filled the lot to capacity.

Glancing at herself in her rearview mirror, she smoothed down her hair. "Why didn't you tell me I look like a scarecrow?"

He chuckled. "You're fine."

The two got out of her truck and strolled past a row of motorcycles. At the entrance they approached a bald, beefy guy who wore a black T-shirt emblazoned with white words: SECURITY, ID REQUIRED, NO GANG COLORS AND NO ASSHOLES OR WE'LL REFUSE SERVICE.

"Hello," she said, whipping out her driver's license.

He studied the card, then waved her into the building.

Jeremy lifted aside his suit jacket to reveal his shiny detective's badge.

"Have a nice evening, sir," the guy said.

Reese winced as they entered the dark establishment throbbing with death metal music. She headed over toward the bar where six heavily-tattooed guys in jeans and leather jackets stood talking and drinking.

Her gaze drifted toward the hideous stuffed vulture in a nest perched on a shelf above a display of booze bottles.

Jeremy leaned down and whispered in her ear, "I assume that feathered freak must be the bar's mascot."

She snickered. "I believe you're right."

Reese sidled up to the counter and hiked one boot on the metal footrest. She pulled a $20 from her purse and waited for the bartender to approach.

One of the bigger fellows in a black doo rag decorated with red and orange flames turned and winked at her. He had a giant brown and gray beard that brushed his black T-shirt and a silver stud piercing his left brow. Muscles bulged from his arms and his chest looked as broad as a barrel.

"Ah, little lady no need for that," he said. "I'll cover it. What are you having?"

"Thanks, but I'm buying for myself and my friend here." She nodded toward Jeremy, who smiled at doo rag.

My mistake," he said with a grin. "Reaching for a cigarette hanging on an ashtray, he took a long drag.

"No problem," Reese said.

"Keep an eye on this one," doo rag told Jeremy. "Somebody's gonna snatch her away from you if you don't watch out."

"I'll keep that in mind," Jeremy said.

"There's an open table," Reese told Jeremy. "Let's play some pool."

She led the way through the smoky establishment, her cheeks stinging as she realized doo rag thought she and Jeremy were a couple. She placed her beer bottle on a narrow counter then eased up to a pool table covered in stained green felt.

A giant fluorescent light fixture suspended above the pool table illuminated the surface. Nearby, a large fiberglass shark with lights inset in its belly had been placed on two hanging chains.

You can never have too much light for pool, Reese thought as she studied it.

At another pool table nearby stood a man, probably in his late thirties, wearing leather pants and a black T-shirt. Eyes narrowed, he took his time leaning over the table to line up the colorful balls before he aimed and took his shot.

A small woman, her mousy brown hair in a braid, stood behind him, and Reese wondered if she was old enough to be in a bar. If so, she must be barely legal. She wore a pink sundress and sandals and giggled a lot.

A server came by and the two ordered nachos.

"How does 8-ball sound to you?" Jeremy asked.

"Rack 'em up," she said, trying to focus on having a nice night, rather than worrying about her cases.

As they hit the balls with cue sticks, smacking the objects together, they also joked with each other. Reese eventually relaxed. Unfortunately, her ears seemed nearly numb from the clanging music. If she came to the bar very often, by the time she was 60, she'd probably need hearing aids.

Reese talked about her visit with Jayla Weeks and what she had begun to suspect about Hunter—that he was running a life insurance scam by killing his wives. It made sense, especially since his parents had cut him off from any financial support. Jeremy believed in her theory, but he said they would need hard evidence to prove it.

When they decided to end the evening, Reese wondered if Jeremy considered this a date. Nah, she decided, this was only a friendly game of pool with a co-worker. Nothing more.

She and Jeremy high fived and laughed, then took good-natured jabs at each other about their game prowess, or lack thereof. They'd each only had the one beer, and had consumed ice water afterward, so their minds were clear.

"Let's do this again soon, Reese," Jeremy said, his dark eyes sparkling.

"I'd like that," she said, glancing at her watch, surprised that two hours had gone by. She was tired, but felt strangely energized after spending time with Jeremy.

"I'm going to see if Hunter's answering his phone yet." Jeremy whipped out his cell phone and dialed. After a bit, he clicked off the call and frowned. "Still no answer."

"Maybe he's out of town," Reese suggested.

"Before we call it a night, let's swing by Hunter's place. If he's home, I'd like to ask him a couple of questions."

Reese had a good idea of what Jeremy hoped to accomplish. "Do you think he'll slip and say something incriminating?"

"It's worth a try, don't you think?"

"Sure," she said.

"I just can't stop thinking about your theory," Jeremy added as the two of them put away the pool cues and the colored balls. "I'm curious."

"Me, too."

They walked outside into the warm, smoky air. From the distant train tracks came the sound of a locomotive sounding its lonely whistle.

A man ambled across the pothole-riddled road and past a gnarled cottonwood tree. He wore a brown leather vest, jeans, boots, and a safari hat. He smiled at them, showing off his friendly, tanned face.

"G'Day folks, are you enjoying the warm weather?" he asked them in what sounded like a New Zealand accent. "Although, it's a bit smoky from yon wildfires that I understand are raging south of the area."

Reese had lived with a family in Auckland for a semester as a high school foreign exchange student, so she had become familiar with their dialect.

"Hello," both Reese and Jeremy said.

"Are you going to The Vulture's Nest?" Reese asked.

"Indeed, I'm meeting a friend there," he said. "He told me I couldn't visit Meadowlark Valley without seeing the famous biker bar. But I'm lost. Can you help me?"

"It's right across the street," Jeremy said, pointing.

The man narrowed his gaze and looked over at the building. "Ah, there it is! Right in front of my eyes. Thanks mate."

Reese unlocked the Bronco doors. She and Jeremy climbed in, they buckled up, and she drove toward Hunter's house.

"What if he's not home?" she asked.

"I'll drive over again tomorrow."

"Want me to go with?"

He rested his hands on his knees. "Sure."

Reese got anxious again thinking about her and Jeremy, then told herself to stop being ridiculous. It was always better to question a suspect with a partner, if it was possible.

When she pulled up in front of Hunter's house, she immediately spotted his SUV in the driveway. The lights inside the house were also on.

"Looks like we're in luck," she said as she parked along the curb.

They got out of the truck and walked up the sidewalk, then onto the porch. Jeremy rang the doorbell and stood back. Side by side, they waited for Hunter to open the door, but he never did.

"I swear it looks like he's home," Jeremy said.

"Maybe he looked out a window and saw us," Reese said. "And he doesn't want to talk."

"Yeah, maybe." Jeremy pointed to right side of the house. "You go around that way and I'll go in the opposite direction. It's still light enough outside to make out anything suspicious."

"Got it." Reese said.

"Don't take any risks," Jeremy warned. "Come get me if something seems off."

Reese walked onto the driveway, stopping to look inside Hunter's SUV. It was full of fast-food wrappers and other trash, but there weren't any telltale signs of trouble.

She continued walking around the house, peering into the bushes and flowers so she didn't miss anything. Stepping over a decorative split rail fence, she went around the back of the house. The sound of running water caught her attention, and she noted the screen punched out of an open window.

Yellow Chrysanthemums sat directly beneath it, crushed and mangled as though they'd been stepped on. Reese leaned over and noticed a hammer covered in sticky blood. Dried red streaks marred the surrounding blossoms and leaves, and the screen laid on the lawn.

When Jeremy rounded the corner of the house, she pointed out what she'd found. "Have a look at this!"

Hurrying over, he hunkered down to study the ground. "We'd better look inside to see if someone's hurt."

Or dead, Reese thought, but didn't say it aloud.

Jeremy walked up to the patio door with Reese following. Fortunately, it wasn't locked and he opened it. He unholstered his gun and held it at the ready as they entered, searching the front room and the kitchen. Hearing the water again, Reese walked down the hallway and opened the door to the bathroom.

Steam rolled out past her, fanning her with moist heat as she called, "Hunter, are you in there?"

Jeremy scooted around her and stepped into the moist confines. "What's going on, man? Are you okay?"

Still no answer.

Reaching for the shower curtain, Jeremy nodded to Reese and began to pull it aside.

She watched tensely until Hunter's body appeared. His head rested on the side of the tub, one side bashed in and bloody. The rest of his large body lay under the shower, pale and gleaming from the hot water. Swallowing bile, she whipped her cell phone from her pocket and punched in 911.

"He's dead," Jeremy said as he checked for a pulse on Hunter's wrist. "Call—."

"On it," Reese told him, cradling the cell to her ear. To the operator, she said, "I'm reporting a homicide."

Chapter Twenty-Three

The shrill cry of sirens sounded in the distance, becoming louder until red and blue lights flashed through the front window of Hunter's house. Jeremy opened the door and ushered in two police officers, one of whom was Allison Berry, the officer on duty the day Ford had been attacked in his store.

"The crime scene investigators are on their way," the red-headed officer said.

"The body's in the bathroom," Jeremy said as he led the way down the hall, with the officers following.

Reese began strolling around, looking closely for any clues about the identity of Hunter's killer. Pillows on the couch looked haphazardly placed, but nothing else in the living room appeared out of order.

In the kitchen, she studied the counters, which held typical appliances like a toaster, a blender and cannisters. On the table were two wine glasses, indicating there had been another person here earlier.

Leaning closer, Reese studied the glass with a dish cloth placed next to it. The rim appeared to have been wiped clean. Obviously, the killer had attempted to destroy fingerprints and any traces of DNA.

With a pen she withdrew from her purse, she opened cupboards and perused the contents. A bag of rat poison pellets rested on a shelf in the pantry. Nearby sat boxes of wheat squares and sugar rings. Reese frowned. Who in the heck stores pesticides near cereal?

A man who sprinkles it in his wives' smoothies, she thought.

When she heard vehicle motors, Reese went back to the front room and parted the curtains. A black CSI van had parked along the curb, along with a black county coroner van.

She went into the living room, introduced herself as they entered and told them where the body was.

One of the workers went back to talk to the officers, then rejoined his team. Before long, the workers had looped their yellow crime scene tape outside and began processing the area.

Reese wandered upstairs to where the bedrooms were located. In one, she found an office with a wooden desk and matching file cabinets. She reached into her purse and fished out a pair of blue plastic gloves.

Opening the top file drawer, she rifled through a couple of manilla folders. They contained personal information like birth certificates, passports, etc. Other folders held utility bills, heating bills and the like.

The bottom drawer was locked, so Reese pulled out a lock pick from her purse and wedged it open. Now she could get to the folders that contained information about Hunter's sign company, Ad Pro. At the very back of the drawer, four files were labeled in thick block print with the names of Lisa Tremblay, Jayla Weeks, Bella Northwood, and finally, Ivy Drake.

Reese removed the files and spread them out on the desk.

"What'd you find?" Jeremy asked as he sauntered into the office.

"Come see," Reese told him.

He eased up alongside of her and studied the folders.

"Let's look inside," he said, reaching for Lisa's folder.

Reese opened Bella's file. Tucked inside was a life insurance policy Hunter had taken out on her for $500,000. A yellow sticky note pasted to the top read, TO BE PAID. Additionally, several tresses of brunette hair tied with a pink bow had been taped to the top.

"What do you know?" Jeremy held up a similar life insurance policy with Lisa's name on it, in the amount of $600,000. The yellow sticky note on it read, PAID. More brunette hair tied with a blue bow had been taped on it.

"Incredible," Reese said.

"Look at these," Jeremy said as he opened the two remaining files and pulled out life insurance policies for Jayla Weeks and Ivy Drake, each one worth $500,000. In similar fashion, they held clumps of hair with a yellow ribbon and a green ribbon respectively. Jayla's sticky note said, CANCELLED. Ivy's policy bore another note that said, PENDING.

"You guessed it," Jeremy said. "Hunter was operating a life insurance scam."

"I got lucky."

"Gut instinct," Jeremy said.

"I don't think Hunter made a killing running Ad Pro, but it seems that his life insurance scam paid off," Reese said.

"With Lisa Tremblay, at least it did," Jeremy said. "Luckily for Jayla Weeks, she left him before he could poison her."

"True," Reese said. "Bella's life insurance settlement would bring in some significant cash, but now that he's deceased, he won't be able to collect."

"Right," Jeremy said. "I'll check with Lisa Tremblay's family, though. Considering what we just found, and your suspicions that Hunter's been poisoning his wives, they may want to have her body exhumed for testing."

"If I were her mom or maybe her sister, I'd want to have it done. Then I'd know why she died."

"Me, too," Jeremy said.

"By the way, I found Hunter's favorite ingredient for his smoothies—rat poison—in the kitchen pantry."

"Sick bastard," Jeremy said, making a face.

"Poor Ivy," Reese said. "She was Hunter's next victim."

"It's too late tonight to go talk to her, but we should stop by her place tomorrow," Jeremy said. "Will you have time to go with me?"

Reese thought about the idea. "I'd planned to write up Bella's accident report for the department. Can you wait a bit longer for it?"

"Yeah, you can turn that in later. I'd rather have you with me tomorrow."

"I'll ride with you, then," Reese said.

"I also need to notify Pearl and Walt Northwood about their son's death. I'd rather talk to them in person than call."

"I agree, it's heartless," Reese said. "I always preferred the personal touch, too."

Jeremy ran a hand through his thick hair. "We'd better stop by the Presley's place to tell Naomi and Ian."

"We can also ask about how Ford is doing." Reese collected her lock pick from the desk and dropped it into her purse. Then she peeled off her gloves and dropped them into a wastebasket.

"I'll pick you up at nine tomorrow morning," Jeremy said.

"That'll work," Reese said. "Meanwhile, I'm bushed. I'm going to head home to get some sleep. Will you be able to catch a ride back to the station?"

"No problem," Jeremy said.

"Good."

"Hey, thanks for your help tonight," Jeremy said.

Reese tossed Jeremy a smile, then left Hunter's house and headed to her Bronco. She started up the engine, then drove home, weariness sifting through her. After parking under her carport, she let herself into her place.

Feeling as dead as a zombie, she tossed her purse on table, then undressed as she headed to her bedroom, leaving a trail of clothes behind her. While she crawled under the covers, Bo jumped up beside her, kneaded her shoulder with his paws, and began to purr.

Before long, she drifted off to sleep. Her dreams consisted of rafting down the river and going over a waterfall again. This time, she didn't turn into a mermaid at the end.

Bella stood on the bank waving to her. Reese managed to make her way over to where her friend stood. As she struggled to get out of the water, Bella reached down and helped her onto solid ground.

"I need your help," Bella told her earnestly. "You've got to save me. You're the only one who can."

Reese awakened with a jolt, repeating the dream in her mind. It had seemed so real; however, she knew it was just her imagination playing tricks. *Again.* Bella was dead, no matter how much Reese wished she wasn't.

She stretched out on the mattress and stared at the darkened ceiling until drowsiness pulled her into the realm of Morpheus. Because she'd recently encountered Hunter's dead body, and she wondered who would have taken his life, troubling dreams continued to plague Reese.

Her slumber was far from restful.

Chapter Twenty-Four

When her alarm rang the next morning, Reese dragged herself out of bed and yawned. Bo also yawned and stretched, then he looked at her and meowed.

"Good day to you, sir," she told him, wondering if she was the only person on the planet who talked to her cat as if he was a human being.

She threw her bed together as best she could with Bo still curled up on the covers, then she headed to the shower. After a good soak, she dressed in jeans, boots, and an embroidered drawstring blouse.

Yawning again, she prepared the coffee pot and turned it on. She longed to swing by Starbucks, but didn't want to take the time this morning. By the time she'd finished eating an apple for breakfast, the brew was ready. Pouring herself a steaming cupful, she entered her office. At her desk, she fired up her computer, brought up the internet, and logged into her email.

She scrolled through messages until she noticed one from someone named Doug Marsh. She opened it, anticipating he might be a potential client.

After clicking the message, she read:

Hello, I'm a senior at Meadowlark Valley High.

Reese sighed, expecting the typical request for a job shadow because he was working on a project about private investigators.

I'm responding to the newspaper ad you placed, asking for anyone who was at the Trout River on the day Bella Northwood drowned to contact you. I was there, and I'm pretty sure I saw her after the accident. If you can, meet me at the abandoned cabin off of Wilderness Way this morning at 7 a.m.

Reese frowned. It'd be amazing if Bella had made it out of the river, but she knew that was impossible. Maybe Doug had seen someone who looked like her. Nevertheless, she owed it to him to see what he had to say. He'd gone to the trouble of responding to her ad.

Picking up a pen, she chewed thoughtfully on the cap.

Jeremy would be coming by in a couple of hours, so she had to make it a quick trip out to the river. Bottom line, she wasn't going to pass up the opportunity to hear Doug's story. If he was playing games, and she felt threatened, she had pepper spray and she knew how to use it.

Grabbing her purse and keys, she left the house and walked to her Bronco parked in the carport. Climbing in, she drove out of the city and toward the Trout River. A smoky pallor filled the sky above the prairie bluffs. The mountains, although nearly hidden by haze, were still visible on the horizon.

Familiar landscape passed by, including the KOA Campground and the Trout River Sporting Club. She'd heard their dining room served great rib eye steaks, but she'd only been there once when a boy had treated her to dinner before the senior prom.

Through the trees, she spotted the river's blue waves rushing past the grassy banks. She turned on Wilderness Way and headed west toward the dilapidated cabin located further down the road.

Local legend claimed that a prospector had built the shack for himself and his family as he searched for gold. He didn't strike it rich, however. Eventually, he'd moved he and his family back to Meadowlark Valley where he'd opened a blacksmith shop. It was a typical tale of the old west and the resilience of local settlers.

When she spotted the log structure located on a rocky knoll, she pulled off onto a dirt area and parked next to an older model sedan. The rusty green paint and dented fender gave it a vintage look.

Stepping out of the Bronco, she pushed her keys in one of her jeans' pockets and her cell phone in another. Then she withdrew a small black cylinder of pepper spray from her purse. Cautiously, she approached the log building.

A small patch of yellow leaves in the top branches of a nearby aspen tree indicated the nights were getting colder. During the next few weeks, groves would begin to show autumn hues of crimson, orange and brown. The surrounding pine and spruce trees would remain evergreen, even when they were coated with winter snow.

Standing on the rickety porch of the cabin, she called out, "Doug? Are you in there?"

Someone shot out from behind the cabin, racing away at top speed. A female with long red hair, wearing a plaid poncho, Reese noted.

"Stop," she shouted.

The girl looked over her shoulder at Reese, but continued running through the tangled weeds. She whipped around a corner and disappeared from view.

Worried about Doug, Reese hurried inside the dark front room. With only one dirty window in the place, there wasn't much light.

As she stepped across the floor, her boots crunched on dead leaves, dry grass, and food wrappers. Musty, mildewy odors assailed her nostrils. Her toe hit something and it skittered across the floor. She noticed it was only an empty soda can.

Spiders had claimed the abandoned place as their own, draping cobwebs from all corners. Creepy, crawly little beasts, she thought, hating the idea that one might spin a silken strand and parachute down on her head.

She shivered. Those critters were the bane of her existence.

"Doug, it's Reese Golden," she called. "Are you in here?"

Entering another room, she noted more debris littered across the floor. Then she spotted the unmistakable outline of someone slumped in a corner.

"Doug!"

Hurrying over, Reese knelt down. She examined the young man, noting he had a bleeding gash on his forehead. He moaned, and Reese's heart skipped a beat as he moved his head.

"You're going to be fine," she assured him. She grabbed her cell and started to punch in numbers

"Who are you calling?" He grabbed her arm, glaring at her.

"911."

"No." He sat up and ran his head through his sandy-colored hair. "I'm fine."

"Someone smacked you in the head. You're bleeding."

He reached up and wiped his face on his hoodie sleeve. "There," he said, wincing. "That should take care of it."

"You need a doctor." Reese scowled at him. "You might have a concussion."

He stood and brushed off his clothing. "It's nothing worse than I've gotten playing football. I'll live."

"But—"

"My mom'll kill me if she finds out I'm here. I'm supposed to be grounded."

"I don't think she'd would, especially knowing you've been attacked."

"I know the girl who hit me," Doug said. "She's from my school. I don't want her to get in trouble."

"The redhead?"

He nodded. "I think she's homeless, and she was staying out here. I must have startled her, because she grabbed a stick and clocked me."

"That's concerning," Reese said, spotting the branch at his feet.

"She only shows up at school once in a while," Doug explained. "I'd have given her a ride today, but she took off before I could offer."

"Probably scared," Reese said.

"I feel sorry for her."

"She's not safe living on her own," Reese said. "Tell a counselor at your high school you found her sleeping out here. Do you know her name?"

"I think it's Nikki."

"I'm sure the school can help her."

"Good idea," Doug said.

The dark, damp cabin interior made Reese shiver. "Let's go outside to talk."

"Yeah," he said, rubbing his head. "This old place gives me the creeps."

Chapter Twenty-Five

Outside, Reese headed to her truck and opened the passenger door. She reached into the glove compartment and produced a packet of wet wipes and a bottle of water. She handed them to Doug, who drank liberally, then used several wipes on his face and hands.

"Thanks," he said, tossing them on the ground. Reese scrounged around in her truck, grabbed a grocery sack and held it out.

With a grunt, Doug leaned over, collected his trash and dropped it into the bag. "You're as bad as my mom."

"We shouldn't litter." Reese tied the top, threw it in her truck, and brushed off her hands.

Doug leaned against a tree, whipped his cell phone from the front pocket of his hoodie and began scrolling.

Annoyed that he'd brought her out here to talk and now stared at his phone, Reese asked, "Did you tell anyone you were coming here today?"

He looked up. "Just my friend Colton Drake. He lives next door to me and we've been buddies for a long time. He was at the river partying with me and my friends the day I think I saw Bella."

"The day she drowned?"

"Right."

"Is his mom Ivy Drake?"

He nodded.

Hmm, Reese thought. Colton had probably told his mother that Doug thought he'd seen Bella after she was supposed to have drowned. She wondered what Ivy thought about that.

Reese crossed her arms over her chest. "What did you want to tell me, Doug?"

"Sorry." With a guilty look, he pocketed his cell phone. He sat on the ground, elbows resting on his knees. "Like I said before, I was at the river the day Bella drowned. School was getting ready to start up, and since this is our senior year, me and some friends were celebrating."

"Okay."

"That's the reason I'm grounded, by the way. My mom found out."

"Not good to piss off the parents." Reese sat on a tree stump and stretched out her legs.

"No shit—I mean no kidding. Yesterday my mom mentioned the newspaper ad you placed, asking people who might have seen something that day to contact you. I almost didn't do it, but I decided I should anyway."

"What happened?"

"My girlfriend and I went for a short hike and we were, well, you know, making out."

Reese was amused at how red Doug's face became, but she didn't want to embarrass him by smiling. She pasted on her best poker face.

"Gina and I were in the woods across from this cabin," he continued. "We heard someone crying and when we looked around, we noticed a soaking wet woman in a life vest running from the river."

Reese tensed. "What did she look like?"

"She was tall and had long dark hair. I swear she looked like Bella. I know her from church. Gina and I both decided we should try to catch up to her and see if she needed help. When we did, she told us she was fine and that she left something on the stove, or something like that. She seemed so upset, her words came out all jumbled."

"She said she left something on the stove?" Reese asked, completely puzzled.

"Yeah."

"Maybe the woman you saw had been cooking before coming to the river."

"Right, that's what me'n Gina thought too. Weird, huh?"

"What happened next?"

"She took off running again. She headed toward an old, beat-up orange truck parked in the underbrush not far from the road. She pulled keys from her pocket, got in and drove off. I swear I've never seen anyone move so fast."

"Did you get a license plate number?"

"No."

"Which way did she go?"

Doug pointed south. "It's been so dry around here that the dirt mushroomed up around her like a giant thunder cloud."

Reese recalled the orange truck she and Kiki had seen parked in this area on the GPS map.

"Thanks, Doug," Reese said.

"Do you think we actually saw Bella?"

"I don't know, but I appreciate you sharing your story with me."

"What will you do now?" Doug asked.

"I'll let the cops know," Reese told him. "I'm working with them on this case."

He shook his head. "I heard her family held a candlelight vigil. Why wouldn't she want them to know she was alive?"

"She may not have been Bella," Reese said. "You didn't talk to her for long. And she was dripping wet."

"I guess." Doug stood up. "Just don't tell my mom what we talked about. I'm already in hot water for partying at the river that day. If she knew I was out in the woods with Gina, well, you can imagine how much more trouble I'd be in."

Reese stood up. "I promise, I'll never mention it to your mother. I don't know her, anyway."

"She's the high school principal."

"Wow."

"It really sucks when your mom's in charge."

They both laughed.

Reese glanced at her watch. "You probably need to get to school."

"Yep," Doug told her as he raced to his car.

Reese watched as he drove away, her mind working overtime. Immersed in this woodsy area, listening to the birds call and insects buzz, she wondered if Doug and Gina had actually seen Bella.

It didn't seem likely, but she decided she needed to have another look at Bella's journal, the one Clara had given her. Then she needed to give it to Naomi. When Ford got out of his coma, he would probably appreciate having his daughter's writings. Hopefully, the journal would comfort him, rather than evoke painful reminders that his daughter was gone.

• • •

Thoughts in Reese's head swirled like a merry-go-round as she drove back into town. Jeremy was parking his dark blue SUV along the curb in front of her house when she pulled under her carport. Grabbing her purse, she jumped out of her Bronco and walked toward his vehicle. Opening the passenger door, she climbed in.

"Where've you been?" He asked. Along with his polished boots, he wore a gray corduroy jacket, jeans, a white shirt, and a braided leather bolo tie secured with a silver and turquoise slide.

"You've really got your western detective look down, don't you?" Reese ran an appreciative glance over his attire.

"I asked you a question first," he said.

"I don't recall whether I told you I placed an ad in the local newspaper, asking people to contact me if they were at the Trout River the day Bella drowned."

"You didn't," he said.

"I always like to gather eyewitness accounts of incidents. Anyway, this morning, I met with a person who believes he saw Bella after she fell in the river."

"That's doubtful."

"My thoughts exactly. But I heard him out."

"What did he say?"

"He encountered a drenched woman wearing a life jacket hurrying through the woods She got in an old orange truck parked near the road and drove south."

"Can't do much with that," Jeremy said.

"I know," Reese agreed. "

"Nice he contacted you, though."

"Yes, it is."

Jeremy started the engine and drove down the street. "First stop we're going to make today is Ivy Drake's house. She should know Hunter is dead, especially since she'd have been his next victim."

"I bet she'll be surprised," Reese said. "When I saw them together, they were pretty lovey-dovey."

Jeremy rubbed the back of his neck. "Today's going to be a long one."

"I figured as much."

"You okay with that?"

"That's the story of my life right now—long days."

"Ivy lives in Elk Haven Estates, right?"

Reese nodded. "She's at 5632 Mustang Lane."

Jeremy headed north toward the bluff overlooking the city, where the exclusive neighborhood showcased its sophisticated homes and stellar landscaping.

"By the way, do you have any other suspects to question about the assault on Ford?" he asked.

"Just Hunter. I still suspect the two of them fought because Ford learned about Hunter's affair with Ivy."

Jeremy nodded. "If I found out my daughter's husband had been cheating on her, I'd be livid."

"It's all a moot point now since Hunter's dead," Reese said. "If Ford comes out of that coma all right, hopefully he can tell us who put him in the hospital."

Upon reaching Ivy's neighborhood, a carved sign on a hill announced that visitors had found Elk Haven Estates. Reese didn't recall seeing that the last time she'd been here. She did, however, remember the tall trees, emerald green lawns and shrubs surrounding the beautiful homes lining the streets.

Jeremy gave a low whistle as he studied the display. He turned into Ivy's circular driveway and continued toward the Georgian style country house constructed of pale white stone. Once again, Reese found herself impressed with the splendid cottonwood trees, the flowering bushes and the bubbling fountain.

She remembered following Ivy out here after the candlelight vigil. That's when she'd spotted Hunter and the widow in the throes of passion.

Jeremy parked in the driveway and Reese got out of his vehicle. She followed him to the front door and waited as he pressed the doorbell.

A few seconds later, Ivy opened up. She wore a matching, cream-colored, two-piece pantsuit patterned with green palm fronds. Her dark curls cascaded down her back and the large diamond on her wedding ring flashed in the sunlight, as did her bejeweled white sandals.

Ivy glanced at the detective badge on Jeremy's belt, and her eyes widened. "Good morning, officers," she said.

"Detective Savage is with the police," Reese said, touching his arm. "I'm a private investigator."

"I see," Ivy said. "How can I help you?"

"We need to talk to you about something," Jeremy said. "May we come in?"

"Of course," she said, standing aside so Reese and Jeremy could enter.

"Please have a seat in my living room," Ivy said as she walked into a lavishly decorated sitting area.

Reese perched on a long white couch, and Jeremy took a place next to her. Looking uncomfortable, he scooted around, trying to wedge between the multitude of champagne-colored pillows.

Reese tried not to smile. Most men she knew hated pillows.

Pale silver ceiling-to-floor curtains edged tall windows. A tall stone urn in one corner held a bouquet of icy white flowers, a white and gold rug covered the marble floor and a round glass table held a lit candle, a couple of books and a delicate China tea set.

Holding out a slender hand, her nails adorned with a French manicure, Ivy pointed toward the lone teacup on the glass table. "I'd just sat down for some tea," she explained. "I'd have planned to serve the two of you, but I didn't know you were coming."

"We're sorry to interrupt you, Mrs. Drake," Jeremy said. "We have something important to tell you, and it can't wait."

Ivy sat down on another couch across from them. "What is it?"

"Hunter Northwood is dead," Jeremy said without fanfare.

Ivy's face went pale, until it looked nearly as frosty as her living room.

"We're sorry to spring it on you like this," Reese said. "You may be wondering why we are telling you this, but we know you and Hunter were...close."

Ivy sighed. "We tried to be discreet, considering his wife's recent death."

"We understand, ma'am," Jeremy said. "We still thought you should know."

"I'm d-devastated," Ivy said, her lower lip trembling. She withdrew a lacy white handkerchief from her pocket and dabbed the tears on her cheeks. "What happened?"

"We found him last night," Jeremy said. "That's all I can tell you at this time. The coroner will release an official ruling about the cause of death."

Ivy stood, walked over to the large windows and looked out, her back to Reese and Jeremy.

"I hope you don't mind me asking how you became acquainted with Hunter," Jeremy said.

Ivy turned back around to face her guests.

"Hunter and I have been in love for years," Ivy said. "We were in college when we met, and we were young. We planned to marry, but his parents were furious when he told them. They warned Hunter that I wasn't good enough for him and that if we wed, they would cut him out of their family trust."

"That must have been difficult for you," Reese murmured.

"I was mortified," Ivy said. "And it hurt me deeply."

"I'm sure it did," Reese added.

"Hunter dropped out of college and disappeared. I didn't know where he was for a long time, then he finally called. He said he'd been wandering the countryside, doing odd jobs. I believe that's when he got into drugs and started gambling. We didn't talk again after that. I graduated and moved back home to Meadowlark Valley to work, which is where I met Henry—Dr. Drake. He was a wonderful man, and a great father to our son, Colton."

"My condolences on his passing," Jeremy said.

"Please accept my deepest sympathies," Reese added.

"Thank you both," Ivy said. "The saddest part of all this is that Hunter's parents wound up disinheriting him after all because of his unsavory lifestyle. After that, he married other women that Pearl and Walt also considered 'unsuitable.' "

"Do you have any ideas about who would want to murder him and why?" Jeremy asked.

"No." Tears running down her face, Ivy came back and sat down on the couch across from Reese and Jeremy. "I suppose I should tell you my little secret since you'll probably find out anyway."

"What is that?" Reese asked.

"As you know, Hunter and I had resumed our friendship."

"How long ago?" Jeremy asked.

"After Bella died. Hunter was understandably upset, and I wanted to comfort him."

Reese realized that blew apart her theory that Hunter and Ivy's affair had been the reason that Ford and Hunter had quarreled. Then again, perhaps they'd quarreled because right after Bella's death, Hunter had immediately turned to another woman.

"You see, since Hunter and I had both lost our spouses, we didn't want to be apart any longer. We went down to the courthouse yesterday morning and were married by a justice of the peace."

"You're Hunter's wife?" Jeremy raised his brows

Ivy held up her left hand. "Yes, and this is the wedding ring he gave me."

Reese and Jeremy exchanged a knowing glance.

"We have reason to believe Hunter planned to poison you to death, as we believe he did with his first wife, in order to collect a life insurance settlement," Jeremy said.

Ivy pressed her hands against her chest, her eyes flashing. "No! He wouldn't do that!"

"We found a life insurance policy on you in the files at his house, and of course, he's named as the beneficiary," Reese said.

Ivy shook her head. "I can't believe it."

"It's the truth," Reese said.

"One more question," Jeremy said. "Where were you between seven and nine o'clock last night? And where was Colton?"

"Why?" Ivy frowned.

"It's just a standard question," Reese told her.

"A standard question for a murder suspect," Ivy said in a huff. "I can assure you I did not kill Hunter. It was our wedding day, after all."

"I understand," Jeremy said. "Still, I need to know where you were."

"I was here at home with Colton. We were watching TV."

"And he'll be able to back that up?"

"Absolutely. We were watching some ridiculous show about a bachelor picking his bride." Ivy stood, glaring at both Reese and Jeremy. "I'd like you both to leave now."

"One more question," Jeremy said. "Why didn't you and Hunter go somewhere for your honeymoon?"

Ivy placed her hands on her hips. "We didn't want to upset anyone, considering Hunter had just lost Bella. Besides, the gossips would have had a heyday. We decided it would be better to wait a while, then quietly announce our marriage."

"I'm surprised he wasn't at least with you last night," Reese said.

"Hunter said he had some work to finish up at his place," Ivy said. "He was going to come over later in the evening, and we were going to tell my son we were married. But Hunter never arrived. I called, but he didn't answer. I assumed he'd gotten caught up with a project and he'd decided to come over to my house the next day."

"That takes care of what I needed to know for now." Jeremy glanced at Reese. "Do you have anything else to ask?"

"No," Reese said.

"This is such a shock," Ivy sobbed. "I need to be by myself to process everything."

Reese and Jeremy stood at the same time.

"We'll head out now," Jeremy said. "But please, think about who might have held a grudge against Hunter or who may have disliked him enough to kill him."

"I will," Ivy said in a shaky tone.

Jeremy placed one of his business cards on the glass table, and Reese plopped down one of hers.

"Call either of us if you think of anything else," he said. "Even if it seems trivial."

"I'll do that, Detective Savage," Ivy said. "I appreciate you coming to tell me about Hunter, even if I was put off by your line of questioning."

"It's understandable, especially at a time like this," he said.

Reese walked alongside Jeremy as they left the front room. Next to them, Ivy cried softly into her handkerchief.

"Is there anyone you'd like us to call?" Reese said. "I hate to leave you so upset."

"No, I'll be all right. Just go, please." Ivy continued dabbing at her red nose. "I'm going upstairs to get some rest. I believe you two can let yourselves out."

"Of course," Reese said.

Ivy started walking up a staircase, her sobs echoing down the hallway.

When Ivy was out of view, Reese turned to Jeremy. "I know Doug's story about seeing Bella after she drowned might seem farfetched, but I'm going to follow up on it."

Jeremy eased toward the entrance and reached for the doorknob. "How are you going to do that?"

"Remember Bella's journal, the one Clara Washington gave me? I've been reading through it as I have time. I'm hoping she left a message in it that could give me a clue about what's going on."

"You don't really think Bella made it out of that river alive, do you?"

"I can't say. But I want to investigate it."

"If Bella had survived, why wouldn't she have let someone know?" He shook his head. "Why in the hell wouldn't she tell her family, instead of letting them suffer through the grief of losing her?"

"That's what I want to find out."

"You can go chasing after ghosts if you want," Jeremy growled. "As for me, I've got work to do."

Reese and Jeremy walked outside and he closed the front door. As they approached Jeremy's SUV, he asked Reese, "Do you buy Ivy's story?"

"Seems reasonable enough to me," Reese said. "Apparently she and Hunter had kind of a Romeo and Juliet thing going on. It's sad."

"Yeah, I guess," Jeremy said. He opened Reese's door, allowing her to climb up and take a seat before he closed it. On the driver's side, he hopped in, started his engine and drove away from Elk Haven Estates.

Reese withdrew a notebook and pen from her purse and jotted down information about their visit with Ivy. Writing down thoughts clarified the jargon in her mind, and helped her to color outside of the lines and think of different ideas.

"What are you doing?" Jeremy asked.

"Documenting our conversation with Ivy. You know, since both of her husbands have died, maybe we should start calling her the black widow?"

Jeremy chuckled.

Chapter Twenty-Six

"The Presley's live outside town near Cactus Lake," Reese said. "They have a small farm."

Jeremy gripped his steering wheel. "I'm slowly learning my way around and I know where that is," he said.

"Stick with me, kid," Reese said. "I'll show you the ropes."

Jeremy drove down the main thoroughfare past businesses, then continued out past town toward a low range of mountains.

"Naomi and Ian should hear about Hunter's death from us, not from TV news," he said.

"Good call."

"I'd also like to ask them what they were doing yesterday evening."

"You seriously don't believe they had anything to do with Hunter's death, do you?"

He shrugged. "Remember, I said we can't rule out anyone."

"You're right," Reese said. "Maybe I'm losing my edge since I left the DPD."

"I doubt that," Jeremy said. "Being in the private sector now, you look at things differently."

"There is definitely a cop mindset when you're on the job," Reese agreed.

"Do you ever wish you hadn't resigned?" Jeremy asked.

"Sometimes," Reese said. "I still have dreams where I'm on the job, chasing the bad guys. Then I wake up and realize that part of my life is over."

They rode in silence for a short time, then Reese noticed the dark brown bi-level set amidst low hills and green rolling pastures full of angus cattle. A large barn sat on a knoll and several outbuildings dotted the fields. Fenced enclosures held grazing livestock.

"Right there," she said, pointing at a dirt road leading to the residence. "I dropped by Bella's place a few times when we were in high school. We studied together."

"Sure, you were studying," Jeremy said jokingly as he parked along the curb and turned off his engine. "You were probably talking about boys."

"They were discussed," Reese admitted. "But we always got good grades, so there must have been some studying going on."

They got out and walked up to the house, surrounded by combination of grass and xeriscaping, which probably made the landscape easier to maintain. It wasn't as smoky out here, and Reese could actually smell the loamy pastures, rather than a distinct campfire scent. Before either of them could ring the doorbell, Naomi opened the front door.

"Come on in," she said as she led them up a short staircase and into a living room. The beaded fringes on her suede vest rattled as she walked. "I was just on my way to the hospital to be with Ford."

"How is he doing?" Reese asked.

"The doctors are talking about bringing him out of the coma today or tomorrow," Naomi said.

"That's good news," Reese said.

"Yes, thank God," Naomi said. "Any updates about who attacked him?"

"We're still investigating," Jeremy told her.

"I hope you find out who did it," Naomi said. "Right now, though, I'm just focused on my husband's recovery."

"Have a seat," Naomi said as she sank into a leather recliner.

Reese sat down on the brown suede couch and Jeremy sat beside her. The furnishings were simple, with nothing ostentatious in view. A working family's home, Reese decided.

"I'll keep this simple since you're on your way out," Jeremy said. "We wanted to let you know that Hunter Northwood is dead."

"What?" Naomi gripped the arms on her chair, her knuckles white.

"He was discovered last night in his home," Jeremy added.

"An accident?"

"We're looking at murder," Jeremy said.

"Oh, no," Naomi said. "That's unsettling. What happened?"

"I can't release that information," Jeremy told her.

"Did you and Hunter get along well?" Reese asked.

"He wasn't my favorite person, even though he was my son-in-law. Ford and I didn't like the way he treated Bella."

"Why?" Reese asked.

"He talked down to her. Condescending, is the word. Poor Bella. Even though they'd only been married a few weeks, our girl didn't seem happy."

"Do you believe she regretted marrying him?"

"She never mentioned it out loud, but she seemed uncomfortable about something. Especially toward the end before..." Naomi sighed. "I guess we'll never know what was bothering her."

"I have to ask this, Naomi," Jeremy said. "Where were you between seven and nine in the evening yesterday?"

"At my bridge club," Naomi said. "I needed a break from the hospital, so I went to the game last night. As soon as it was over, I went back to be with Ford. The rooms have couches that make into beds, so I've been spending the nights there."

"Are there people who saw you playing bridge?" Jeremy said.

"You can check with Myra Cross, the club president," Naomi said. "She hosted the game at her house. The ladies and I finished our game around ten o'clock."

"And you drove straight from there back to the hospital?" Reese asked.

"Yes."

"Thank you, Naomi," Jeremy asked. "Where is Ian? Can we talk with him, too?"

"He's out of town," Naomi said.

"When did he leave?" Jeremy asked.

"Yesterday morning I drove him to the Laramie Regional Airport," Naomi said. "He's in San Antonio at the Seguin Rodeo."

"Participating in a bull riding contest?" Jeremy asked.

"Yes," Naomi said. "I hope he doesn't come home with a broken back or something else just as bad. So far, he's been lucky as far as getting terribly injured."

"I'm surprised he'd leave with Ford in the hospital," Reese said.

"Believe me, he didn't want to," Naomi said. "He's been worried sick about his dad. But I convinced him to go."

"Why is that?" Jeremy asked.

"Unless you make it big in the rodeo circuit, there's not much money to be made with that lifestyle. Ian can't afford to miss a chance to compete and possibly win a prize purse, even if it's a small one."

"Rodeo is a tough life," Reese said.

"It certainly is," Naomi said. "But we could never convince that boy to pursue a different career. If Ian doesn't get hurt, which I pray he never will, he's only got a few more years that he can compete. Most riders retire in their early thirties."

"Naomi, do you know of anyone who would want to hurt Hunter?" Jeremy asked. "Maybe he'd offended one of his customers or a business competitor?"

"I don't know anything about Hunter's sign company, just that he didn't make much money at it," Naomi said, rubbing her hands up and down her legs. "He worked long hours, but it wasn't very lucrative. From what I understand, he and Bella lived mostly on the income she made from the sale of her paintings and her job at the rec center."

"She taught swimming, didn't she?" Reese asked.

"Yes," Naomi said. "She was born under the sign of Pisces, so it's no wonder she was a good swimmer. In the end, unfortunately, not good enough to save herself."

Chapter Twenty-Seven

After talking with Naomi, Reese and Jeremy headed back out to his SUV and buckled into their seats. Jeremy drove until he turned onto the highway and drove north.

"Have you ever been to the Flying W Ranch?" Jeremy asked.

"No, I've only seen photos. It's huge, from what I understand."

"I've heard the same," Jeremy said. "I also heard that the Northwood family is a longtime member of the Wyoming Stock Growers Association."

"No doubt," Reese said. "There was a presentation at the Smythe Museum in town when I was a kid and my class went to see it. It talked about the families who settled Meadowlark Valley. Northwood ancestors came west in the early 1870s, bought up a bunch of land and developed their ranch. They've been one of the state's main cattle producers since time began, so it seems."

"They have lots of influence," Jeremy said.

"Somehow, they manage to get what they want," Reese said. "I have no idea how that works, but I've heard it all the same."

"Even if it breaks the law?"

"I can't say," Reese said. "I'm only curious what it would be like to have that much power."

"Would you want that kind of power?"

"Not really," Reese admitted. "It's incredible though, that if you throw enough money around, how people will find a way to bend rules."

"I've seen that plenty," Jeremy said.

"Me, too," Reese added. "Still, even with all their money, the

Northwoods couldn't keep Hunter in line. They couldn't buy their son out of a drug and gambling addiction."

"That's why I'm worried about ever having a family," Jeremy said. "Society has gone to the dogs and there are so many temptations for kids these days. It's scary."

"My grandmother always said that in the end, we have to have faith."

"Faith in what?" Jeremy gave her a curious glance.

"Faith in life; faith that everyone will eventually choose better paths. Whether it's in this world or the next."

Jeremy fixed his gaze back on the road. "That still doesn't give me a warm fuzzy about bringing a child into this mess."

"It's a choice," Reese responded. "You also have to have faith in yourself that you can guide your children and give them what they need to survive and do the right thing."

Jeremy didn't say anything else, but he seemed to be mulling over what Reese had said. Through the windows, she watched as the rolling brown prairie on either side of the Trailblazer turned from wildflowers and sagebrush into rocky hills.

Yucca plants were more prevalent here, and the spiky leafed plants thrust skyward a stem full of creamy white blossoms. Distant purple mountains were draped with white, since in the higher elevations it had gotten cold enough during late summer to collect snow.

Overhead, the sky was much clearer than it had been when they left Meadowlark Valley. The foothills still held the green of summer, and the rangeland stretched beneath the sun, covered with grass and grazing Texas Longhorn cattle. A curious breed, Longhorns, with their lengthy, curved horns. They came in an array of colors, and Reese studied the variety of brown, ochre, and black combinations.

Bunchgrass and bushes sprang up by a stream that meandered near the road, then low-slung outbuildings began to appear, along with an old wooden barn covered in peeling red paint. A newer style barn made of metal also stood nearby, along with a windmill that whirled in the breeze. Livestock pens and corrals also appeared in the fields.

A flat-roofed, Santa Fe-style home sprawled up ahead with pine, spruce and aspen as a backdrop. A blue lake nestled behind it with fingers of land stretching out toward the depths.

"It's beautiful up here," Reese said.

"Sure is," Jeremy responded.

After passing a mile marker, Jeremy turned down a dirt road. The Trailblazer bumped along the gravel as he headed toward the ranch house. Made of an earthy color of adobe, reminiscent of the desert, the home seemed warm and inviting.

Jeremy drove beneath a tall timber gate with a wooden sign that read: Flying W Ranch. Wagon wheels propped against the poles on either side of the gate gave off definitive western vibes, along with the blue green sagebrush.

Beside the road, a wood-slatted ranch wagon sat, along with an old plow. Tall sunflowers growing nearby waved in the breeze. At the house, Jeremy parked in the large gravel courtyard. Nearby sat a couple of large dusty trucks and an older sedan.

Reese got out of the Trailblazer and walked toward the porch, which was supported with heavy timbers extending through the thick house walls. She walked past several large, terra cotta pots full of red geraniums and knocked on the heavy front door which bore decorative iron bands.

Jeremy walked up behind her and stood with his thumbs hooked through his belt loops. His expression was pensive as they waited. Reese tried knocking again, then rang the doorbell—something she probably should have done in the first place.

Finally, Pearl opened up. Dressed in a prairie skirt, she wore sandals and had a lacy shawl draped around her shoulders. Her dark hair, streaked with gray, had been arranged in a lose knot atop her head.

"Pearl Northwood?" Jeremy asked.

"Yes," she responded, with a curious glance at the two of them. "What can I do for you?"

Jeremy introduced himself, as did Reese.

"We're here about your son, Hunter," Jeremy said. "Is your husband home?"

"Yes, please come in," she told them, standing aside to let them in.

A multi-color Southwestern-style rug spread across the dark red tile in the entry area and a heavy iron chandelier gave off light.

"Walt, come here," she called. "People from the Meadowlark Valley Police Department are here. It's about Hunter."

Tall, with a muscular form and tanned face, Walt stepped through an archway into the entry area. He'd most likely just come inside since he wore dusty boots, worn jeans and a worn blue work shirt bearing sweat rings under the arms.

"Why doesn't that surprise me?" Walt said with a chuckle. "What's he done now?"

Jeremy introduced himself to Walt and Reese introduced herself, explaining she was a private detective from Meadowlark Valley.

"First, come in and have some ice tea with us," Pearl suggested. "It's miserably hot today."

"That's not necessary, ma'am," Jeremy said.

"Nonsense," Walt insisted. "Besides, I don't want to stand out here and shoot the breeze with you. Come in and take a load off."

Pearl led them through another archway into a living room, the tile floor covered by another colorful Southwestern-style carpet. A black leather couch sat near a corner beehive fireplace flanked by two heavy wooden rocking chairs with patterned cushions. Desert paintings and tapestries covered the white walls.

She pointed toward the carved, espresso wood dining room set in another area, with a large kitchen visible beyond. A tray containing a pitcher of iced tea and two glasses sat on the table beside a bouquet of flowers.

"I'll fetch two more glasses," Pearl said as she left the room.

"Have a seat," Walt said, nodding toward the chairs.

Both Reese and Jeremy took places at the table, and Walt sat across from them. He poured iced tea in the two glasses on the table and handed one to Reese, and the other to Jeremy. Pearl returned quickly and poured iced tea in the glasses she'd brought, handing one to her husband and then taking one for herself.

"What can we do for you today, Detective Savage? Ms. Golden?" Walt shifted in his chair.

"I hate to tell you this, and there's no easy to say it, but we found Hunter dead in his home last night."

"What?" Pearl's mouth dropped open and tears filled her eyes. She began sobbing, but placed a hand over her lips.

"Hell, what happened?" Walt asked.

"We aren't entirely certain yet," Jeremy said. "We're still investigating. The coroner will have to file the official report before we can release any information."

"My p-poor boy," Pearl said. "I suppose his body's in the morgue?"

"Yes," Jeremy told her.

"I guess we've got a funeral to arrange," Pearl said. "With Bella gone, it falls to us."

Walt muttered something, then said, "I knew that boy would come to no good."

"Why do you say that?" Reese asked.

"He gave us a lot of problems to deal with," Walt said. "But your kids are your kids, you know? You take care of 'em no matter what."

"We cleaned up a lot of his messes and paid off the debt he kept accruing, until we cut him off," Pearl said. "Otherwise, he'd have expected us to always fix his troubles."

"It wasn't easy, but we had to be firm," Walt said.

"We thought he'd turned his life around," Pearl said. "Well, we'd hoped anyway."

"What do you mean?" Reese asked.

"With his doping and gambling, he led a miserable existence," Walt said. "Then he seemed to settle down some—got married and began his sign business."

"Where did the money come from for him to start it?" Jeremy asked.

Pearl and Walt looked at each other, and Walt nodded.

"From us," Pearl said. "But we told him it was the last he'd ever see from us unless he made good use of it."

"I understand his first wife died," Reese said.

"That was a sad, sad day," Walt said. "Me'n Pearl figured Hunter would get depressed and return to his old ways when Lisa passed away. Surprisingly, he buckled down and kept going."

"Then he married Jayla," Pearl said. "She wasn't good enough for him, of course, none of the women he married were. Jayla took off not long after the wedding, and that was that."

"After she divorced Hunter, we don't know where she went," Walt said.

"We thought sure he and Bella would stay married, despite the fact that the Presley's live a completely different lifestyle than we do. She was a sweet girl, even though she did come from a lower class of people."

Reese raised her brows, but Jeremy didn't flinch a facial muscle.

"Awful, what happened to the Presley girl," Walt said. "And now, Hunter's dead, too."

"Is there anyone you believe would want to hurt your son?" Jeremy asked.

"Hunter used to gripe about a guy named Whit Turnbull," Walt said. "But it was only about a sign Hunter had made for his business. Whit didn't like the way it turned out, but Hunter reimbursed him."

"That doesn't sound worth murdering someone over," Reese said.

"It sure doesn't, and I hope whoever hurt our son rots in hell," Walt said.

Pearl winced.

"Where were the two of you between seven and nine in the evening?" Jeremy asked.

"Why?" Pearl asked.

"If you're getting at the idea that possibly Pearl or I killed our boy, you're barking up the wrong tree," Walt said with a huff. "Besides, we were at the McNabs' barbecue all evening."

"What time?" Jeremy asked.

"I don't know, let's see," Walt said. "Probably got there around five and headed home about ten o'clock. You can check with Earl and Hester, they'll vouch for us."

"I can't believe you asked us that," Pearl said. "It's offensive that you'd even consider the possibility that we'd murder our own son."

"We had to check," Reese said. "It is possible he asked for help from you and Walt one time too many and you were getting tired of bailing him out."

Pearl and Walt both narrowed their gazes at Reese.

"What about Hugh?" Reese asked. "Where was he last night?"

"Here at our ranch taking care of the livestock," Walt said.

"Was anyone with him?" Reese asked.

"The town veterinarian from Brush," Pearl said. "She handles our stock if one of 'em gets sick. The two of them have been seeing each other for several months."

"Do you know when she left last night?" Jeremy asked.

"She was gone when we got home," Pearl said. "You'll have to talk with Bonnie Jo about the exact time she went home."

"Bonnie Jo?"

"Bonnie Jo Bishop," Pearl said. "She's the vet."

"Is Hugh around today?" Jeremy asked.

"He's out mending some broken fences," Walt said. "I was just out there with him. The sun about withered both of us like dried grass."

"Have him give me a call as soon as he can," Jeremy said, placing one of his cards on the table.

"Or me," Reese said, placing one of her cards beside Jeremy's.

"One last thing," Jeremy said. "We have reason to believe your son was poisoning his wives in order to collect on life insurance policies he'd purchased."

"Holy hell," Walt said. "It's hard to admit, but I believe he'd do something underhanded like that. I know he got a large life insurance settlement after Lisa died."

"We did our best raising Hunter," Pearl said. "But we could never seem to help him see the world in a reasonable manner. He had no concept of hard work and honesty. Thought everything ought to be handed to him."

"That's why we cut him out of our will," Walt said. "It had to be done, otherwise he'd have bled us dry."

"I realize this isn't an easy time," Jeremy said. "We appreciate you talking to us."

Reese exchanged a glance with Jeremy, and he nodded, which she took as an indication that he was finished here. Rising, she eased toward the archway leading into the spacious room.

"Thanks for your time," she told the Northwoods. "Please know you have our deepest condolences."

"We'll let ourselves out," Jeremy said as he got up.

Walt rose, along with Pearl. As he placed his arm around his wife's shoulders, he said, "As soon as you find out who the bastard is that killed our son, you let us know."

"Will do." Jeremy walked with Reese down the tile hallway and toward the entrance. They left the house, and Reese closed the door behind them.

As if they had fire nipping at their boot heels, they both hustled toward Jeremy's Trailblazer and got in. Jeremy released a growl as he backed out, turned down the gravel road and drove away.

"I hate informing families that a loved one is dead," he said.

"That was always my least favorite part of the job, too," Reese said.

"Death's inevitable, but after a while, it's a drain to be so close to it."

"I know," Reese said.

"Thanks for coming with me," Jeremy said. "Makes it easier."

"Hey, what are friends for?" She smiled at him.

He gave her a quick, appreciate glance, then turned to watch the road. As he reached up to rub his neck, he said, "I'll follow up with Bonnie Joe Bishop, Hugh Northwood and Whit Turnbull to make certain they all have solid alibis."

"Let me know if I can help with anything else," Reese said.

"You're keeping track of the hours you spend on police work, right?"

"I am," she told him. "I'll shoot an email to you with my time."

"Good." Stroking the stubble on his chin, he said, "When

things aren't so busy, the two of us should go out to dinner."

"To talk about business?"

"Uh, yeah," he said. "And whatever else comes up."

She studied her hands, unsure of how to respond. "Are you sure you want to do that?"

"Why not?" He gave her a surprised look.

"I come with a lot of emotional baggage."

"We all have it," he said.

"Still, I don't think you want to know me that well," Reese warned. "My life is...complicated."

Jeremy met her gaze. "Hey, you don't get to tell me who I want to spend time with."

Reese squirmed and fiddled with her seat belt. She typically preferred to keep to herself. Making time to hang out with her friend Kiki was enough. A relationship with Jeremy would take a lot of care and feeding. Uncertain if she could handle the emotional toll, she watched the landscape rolling past the window.

Take it one step at a time, she told herself.

Chapter Twenty-Eight

When Jeremy dropped Reese off at her house, she watched as he backed down the drive. She unlocked her front door and stepped inside, smiling as Bo jumped off the couch, padded over, and rubbed up against her legs. She scratched around his ears and he buried his face in her jeans, meowing.

Something prompted her to look out the front window, and she watched as Jeremy started to drive away. He waved at her, and she waved back. A tight feeling gripped her abdomen. She hesitated to get involved with him, even though it tempted her. It might jeopardize their working relationship.

Glancing at her watch, it occurred to her that going to Kiki's meditation class would be a perfect solution. Sitting here by herself and stewing about her life wouldn't resolve anything.

Grabbing her truck keys from a hook on the wall, she went back outside and got into her Bronco. Doing her best not to speed, she made a beeline to The Celestial Eye and parked in front of the green and white Gothic-style cottage.

The inside of her truck might be a hot mess, but there was a method to her madness and she had good reasons to carry the jumble of items strewn throughout her vehicle. Spur of the moment decisions often worked out because she found herself prepared for most anything.

Since her oversize handbag also held her exercise clothing, Reese jumped out of the truck, locked her door and headed up the steps. On the porch, pots of white petunias and ferns greeted her once again, impressing her with their waterfall of blossoms.

She entered the shop, her gaze sweeping past the familiar

displays of crystals, incense, and mystical wares. Calming music filled the air and the typical spicy scents wafted into Reese's nostrils.

Kiki had been right about the benefits of attending these meditation classes. They always put her in a good mood and helped her release her frustrations—at least for a short time.

"Wow, you're early," Kiki said as she emerged from a back room. Barefoot and wearing an ombre red and pink yoga outfit, she studied Reese.

"You should be happy I'm taking your advice," Reese responded. "I've got a lot of things on my mind and I hope your class will help me make sense of everything."

"Well, kiss my grits," Kiki said, laughing. "You know where you can change clothes."

"I do."

"I'll be in the meditation studio," Kiki said. "And hurry. I want to tell you about this new guy I met."

"Yes, ma'am."

In the bathroom, Reese slipped on black yoga pants and a gray crop top. Padding barefoot into the meditation studio, Reese approached Kiki who sat beneath the giant mandala wall decal.

The lush plants, a pagoda-shaped incense burner with fragrant blue smoke rising from it and the bubbling sound of the water fountain set a comforting, tranquil scene. After the day Reese had experienced, she welcomed the Zen environment.

Kiki pushed a blue cushion toward Reese.

"Thanks." Reese plopped down on it and hugged her knees. "Spill."

"His name is Brett and he's so nice. We're going out this weekend."

"That's cool, where'd you meet him?"

"At the bank, of all places." Kiki quickly dished about the new man in her life. "We could double date; except we'd have to find somebody for you."

"No worries on that account," Reese said. "You two should enjoy yourselves."

Kiki grinned. "Maybe you and Jeremy could go out with us."

"What makes you think we'd do that?"

Kiki glanced at her nails. "It's just an idea."

"Sure. You're trying to play matchmaker."

"I sensed a spark between you two."

"We work together. That's all."

"I think the lady doth protest too much."

"Whatever." Reese tugged a loose black thread from the seam of her pants. "Don't read too much into things."

Kiki sighed. "You can't say I didn't try."

"I appreciate your efforts, but do me a favor and lend your services elsewhere," Reese said. "Things are fine the way they are."

"You know what they say about all work and no play," Kiki warned.

"I love my work," Reese insisted. "In fact, this morning I spoke to a young man who was at the river the day Bella had her accident. He said he saw a drenched woman in a life jacket running through the woods. He swore it was Bella."

"Does he know her?"

"He said he does."

"That's weird." Kiki's eyes widened. "What happened?"

"He asked the woman if she needed help, but she turned it down, got in an orange truck parked by the road and drove off."

"Convenient she had wheels nearby."

"Like she'd planned it all out," Reese said. "Remember that GPS map we found online that showed an orange vehicle parked near the river?"

"Yes, and it was dated the same day Bella had her accident. You don't think this guy really saw her, do you?"

"It's difficult to believe that he did, but I keep thinking about it."

"Did you tell Jeremy?

"Yes," Reese said. "He thinks it's crazy."

"Could be that the woman just resembled Bella."

"I thought that, too," Reese said. "When I was working on Bella's accident report for the police, I visited with Clara Washington, the choir director at church. She and Bella were good friends. Before I left, she gave me a journal Bella left with her a while back. I need to take a look at it when I get home."

"What do you hope to find?" Kiki asked.

"I don't know."

"You'll find the answers you need," Kiki said. "You always do.

When people began to shuffle into the classroom, Kiki stood up and greeted them in her friendly, welcoming fashion.

Reese noticed a few men had even joined the session this time. Good for Kiki, she seemed to be getting the word out about her business.

Everyone sat on the floor, crossing their legs in a typical "yoga" pose. A petite redhead entered the classroom, looked at Reese, then came over to sit down beside her.

"Didn't we meet at the candlelight vigil?"

Reese remembered the sobbing little boy staring at Bella's photo and how he'd cried about missing his swimming teacher.

"Yes, we did. You're Craig's mom, right?"

"That's right. I'm Genevieve Lane. You can call me Genie."

They shook hands.

"It's nice to know you, Genie. And I'm Reese Golden."

"Nice to know you too."

"Is Craig feeling any better?"

"He still misses Bella terribly."

"The community has suffered a terrible loss," Reese said.

"It's strange, you know, but my son claims that Bella told his class that if she ever had to go away, she would always remember the kids."

"That is random," Reese said, wondering why Bella would say such a thing.

Genie shrugged. "Maybe not so much. They say people often sense their deaths."

"I've heard of that, too."

"Either way, it gives Craig comfort to remember her words," Genie said.

"Did Bella mention to the parents of her class she might be going somewhere?"

"No, she didn't. She only talked to the kids."

"Welcome to our meditation session," Kiki spoke up. "As your wellness coach, I hope I can help you to find your personal power in order to journey to your inner bliss."

Reese turned her attention to the meditation session, as did her fellow class attendees. She listened to Kiki's soothing voice and pushed aside her concerns in order to concentrate on being in the moment.

Chapter Twenty-Nine

When Reese returned home that evening, she went into her office to look for Bella's red leather journal. She found it on her desk beneath a couple of notebooks. Clutching it in her hand, she headed into the living room.

She switched on the TV for background noise, then settled on the couch, legs tucked beneath her, to thumb through more of the pages. Curlicues and swirls swept across the pages, along with diagrams of local wildflowers colored in red, purple, and yellow pencil. There were sketches of the solar system, hearts, creative designs and patterns.

Thumbing through the remaining pages, she studied Bella's illustrated short poems and other writings. One rendering featured twinkling gold stars and said: **You belong to the universe.** Another poem surrounded by various artistically rendered suns read: **Sunshine follows bright souls like shadows follow trouble.** Bella's next poem, surrounded by pieces of wrapped candy, bore the lines: **You are sweet and you are loved; ignore those who tell you otherwise.**

The heartfelt words seemed to express Bella's innermost thoughts. Reese believed her friend had been searching for recognition and validation, which she may have felt was missing from her life. She recalled Naomi saying Hunter was condescending toward her. Had he made her feel inadequate?

She continued to read the emotions Bella had secretly shared in the journal. On the last page, Bella had addressed Clara in a note.

"If someday you no longer see me, please know I am nearby in spirit. Life is a journey that often takes us in many directions. Most important of all is for us to be free from hate and manipulation.

Love, Bella—your good friend

9 – 13 (__) 19 – 1 – 6 – 5 (__) 9 – 14 (__) 20—9 – 13 – 2 – 5 – 18 (__) 3 – 15 – 22 – 5.

Bella's cryptic note promised an answer to something, she felt certain. Reese decided it must be buried in the words and numbers.

What had Bella been trying to tell Clara?

Reese studied the message with a critical eye. *Life is a journey* could be Bella's way of saying she was going somewhere. *Free from hate and manipulation* could mean she wanted to leave Hunter.

The message left a lot to interpretation, yet Reese tried to make sense of it. The numbers confused her. What did they represent? Maybe it was an algebra formula? She decided it wasn't that. Besides, she sucked at math.

Yawning, she picked up her iPad sitting on an end table. After bringing up the internet, she looked up encoded messages. A variety of information filled her screen, and she eagerly scanned through it. She learned the practice had been around for thousands of years. Once civilizations evolved language, codes and cyphers were used to obscure messages.

Greeks and Egyptians used encryption for private messages, as did other cultures. The practice became especially handy during wartime in order to send things the enemy would not understand, such as troop movements and locations.

"I'm lost," she muttered.

She glanced at Bella's writing again, then the numbers, and looked up numerical cyphers. There was so much to read, her head began to ache. Leaning back against the couch, she closed her eyes, her intent to only take a break.

A dream transported Reese to another world, one where swirling mist and water mingled. She floated in the rippling blue depths of a lake. The sinking sun, obscured a blaze of red and orange, urged her to return to shore where sandy beaches awaited.

Slowly, she stroked through the waves, trying to reach land.

Yet, no matter how hard she swam, she didn't get anywhere. Spotting a boat, she surged toward it, believing it could take her where she wanted to go.

A silver fish jumped out of the lake and shouted, "No, don't leave me! I need your help."

When Reese recognized the voice as Bella's, she stopped swimming. She watched as the fish splashed back under the surface of the water. Then Bella emerged, her long hair wet and streaming down her back.

"You need to find me," Bella said as she moved her hands through the waves and began to tread water. "There's danger in the midst. You can't give up."

"Where are you?" Reese managed to say, even though her words came out slurred.

"Find me," Bella insisted. "Time's running out."

In the wee hours of the morning, Reese jolted awake and looked around the room. The TV blared an infomercial about skincare and Bo had jumped off the couch at some point. He now lay in his carpet-covered cat tree in the corner.

Blinking to clear her gaze, she went into the bathroom and splashed water on her face, which revived her. On the couch again, she brought up the internet on her iPad and resumed her search. Information about using a matrix to code numerical messages caught her eye, and she clicked on it.

Reese read further, feeling like she'd finally found something that might help her with Bella's numbers. She spent the next half hour going through various combinations, trying to figure out the significance.

Finally, it occurred to her what the key might be. She grabbed a piece of paper and a pencil on the end table and jotted down what she believed could be Bella's code: 1 equaled A, 2 equaled B, and so on throughout the 26 letters of the alphabet.

Eagerly, she read Bella's words, "I'm safe in Timber Cove."

Stove and cove rhymed. The woman Doug and his girlfriend had seen could have muttered the word cove. Had that woman actually been Bella?

"Bo, guess what? I think I solved Bella's riddle," Reese said to her cat, who yawned and stretched, then stared at her from his feline perch.

Reese rose up from the couch and began to pace. She could have kicked herself for not looking through this journal sooner. The question still remained, why had Bella pretended to drown the day of her accident? It made no sense, and Reese still mistrusted her instincts. Yet, something urged her to go forward with the idea.

She pulled up a Wyoming map on her iPad and spotted the location of Timber Cove. Once upon a time, it had been a hopping tourist destination in the middle of a forested mountain area. Reese and her family had stayed there when she was a kid. They'd ridden horses, hiked and fished in the summer. In the winter, they had gone cross country skiing and raced snow mobiles.

These days, the land must be overgrown with tall grass and weeds. Stores and cabins had to be in dilapidated condition from lack of maintenance. The best place to spend time back then, the dance hall, had probably been left to mice and ghosts.

Reese looked for an update to the Rockrimmon Peak wildfire. On the Wyoming Forestry Division's online site, a message said it was still mostly uncontained. Reese noted that the conflagration was creeping toward Timber Cove area.

Reese realized Bella's message could have been written long ago, as some sort of game. Nevertheless, she decided she needed to take a road trip. Since it was too early to call Jeremy, she texted him her plan to check out Timber Cove, hoping he might be awake.

To her surprise, he texted back and told her to stay put. **Don't go! Wildfire is too close. Foolish to think Bella's alive.**

Reese stood by the front window, studying the neighborhood as she contemplated Jeremy's warning. Despite his concerns, it wasn't like her to ignore intuition. Bo lifted his dark, furry head, watching her with curiosity as she stormed into the kitchen and started the coffee.

Next, she headed into the bathroom, took a good hot shower, then went to her bedroom to pull on jeans and boots. She finished by pulling on a red tank top and a plaid chambray blouse.

Out in the kitchen again, she dropped some granola bars and bottles of water into her purse. She poured hot coffee into an old thermos and screwed on the lid. Then she poured a measure into her travel mug. By now, sunrise filled the hazy eastern horizon with salmon and orange light, which shone through the kitchen window. It illuminated the white café curtains with a warm glow.

After collecting her phone and keys, along with her purse, she plopped her cowboy hat on her head. When she walked outside to her truck, she dropped the mug in a cup holder, then placed everything else on the passenger seat. Sensing a presence ease up behind her, she spun around.

Ivy Drake stood there in a sleek black pantsuit, looking as fashionable as ever, despite the early hour.

"Wow, you scared me," Reese said, pressing a hand to her chest. She'd been so preoccupied with her mission; she hadn't even bothered to look around.

Ivy smiled, dimples showing in her cheeks. "I wanted to let you know that after our visit yesterday, I remembered something Hunter told me a couple of weeks ago."

"What?"

"We ran into each other at the Western Moon Café one day. He mentioned that Bella had been very sick lately, and he believed she was dying. You and Detective Savage believe he'd been poisoning his wives. He was probably poisoning her."

"It's a theory," Reese said.

"Do you suppose Bella couldn't save herself from drowning because she was too weak to swim?" Ivy conjectured.

"It crossed my mind," Reese said.

"That concerns me," Ivy said. "Especially considering I know now that he'd planned to do the same to me."

"Did Hunter say anything else that day at the Café?" Reese asked.

"He wanted to start seeing me again. He said he'd never really gotten over me and missed us being together."

Reese thought about the rat poison she'd found in Hunter's cupboard and decided he probably had been lacing Bella's smoothies with the pellets. That was his modus operandi. No wonder he began pursuing Ivy, even while his current wife was still alive. He assumed the poisoned smoothies would kill Bella before long, making him a widower who was free to play the field.

"Did you mention this to Detective Savage?" Reese asked.

"Not yet," Ivy said. "I plan to stop by the police department later to talk with him."

"Good idea."

Ivy leaned against the side bumper of Reese's truck. "Where are you going?"

"Why do you want to know?"

Ivy shrugged nonchalantly. "I'm just curious is all. I didn't mean to pry."

Reese climbed into her truck, closed the door and rolled down her window.

"I think we started out on the wrong foot with this conversation," Reese said. "I'm busy, and every minute counts in my schedule."

"I get it," Ivy said.

"I planned to get to the rec center early and get in a good workout before I start my day." Reese realized she wasn't dressed for that, so she added, "I've got my gym bag packed with everything I need, so I'm ready to rock."

"I don't see a gym bag," Ivy commented.

"It's in the back of my truck."

"Oh, there it is," Ivy said as she glanced in the Bronco's back window.

"I keep it in my truck so it's always handy," Reese added.

"I'll be on my way, then," Ivy said. "Let me know what kind of progress the police are making on Hunter's case."

"I will," Reese said.

She watched as Ivy sauntered down the driveway and over to the other side of the street to get in her sportscar. When she drove off, Reese decided she'd better own her lie and actually get her butt over to the gym.

Chapter Thirty

At the Windflower Recreation Center, Reese parked in the lot, grabbed her purse and went inside. She waved at Karen standing at the front counter, noting her hair highlights today gleamed hot orange. After fishing out her membership card, she held it up.

"I swear." Karen shook her head, judgement written in the lines of her face. "Didn't anyone ever tell you to wear workout attire to the gym? You're not supposed to show up in boots and a cowboy hat."

Poor Karen, she just couldn't resist criticizing. Rather than taking offense, Reese chuckled and held up her oversize purse. "I've got clothes and shoes to change into."

"Of course," Karen said.

After passing through the turnstile, Reese headed down the hall. She entered the pool area and sat on a bench. As people paddled around or swam laps, she pulled out her cell and caught up on her email.

After about a half hour, precious minutes she hated to waste, Reese began the trek back to the entrance. Karen stared at her suspiciously as she walked past the counter, but Reese simply smiled at her. She walked into the warm light of day and glanced around the parking lot, then scanned the streets.

You're paranoid.

Ivy's vehicle was nowhere in sight. Reese decided she'd been silly to believe Ivy would actually follow her. What would be the point?

Nevertheless, she decided to keep a close watch for any tails as she drove to up to Timber Cove. She climbed in her Bronco, started the engine, and wheeled out of the rec center parking lot. After several cautious glances behind her, she headed toward her destination.

After exiting onto the highway, she drove south into the hazy yellow distance. As she listened a local talk show on the radio, the prairie transformed from swells of waving grass into reddish bluffs and plateaus. Late summer wildflowers of yellow, pink and blue dotted the rugged landscape.

As Betty climbed high into the Medicine Bow Mountains, Reese's ears began to feel stuffed. The altitude change introduced different air pressure, which she knew caused the annoyance. Before long, her ears popped, which meant they had finally adjusted.

When the radio program faded into crackling noise, Reese plugged in one of her country music cassettes. As the player blasted oldies but goodies, she hummed along. It didn't take much time before she'd drained dry her travel mug of coffee.

Time passed in a blur of landscape and dusky sky. Spotting the Timber Cove exit, her heart sank. It bore a bright red closed banner. To make certain no one decided to sail down the road, a large sign with orange and white stripes, combined with concrete Jersey barriers, announced the closure and blocked anyone's travel.

Police and fire officials had obviously closed the main thoroughfare because of the wildfire danger. It was a good call, but not for Reese.

"Well, crap," she muttered as she continued driving down the highway. Luckily, she knew of a back road that her family had often used when going up to the cove.

At the next exit, she left the highway and headed down an uneven, barely-used service road. She traveled on that for about 10 minutes before she noted a wooden, hand-carved sign that read, Timber Cove, 2 miles.

Long before the highway had been built with its dedicated exits, visitors had used this old gravel path, which fortunately, officials hadn't closed. It was barely maintained, and she dodged a multitude of potholes that counted like stars in the sky.

"That's why I have you with your trusty four-wheel drive, Betty," Reese said as she patted the Bronco's dusty dashboard. One of these days, she needed to take a break and clean up the interior. In its current state, the vehicle ought to be declared a disaster area.

For the first mile or so, the Bronco bumped along. Then the gravel began to thin and the road became more of a wide dirt trail. Pines, spruce and aspen lined either side, the ground beneath them covered in a carpet of dried leaves, tree needles and tangled undergrowth.

Reese shifted into four-wheel drive as she continued making her way higher up the mountain. Yellow and gray wildfire smoke choked the sky until not even a small patch of blue remained.

Flakes of ash skittered across the windshield and slid off with the truck's uneven, jolting motion. The trees began to thin and a clearing of tall grass appeared. In the middle of it stood the old dance hall. In the distance, the Laramie River glimmered, a bright blue ribbon of water winding through banks covered in thick brush and trees.

Reese pulled into the weed-overgrown parking lot and stopped the Bronco. She crawled out, pressed her hands on her hips and looked around.

Her family had enjoyed renting cabins up here on special occasions. She recalled scrambling over the playground that once stood in front of the main office and wandering in the woods or fishing at the river. Everyone had taken long hikes together, laughing and talking in the bright sunshine. One Easter, they'd even cracked their colored eggs on rocks in order to peel and eat them.

The acreage that made up Timber Cove had originally been owned by an army colonel who retired here in 1886. He built himself a small wooden home, then constructed the dance hall and invited friends and family to purchase lots to build their own resort cabins.

The place offered great opportunities for hunting, fishing, and simply relaxing. Many of the colonel's acquaintance took him up on his offer. Then others came along, requesting to purchase their own parcels of land.

Eventually, as the colonel and his family members passed on, Timber Cove became a resort area owned and operated by various private companies that rented out the cabins. About a decade ago, it was abandoned. No one wanted to purchase the place since it had fallen into disrepair.

As far as Reese knew, it was still for sale. What a shame no one wanted to take it on, but she wasn't surprised. It would take a huge investment to renovate the buildings to make them habitable again.

At present, it remained a ghost of its former glorious self. Once upon a time, there had been a restaurant, a general store, a gas station, a post office, and a couple of tourist shops. Now, nature had reclaimed it with twisted green weeds, thorns, and overgrown bushes.

Considering the ramshackle condition of the cabins, Reese wondered which one Bella might be staying in. If indeed, she had come up here. Reese understood what a farfetched idea it was.

Never one to give up on something easily, she decided since she'd come all this way, she'd pass by each of the cabins to look for any signs of life. That wouldn't take too long. All in all, there were maybe ten of them.

"Might as well get it over with," she muttered as she headed to her Bronco. Later on, she and Jeremy could laugh about her wild goose chase.

Chapter Thirty-One

Reese maneuvered the dirt roads that led to the small log cabins nestled beneath leafy tree canopies. Abandoned and showing signs of neglect, the area still retained a unique, rustic beauty. Gaze narrowed, she scanned for signs of life. She braked occasionally, unable to resist using her cell phone camera to take some shots out of the window.

This high in the mountains, patches of gold and orange leaves revealed night's frosty touch, which hinted at autumn's timely approach. Tall hollyhocks covered in faded red, yellow and pink blossoms proliferated around porches and walls. Birds sailed overhead calling to one another.

Nestled near rock foundations, clumps of daisies and western yarrow bushes sprouted. Thick sunflower stalks shot up in random patches, their reddish orange flowers turned upward to absorb the sun's rays.

Part of Reese wished she had the money to purchase the place. What enjoyment it would bring to revive the vacation spot and bring it back to life. Preoccupied by grandiose ideas of restoring the resort, she studied rock-surrounded fire rings, old metal swing sets, teeter totters, and gravel RV sites.

A flash of orange jutting from behind one of the cabins caught her eye, and she braked. Eager to investigate, she shifted into reverse and backed up. A cottage, surrounded by thick stands of bushes and tall trees, had nearly been hidden by lanky fireweeds with their pink-purple flowers.

She pulled into a dirt parking spot and turned off her truck engine. Stepping out of the Bronco, she closed the driver's door.

Walking behind the cabin, she noted the rusty orange truck, an old Datsun. Was that the same vehicle she'd seen parked by the river? And was it the same one Doug had seen?

Insects buzzed as she circled back around to the front of the building and walked up onto the small porch. After rapping on the door, she leaned over to glance through the front window, but the curtains were drawn closed.

Finally, the door opened.

Reese's mouth went dry at the sight of Bella. She wore a loose green blouse, black capris slacks, and white tennis shoes. Around her neck were purple bruise marks. She had a black eye and her face bore contusions.

The two women exchanged surprised looks. For a second, Reese thought she was having another vivid dream. She almost pinched herself to make sure she was awake.

"We all thought you were dead," she managed to say, still in disbelief.

"That was the idea—to make everyone believe I had drowned."

They hugged, then stood back at arm's length.

"How did you find me, Reese?"

"When I finally finished reading the journal you'd given Clara Washington, I managed to crack your message code. I drove up here, figuring I was on a wild goose chase. I had no idea that the note was real."

"You can't tell anyone I'm here."

"Why are you hiding?"

"It was my dad's idea," Bella said. "He was worried about what Hunter would do to me if he realized I'd taken his burner phone."

"Just so you know, Hunter's dead. You don't have to worry about him any longer."

Bella's jaw dropped. "H-how?"

"Somebody bludgeoned him to death. Of course, the coroner still hasn't released an official cause of death."

"I-I never expected to hear that."

"What was on the burner phone?" Reese asked.

"Proof that Hunter was trying to poison me, and that he'd

poisoned his first wife. He admitted everything to Ivy Drake in a text message. When I was cleaning out Hunter's SUV, I found it."

"What all did he say?" Reese asked.

"Let's sit down first, and I'll tell you." Bella pointed toward two lawn chairs on the porch, and sat in one.

Reese lowered down in the one next to Bella.

"Hunter told Ivy that his first wife Lisa died a few months after they were married. He explained how he put rat poison in the health smoothie he blended for her every morning. After she was gone, he collected a huge life insurance settlement on her."

"I knew it," Reese said.

"Knew what?"

"That Hunter was pulling a life insurance scam. Especially after I went in the office at your house and found all the policies on his wives. He kept them locked in the bottom drawer of a file cabinet."

"I wondered what he kept down there," Bella said. "He warned me to never go snooping."

"He even had a policy set up for Ivy."

Bella's eyes widened. "Does she know that?"

"Jeremy and I told her."

"What did Ivy think?" Bella asked.

"She was in disbelief," Reese said.

"Hunter was sneaky, but his second wife got the best of him," Bella said. "She left him before he could poison her."

"I talked to Jayla," Reese said. "She knew Hunter was trying to kill her, but was afraid to go to the police. She also feared what he or his family might do to her if she accused him."

"In that burner phone text, Hunter told Ivy he'd married me only to play the same insurance scam. The two of them were planning to be together after I was gone."

"You drank his health smoothies?"

"Uh, huh." Bella made a face. "No wonder I felt so sick all the time—they were full of rat poison. Who knows what kind of long-term effects that stuff might have on me?"

"I can't believe Ivy knew what Hunter had been doing," Reese said. "I sensed there was something off about her, but I don't know her well."

"That woman is definitely not trustworthy. She should have gone to the police and showed them the text message."

"A good person would have done that," Reese agreed. "By the way, Ivy and Hunter were married by a justice of the peace yesterday morning."

"Wow," Bella said. "That was quick. It can't be legal though, right? I'm still alive."

Reese nodded. "When Detective Savage and I talked with Ivy yesterday, she said she and Hunter were trying to keep it a secret."

"I can't imagine why she'd want to marry a jerk like Hunter," Bella said, rubbing her bruised forehead.

"Did he do that to you?" Reese asked.

"I threatened to leave him and he laid into me. He even threatened to hurt my family, too."

"He does have a dangerous temper," Reese said. "Well, he did. Tell me, how did your dad get involved in all of this?"

"After Hunter and I fought, he stormed outside and went into his shop. I was really upset, but I grabbed my car keys and drove out to Dad's gas station. Dad was livid when he read Hunter's text message."

"I don't blame him."

"Dad said he'd take the phone to the police. He was afraid that if I talked to them, I'd be in big trouble with the Northwoods. He said it might take a while for the police to arrest Hunter, and he insisted I come up here to be safe."

"What finally happened to the burner phone?"

"Dad carved out a niche under the name plate of the diorama I gave him and hid it there."

"Diamondback Revenge?" Reese asked.

Bella nodded. "He thought I should fake my drowning during the church rafting trip the next day. I didn't like the idea at first, then I finally agreed to do it. After I let myself fall from the raft, I swam underwater for a while, then crawled onto the shore and ran through the woods to the old truck Dad left for me, which he'd packed with supplies. Then I drove up here to stay. Meanwhile,

Dad was supposed to take the burner phone to the police. Once Hunter was behind bars, I planned to return home."

No wonder Ford had been so eager to have Reese find the diorama. He'd hidden critical evidence against Hunter in it. "I bet you were scared."

"I was, and Dad was pissed, but he was ready to do some ass kicking. He can be a real hot head."

"So I've learned," Reese said, thinking of Ford's life-threatening injuries. "You need to know your dad's in the hospital right now. Someone assaulted him and he's in a coma."

Tears filled Bella's eyes. "Oh my God, what happened?"

"I found him at his store the day after your accident," Reese said. "He was in bad shape, but we got him to the emergency room. The police hired me to help investigate the case, and I've been following some leads on suspects."

"Did my dad say anything to you after you found him?" Bella asked.

"All he mumbled was, 'he knows' before he passed out," Reese said.

"Who was he talking about?"

"I have no idea," Reese said.

Bella curled her hands into fists and an angry gleam filled her eyes. "I know Dad can hold his own, but I can't believe someone beat him up."

"He's coming along really good," Reese said. "Naomi said he's going to be okay."

"I still don't like it," Bella said. "Now I understand why he hasn't stopped by to tell me what was going on. He couldn't."

"Your mom and Ian are pretty upset, thinking you drowned. They even held a candlelight vigil for you. I think half the town showed up."

"Gosh, that makes me feel terrible," Bella said, her lower lip trembling. "Dad was going to tell Mom and Ian the truth so they wouldn't worry, but I guess he didn't get a chance. And I owe everyone in town an explanation and an apology."

"That's a good idea," Reese said. "Everyone's been heartbroken."

"Do Hunter's parents know he's dead?"

"Detective Savage and I went up to their ranch yesterday to tell them. They're very upset, but Walt mentioned that he always sensed Hunter would wind up in a bad situation."

"Hunter caused them a lot of trouble over the years," Bella said, running a trembling hand through her brown, shoulder-length bob.

"I got that impression from the way Pearl and Walt talked about him," Reese said.

Reese studied the cabin's exterior, noting it wasn't in bad shape. "Why did your dad suggest you hide up here?"

"Some big corporation bought Timber Cove at the beginning of summer. They've got plans for the place. They hired Dad as the caretaker to keep an eye on stuff. He's been working on weekends to straighten up this cabin to use as his home base."

"That makes sense," Reese said.

Tears rolled down Bella's cheeks. "I suppose I can go home now. Am I in trouble for faking my death?"

"There'll be questions I'm sure, but you won't be prosecuted," Reese said.

"Thinking back now, it was probably crazy of me to pretend to fall off the raft and drown."

"You and your dad were worried," Reese said. "People do crazy things when they're desperate."

"Both me and Dad were also afraid the Northwoods might come after me if I caused their family any trouble."

"I definitely don't blame you," Reese said.

I still feel bad about Mom and Ian," Bella said. "I hate that they've been upset."

"They love you," Reese said. "Once you explain what happened, they'll understand. They'll be overjoyed you're alive."

Bella smiled.

Reese slapped her knees and stood. "That wildfire is moving closer. We need to get out of here."

"I want to be with my dad," Bella said as she rose.

"When we get back to town, the hospital will be our first stop."

Chapter Thirty-Two

At the sound of crunching gravel, both Reese and Bella looked toward the road. A familiar silver SUV pulled in front of the cabin and rolled to a stop.

"That's Hunter's truck," Bella said, her brows furrowed.

Reese peered through the windshield, trying to determine who was driving.

"Did you tell anyone you were coming up here?" Bella bit her lower lip.

"Only Detective Savage," Reese said.

When the vehicle stopped, Ivy Drake stepped out. Wearing jeans and a yellow polo shirt, she walked up onto the porch and stood in front of them. Accustomed to seeing Ivy dressed in haute couture, Reese tensed. Ivy had really let down her hair today— what was she up to?

"Well, well, well," Ivy said, looking like the cat who ate the cream. "What do you know? Bella Northwood is alive after all."

"What are you doing up here, Ivy?" Reese asked.

"I overheard you and Detective Savage talking yesterday at my house when I was walking up the stairs," Ivy said. "You mentioned a journal and something about finding out if Bella was alive. That got me curious."

Reese frowned. She should have waited to talk about her ideas until she and Jeremy were out in his vehicle.

"How did you know I'd come up here?" Reese asked.

"Remember me stopping by your house this morning?" Ivy smiled. "I placed a tracker on your bumper."

"That's illegal," Reese said, recalling how Ivy had leaned against her Bronco.

"It is if the police find out," Ivy said. "Which they won't."

"Go away, Ivy," Bella said.

"On the contrary, I believe I'll stay." Ivy cocked her head to the side.

"What do you want?" Reese asked.

"For things to go back to the way they were," Ivy said, pulling a gun from behind her back and pointing it at Bella. "You need to stay dead."

"Oh my God," Bella said in a frightened voice.

Reese tensed. "Ivy, put down the gun."

"Why should I?" Ivy asked.

"You're upset right now—you don't want to do something you'll regret later," Reese warned.

"Oh, I guarantee I won't have any regrets," Ivy said as she moved closer. "I'll have plenty of money to drown my sorrows in."

"What do you mean?" Bella asked.

Ivy chuckled. "I took a cue from Hunter and purchased a huge life insurance policy on him. I can't cash in if I'm not his wife. Bella, you're in the way. You've got to go."

"You were there the night he died," Reese said, the wheels in her mind churning as she recalled seeing two wine glasses in Hunter's house.

"Yes," Ivy said. "We were celebrating our wedding."

"And you killed him," Reese added.

"I had to," Ivy said. "I swore years ago I would enact my vengeance on him."

"Why?" Bella asked.

"Hunter and I go way back. Twenty years, to be exact. We met in college, fell in love, and I got pregnant. I was thrilled, envisioning the future we had ahead. But he wasn't."

"He left you?" Reese asked.

"Bingo," Ivy said. "He swore his parents would never accept me because I didn't come from a family with money and a pedigreed background. I begged him to reason with them, but he refused because he feared they'd become angry and cut him out of the family trust. He insisted I have an abortion and said he'd pay for it. I would never consider such a thing. Several months later, Colton came along."

"Colton is Hunter's child?" Reese asked, wanting to make sure she'd heard Ivy correctly.

"That's right," Ivy said.

"You worked hard to take care of your son," Reese said, hoping to find a way to reason with Ivy.

"He means the world to me." Ivy took a shaky breath. "When Hunter said he wanted to marry me after Bella died, I jumped at the chance to turn the tables on him. He told me he'd been running a life insurance scam to collect on his dead wives, so I took out life insurance on him and planned to do the same thing. With you dead, Bella, I'll be a million dollars richer."

"You wouldn't really kill me," Bella said. "Would you?"

"I killed Hunter," Ivy said. "I will kill you."

Reese tensed, and Bella's face went white.

Apparently proud of her accomplishments, Ivy bragged, "On our wedding night, I grabbed a hammer out of Hunter's tool chest when he was showering. He thought I was joining him when I got in the tub. He was distracted washing his hair under the shower head. I had the perfect timing."

"You need to turn yourself in," Reese told Ivy, trying not to be intimidated by the gun in her hand. "What you did was wrong, even if Hunter hurt you all those years ago. It was up to the police to arrest him for his murder scheme."

"Hunter's parents would have hired the best lawyers that money can buy and he'd have wound up going free. He never would have paid for his crimes."

"You don't know that," Reese said.

"Whack, whack, whack," Ivy said as she used her free hand to demonstrate a pounding motion. "Hunter screamed like a fool, but I got him good. Now he's rotting in hell."

"The police will figure out you killed him," Reese warned.

"No, they won't," Ivy said. "I made sure not to leave a trace of DNA."

"Are you sure of that?" Reese asked. "People often think they're getting away with the perfect crime, but they really aren't."

"What do you know?" Ivy snarled as she stepped up onto the porch and stood directly in front of Reese and Bella.

"You just confessed to the two of us that you killed Hunter," Reese reminded her.

"Reese is a former cop, so she knows how all of this works," Bella said. "We'll tell the world that you're the murderer."

"What makes you think either of you will leave here alive?" Ivy said with a snicker. "After I've taken care of you two, I'm flying to the Caribbean with my son. After all, he's 18 now—an adult. The rest of our lives will be full of sun, sand, and tropical drinks."

Reese grabbed the nose of Ivy's gun, twisted it down, causing a popping sound. Ivy yelped as Reese yanked the weapon from her and shoved her off of the porch.

Sprawled in the dirt and weeds, Ivy held out her shaking hand and cried, "You broke my damn finger!"

"Oops," Reese said. She hopped down from the porch and held out her hand to help Ivy stand, the gun still trained on her.

In a surprise move, Ivy charged Reese, knocking her down and sending the gun flying into the weeds.

Reese swore as she dove for the weapon.

Ivy grabbed it first and pointed it at Reese.

"Some cop you are," Ivy said, brushing dirt off of her clothes with one hand as she held her aim. "You're a joke.

"That wildfire is growing closer by the second," Reese warned, irritated that her defense skills had become rusty from disuse. "We need to get out of here."

"It won't take me long to do what I need to."

"Really?" Reese asked.

"Yup," Ivy said. "Bella, go put on your life jacket. You're going to drown in the Trout River, just like everyone believes you did. I'll drive you there, hit you over the head with a rock and roll your body in. Easy, peasy."

"You're sick," Bella told Ivy as she headed toward the cabin entrance.

"Don't try escaping out the back door, Bella," Ivy continued.

"While you two were gabbing, I noticed it's nailed shut. In fact, when I checked, the windows are nailed shut, too—lucky for me."

Everything had been locked up tight to discourage looters, Reese realized as Bella stormed inside the cabin. That wasn't good for them.

"What you're doing is wrong," Reese warned Ivy.

"Guess what? I don't care what you think," Ivy snarled. "Now give me your truck keys."

When Reese pulled them from her pocket and handed them over, Ivy tossed them across the street into the bushes.

"Sit," Ivy demanded.

Trying to think of a way she and Bella could escape, Reese plopped down into a lawn chair.

Still pointing the gun at Reese, Ivy went to Hunter's SUV, opened the passenger door and withdrew a coil of rope.

Ivy stepped back onto the porch and began wrapping the rope around Reese's torso and the chair back. Sensing Ivy's lack of expertise in tying up a captive, especially since she could only use one hand, Reese began to squirm.

"Come on, Ivy, you don't have do this," she complained.

"BS," Ivy said.

"This isn't right," Reese continued. The twine fiber smelled moldy and she wrinkled her nose.

Seemingly satisfied that she'd done a halfway decent job of securing Reese to the chair, Ivy set aside the gun and tightened the ropes, then tied a couple of square knots.

"You're a pain in the ass, Golden," Ivy said, wiping her brow with the back of her hand.

"Let me go," Reese growled.

"You're staying put," Ivy said. "You'll have a front row seat to the wildfire when it sweeps through this clearing."

"I can help you," Reese said.

"You won't, you know too much," Ivy said.

"I promise I won't say a thing."

"Of course, you will." Ivy picked up the gun and pointed it at Reese again. "D'ya think I was born yesterday?"

Chapter Thirty-Three

Bella walked out of the cabin gripping an orange life jacket. She looked anxious, but determined.

"Took you long enough," Ivy said to her, then turned toward Reese. "Enjoy your afternoon, I can't say it's been a pleasure to know you."

Ivy walked toward the SUV and opened the door to the cargo space. "This is where you'll sit," she told Bella. "I'm going to tie you up in here so you don't try anything funny while I'm driving."

As Ivy leaned into the back of the truck and began moving around items, Reese struggled to loosen her bonds. She'd begun to make progress when Bella eased over and slipped a pocketknife to her. Reese grabbed it eagerly, wasting no time slicing through the ropes.

As Ivy continued to fuss with the cargo area, she hollered, "Get your bony ass over here, Bella."

Bella moved up behind her. In a sudden move, she dropped the life jacket, revealing a large wooden cutting board.

Reese sucked in a breath, watching and waiting.

Still preoccupied with her task, Ivy said, "Crawl up in here."

Bella held up the cutting board and slammed it against the back of Ivy's head.

The sound of wood making impact with Ivy's skull smacked the air. As Ivy grabbed her head and crumpled to the ground, the gun fell from her hand and landed nearby.

"The gun," Reese shouted to Bella as she finished freeing herself. When ropes slid away from her body, she hustled off the porch and lunged at the weapon.

Bella, who seemed to be in a momentary daze, lowered to her haunches and scrambled to reach for it.

Ivy was quicker. She clamped her hand around the weapon and groaned. Obviously disoriented from the hit to her head, she continued thrashing on the ground.

"Get to my truck!" Bella pulled a ring of keys from her pocket and dashed behind the cabin.

Reese followed.

Bella jumped into the driver's seat of the Datsun as Reese slid into the passenger side.

Bella fumbled to fit the key in the ignition. When the engine wouldn't turn over, she cried out and began pumping on the gas.

"You're flooding it," Reese warned. Perspiration coated her brow as she glanced to see if Ivy had managed to follow them. The woman was nowhere in sight.

"Stupid truck!" Bella protested. "It's an old piece of junk."

The engine made a strange groaning sound, sputtered and died. Realizing it wasn't going anywhere anytime soon, Reese jumped out, and Bella did the same.

"The party's not over yet, ladies," Ivy said, having finally stumbled into view. "Where do you think you're off to?"

Ivy rubbed the back of her head as she aimed the gun at them with an unsteady hand. She also blinked frequently, as though trying to focus.

"Run," Reese shouted, pointing toward a large steel dumpster beside a spruce tree. She and Bella sprinted toward it as a shot rang out. The bullet hit a truck tire, which hissed as air escaped.

Another shot exploded as Reese slid behind the hulking metal. Bella collapsed down beside her, gripping her lower calf.

"I'm hit."

"Let me see."

Bella released her hands and Reese studied the bloody furrow located below her slacks hem.

"A graze."

"Stings like hell." Bella clenched her teeth.

Reese took off her chambray blouse, folded it over several

times and tied it tightly around Bella's wound. She peeked out from the side of the dumpster, watching Ivy approach.

"I brought more bullets to the party, ladies," Ivy said with a chuckle. She held up a small cardboard box and rattled it. "I can play target practice for hours. Don't you think it'd be better if you come out now?"

"Witch," Bella growled.

"We have to make a run for it," Reese said.

"How? Ivy will shoot at least one of us for sure. Maybe both."

Reese picked up a good-sized rock. "I'm going to throw this. Hopefully, she'll be caught off guard and shoot at it. When she does, be ready to run into the woods."

"Got it," Bella said.

Reese silently counted to three, rose up, and pitched the rock. As another shot rang out, she helped Bella to her feet. Together, they darted into the smoky woods.

Chapter Thirty-Four

Reese sympathized with Bella as she managed a limping run, despite the pain she must be experiencing. As the two merged deeper into the wilderness, the trees and bushes concealed them with overhanging branches.

"Face it, you two," Ivy called. "You're not going to get far."

She fired another shot, which hit a nearby tree and sent bark skittering.

Reese and Bella plunged into the endless emerald green vegetation, moving into the boundless forest. Their feet crunched on dead leaves, dry pine needles and pine cones, which she knew gave away their position. Reese bit down on her lower lip, wishing the birds would quit squawking and flapping their wings when she and Bella passed by.

"Where can we go?" Bella asked, drawing raspy breath.

"Feather Creek isn't far," Reese responded.

"Come out, come out where ever you are," Ivy taunted. "I can hear you moving, you know."

Through the trees, she spotted Ivy standing in a clearing, her back facing them. It would be impossible to go that direction, toward the small community. Reese swore silently.

We're so screwed.

She and Bella paused for a second, during which she tried to decide what to do. In the baking, merciless heat, perspiration formed over every inch of her body. She and Bella met each other's gaze, and panic needled her.

If it was the last thing she accomplished in this lifetime, she would get Bella home safely to her family.

In a sudden flash, she remembered scrambling through these woods with her little brother Jesse when her family stayed in Timber Cove. One place in particular had completely drawn them—Gray Rocks Country Store.

After hiking and exploring, they'd often stopped there for soda and candy. The owners, Nellie and Tom Osborne, seemed to get a kick out of seeing them each summer. Reese had even stopped by to visit them a few weeks ago.

Nell and Tom had probably been evacuated like the rest of the residents. Fortunately, Reese had a good idea where they hid the key to the back entrance.

"This way," Reese whispered, helping Bella walk as they began moving up the mountain. She did her best to lead them across grass or dirt, which wouldn't crunch like deadfall.

The smoke became thicker, looking like a gray, woolen scarf stuffed through the trees. Fortunately, a well-worn path snaked its way through the brush so Reese could tell they were going in the right direction. Boulders marked the edges of the trail, jutting out like strange creatures warning anyone who dared approach.

Near a grove of tall, thick pines, they stopped to catch their breath. Reese smacked her dry lips together.

"I know what you're thinking," Bella said, wiping her mouth with the back of her sleeve. "I could sure use a drink of water."

"There's a stream on the other side of the hill." Reese pulled her cell from her back pocket to check for service, but it was still dead. She wouldn't be making any calls just yet.

"No bars?"

Reese shook her head. "We're too far up the mountain."

"Damn," Bella said. She waved her hand in front of her flushed face and strands of her hair lifted in the breeze. "Do you think we've lost Ivy yet?"

"I wouldn't count on it. But it seems we've left her behind a few paces."

Reese leaned over and checked the wound beneath Bella's makeshift bandage. It appeared that the bleeding had stopped. At least that was one positive thing.

"It looks better," she told Bella.

The women pressed forward. When the smoke began to clear, Reese had a better view of the forest. Her waning optimism started to rally.

"How do you know your way around here?" Bella gave her a questioning look.

"My little brother and I used to explore these woods when we spent vacations with my mom and grandparents at Timber Cove."

"They'd let you wander off like that?"

"People didn't worry about kidnappings and abductions as much back then," Reese said.

"That's true."

"We're headed to a little country store up ahead off Grey Rocks Highway. That's where we used to buy snacks. They have a landline we can hopefully use."

"Sorry to get you in this mess," Bella said.

"I'm the one who led Ivy here," Reese said, irritated that she hadn't realized that Ivy was playing one of the oldest tricks in the sleuthing book by attaching a vehicle tracker to Betty.

A tear rolled down Bella's face. "I never should have married Hunter. People warned me he was a snake in the grass but I didn't listen. Looking back, I realize he was too nice, too polished and too attentive."

"He's an expert manipulator."

"I walked right into his trap," Bella said. "I should have seen through him."

"Don't blame yourself."

"Still," Bella said. "I'll always want to kick my butt."

They began moving again, hustling as fast as they could up the slope.

"Here's an example of what you faced," Reese said. "It's like when a fisherman lures in a fish with a fat juicy worm. The fish is lured in and bites the hook. The fish doesn't notice that the hook's got a barb on the tip. After the fisherman reels them in, he smacks them on a rock and then guts them and fries them up in a pan."

Bella made a gagging sound.

"Sorry," Reese said.

"That damn rat poison," Bella said. "It's still bothering me, what's left in my system anyway."

"When we get back, you need to see a doctor."

Bella nodded. "If we get back."

"We have to stay positive, Bella."

"Why did you leave the police department?" Bella asked.

Reese sobered. She really didn't want to get into it.

"I decided I wanted to come home. Starting a private investigation business in Meadowlark Valley seemed like the right thing to do."

"I'm glad you're back," Bella said. "We can get to know each other again, though it depends on whether we get out of this mess alive."

"Don't think that way," Reese cautioned. "You'll jinx us."

Bella smiled, and they continued climbing the mountain, both of them silent. Reese tried to recall all of the outdoor safety items Nell and Tom carried in their store. It didn't take long before an idea of how she and Bella could gain the upper hand formed in her mind.

"I'm sick and tired of letting Ivy play cat and mouse with us," Reese said. "How about you?"

"It sucks being a victim," Bella agreed.

"When we get to the store, we're going to take her down," Reese said.

"We'll turn the hunter into the hunted?" Bella gave her a questioning look

"Yes. Right now, Ivy thinks she's got us cornered."

Bella raised her brows. "What are we going to do?"

"Lay a trap."

Chapter Thirty-Five

Reese and Bella tramped through a leafy meadow so green it could have been located on the Emerald Isle. The wind had picked up more, giving movement to the colorful wildflower stems. Overhead, the sky showed large patches between billowing clouds. The smoke had cleared.

As they climbed a knoll, the musical sound of water washing over rocks tickled Reese's ears.

"I can hear the stream," she said.

"Me, too," Bella said.

Once the waterway appeared, looking very much like a silver ribbon stretched across jade-colored velvet, Reese breathed a sigh of relief. She was parched.

Upon reaching one side of the sandy bank strewn with granite rocks, Reese lowered down and cupped her hands. Dipping them into the cool liquid, she scooped as much as she could and brought it to her mouth.

"That helps," Reese said.

Beside her, Bella lowered down and cupped her hands, then hesitated. "Is it safe?"

"My brother and I always stopped here," Reese said. "We never got sick or grew extra arms or a set of antlers."

"I could drink an entire lake right now," Bella said as she scooped up water and drank.

Reese panned her gaze around the clearing, taking in every feature. If Ivy had caught up to them, now would be a good time to take a shot while they were out in the open, preoccupied with slaking their thirst.

She didn't spot anything unusual, so she relaxed. The makeshift bandage on Bella's leg sagged though.

"I'd like to take a closer look at your wound, Bella."

Bella unwound the material.

"Not bad," Reese said, looking at the purplish graze.

"You should have gone into nursing." Bella removed her sneakers and stepped into the stream, submerging her legs. She dunked Reese's shirt into the ripples and wrung it out.

"No, that's not me," Reese said.

"I'm pretty sure it's ruined," she told Reese, handing over her shirt.

"Not a big deal." Reese tied the shirt to a small branch and picked it up. "Let's get moving."

"Right."

Reese and Bella strode quickly through the meadow and got on the path again. As they crested a hill, a tall wooden structure on stilts appeared amid twisted, leaning pines and boulders. It jutted high into the sky, overlooking the Medicine Bow National Forest.

"That's the Rockrimmon Fire Lookout," Bella said. "My dad brought me and Ian up here one time."

"For a building the Civilian Conservation Corp set up in the 1930s, it's still in good shape," Reese commented.

"Ever gone inside?" Bella asked.

"Jesse and I climbed up there a few times. Great view."

Reese noted the breeze had picked up and now blew steadily. In the sky, thunderclouds mounded like mashed potatoes.

Bella held out her hand. "I felt a rain drop."

"I hope it turns into a downpour," Reese said, feeling moisture on her face. "It'll help put out the wildfire."

"True."

"I'm going up in the lookout," Reese said. "I'll be able to see if Ivy's close. You wait here."

"Hurry," Bella said.

Reese hustled up the slope toward the station, noting the foundation covered in rocks and tangled weeds. She jogged up the stairs, which reached into the darkening heavens.

More rain drops splattered her face. The temperature had lowered, and Reese wondered if they were in for some hail. The conditions were right with cold clouds and hot updrafts. Some of those stones could get baseball size, which hurt like hell if you got caught outside.

At the top, she caught her breath. Moving along the walkway, she looked through the dusty, cracked windows of the wooden shack. An old desk stood in one corner, and several overturned chairs sat on the floor. Torn maps were still attached to the shingle walls.

The panoramic wilderness was amazing, except for the dry brown area ravaged by ash borer beetles. To the east, plumes of gray smoke rose above flickering orange-red flames. A massive sheet of rain slanted over the conflagration, slowly dousing it.

When a patch of bright yellow bobbing up the slope caught Reese's eye, an icy sensation shot through her veins.

Ivy.

She hurried down the staircase and told Bella, "She's right behind us."

Bella took off running, her limp less pronounced. The break had obviously helped her recover some strength. Reese wasted no time following her. Before long, the forest depths swallowed them.

Chapter Thirty-Six

Snow rested on the rocky brown heights of the distant mountains. Reaching above tree line, which Reese figured for Wyoming existed somewhere around 10,000 feet, the peaks never grew much vegetation.

"Stop," Bella rasped as she slid to a stop and leaned over, grabbing her knees and taking deep breaths.

"Almost there," Reese managed.

After a brief rest, they headed down a dirt trail where a heap of dead trees blocked their path. Reese and Bella scooted around the tangled mass of branches and continued trekking.

Boulders appeared on either side of the trail, probably moved there by some ancient glacier. A hawk perched in a tree turned its head to watch them as they ran past.

When Nell and Tom's red log store appeared, a flood of relief pulsed through Reese. She tossed a worried glance toward the trail behind them, relieved not to see Ivy. They weren't out of the woods yet, though. That deranged woman was still hot on their trail.

Reese picked up her pace and Bella followed close behind her.

Their shoes crunched on the parking lot gravel as they approached the establishment. Both of them hustled onto the wooden boardwalk and stopped in front of the building. A huge sign above the door read: Gray Rocks Country Store.

Nearby, pairs of snowshoes and antlers had been nailed to the painted panels. From the porch rafters, hanging pots overflowing with red geraniums and pink petunias swung in the breeze. An American flag hung on a post above a red bench. Two white metal ice machines hulked nearby like guards.

Bella twisted the doorknob. "It's locked. How do we get in?"

"This way." Reese walked around the building and paused in front of the back door. Hunkering down and reaching beneath a large bush, she felt around in the rocks.

For a second, she worried, fearing the Osborne's had found a new hiding place.

"Is there a problem?" Bella asked.

Reese gave her a hesitant smile. "No," she said. When she finally located the heavy brown plastic rock, she felt like she'd hit paydirt.

She twisted the rock apart. Picking up the key inside, she slid it into the doorknob. It didn't budge. Swallowing hard, she pulled back on the knob and tried again. Success! The door opened with a squeak.

"We're in," Reese said.

"Good," Bella said.

"Hello?" Reese called as she walked into the store. "Nell? Tom?"

As she'd expected, all was quiet except for the ticking of a grandfather clock hanging on the wall. The Osborne's, along with everyone else living in the canyon, had left due to the dangerous fire conditions.

A long wooden case with a glass front ran along one wall. Displayed inside were jars of hard candy and other confections like cakes, pies, and muffins. Slabs of fudge, peanut brittle, and divinity sat on trays next to clear spice bottles containing cinnamon, cardamom, sage, and several other varieties.

A landline phone handset rested on the counter top, and she rushed over to pick it up. The line was dead.

"Crap," she muttered.

"Not working, I assume," Bella said in a disappointed tone.

"Nope." Reese flipped a switch on the wall, but the lights didn't kick on. "Electricity's out, too. I figured as much, but I just wanted see."

"What do we do first?" Bella asked.

"We've got to work fast."

"Doing what?"

"I've got a plan," Reese assured her.

Quickly, she walked around, observing barrels on the other side of the store that held packages of flour, granulated and powdered sugar, saltine crackers, and other boxed food. The shelves above held commercially canned soups, vegetables, and beans. Cake mixes, gravy mixes, and all kind of condiments filled the space.

Baskets full of shiny apples on the floor added red and green color. Shelves with home canning jars held yellow-orange peaches, pale white pears, crimson tomatoes, scarlet cherries, and dark green snap beans. Crates held orange pumpkins, butternut squash, and striped green watermelon. Another crate held potatoes and the one beside it held onions.

One area displayed round metal racks of shirts, jeans, jackets, sweaters, and skirts. A wooden shelf held sturdy boots and shoes. Perfumes, creams, bath soap, and lotions were arranged neatly on a doily sitting on the top of an old-fashioned dresser.

Refrigerator cases along the back wall contained milk, eggs, lunch meat, soda, and other food that needed to remain cold. Racks nearby offered bread, doughnuts, cookies, potato chips, nuts, and other snacks.

Stairs took customers to the second half floor, which overlooked the main floor and was edged by a sturdy railing. Up there, a person could find equipment like downhill and cross-country skis, snowshoes, canoes, rafts, and hiking poles. Swimwear and ski suits could also be found.

Frustration coated Reese. All this stuff, and she still couldn't find what she needed. Yet, she realized the items had to be here somewhere.

Hurry, a voice in her head insisted. Perspiration broke out on her brow and she felt like screaming.

"There's so much to take in it makes my head spin," Bella said.

"I know," Reese said, intuition finally sparking. "I bet what we need is in the camping section."

"I'm going to lock the back door," Bella suggested.

"No," Reese said. "We want Ivy to enter that way."

Bella gave her a confused look.

"I'll explain in a sec," Reese said.

She strode over to where a length of artificial grass covered the floorboards. A blue and gray two-person tent had been pitched on top and two folding chairs rested nearby. A grill on a metal folding table held a coffee pot, a cast iron pan, and a spatula. Fake bushes and trees edged the back of the scene.

Walking around the tent, Reese approached the shelves, which held outdoor survival supplies, including small cans of pepper spray and large camouflage hunting nets.

"Perfect," she said as she grabbed one of the spray cans. She set it aside, picked up a net designed for big game hunting and ripped open the package. Shaking out the square of material, she nodded in approval. It would definitely work on Ivy.

Reese planned to leave enough money on the counter to cover the cost of the items. Nell and Tom would understand.

Bella scrutinized the items Reese had chosen. "What's your plan?"

"It's a simple one, but it should work."

"Sometimes, simple is all it takes," Bella said. "What do you want me to do?"

Chapter Thirty-Seven

"Take this." Reese handed Bella the camouflage netting and pointed up toward the second-floor railing. "Station yourself right above the back door. When Ivy moves to a position beneath you, toss that puppy down on her."

Bella's eyes widened. "Just like a wild animal."

"Watch out, though, she'll probably start shooting randomly."

"Got it," Bella said.

Reese held up the pepper spray. "I'll give her a shot of this. That'll cool her jets."

Bella nodded. "Is it legal to spray humans with that stuff?"

"In Wyoming, we're allowed to use it for protection."

"What next?"

"We've got to get the gun away from her. Then we'll keep her subdued until we can get cell service to call the police."

"Do you have a pair of handcuffs handy?" Bella asked.

Reese searched quickly among the items on the shelves, thankfully coming up with a package of sturdy zip ties that she tore open and placed on the camping table. "These'll do the trick."

"Quick thinking," Bella said.

"You head upstairs and I'll use the counter as cover," Reese said. Remember, we'll have the element of surprise. Expect Ivy to show up any second now."

Bella hurried toward the staircase and climbed up.

Reese stepped around the counter and hunkered down. She ripped open the pepper spray package and gripped the can. Her muscles became tense as the seconds ticked by. The grandfather clock sounded like a drum in her brain. Her uneven breathing grated on her ears.

More time passed, then the front door knob rattled.

Bella sucked in a loud breath and Reese's heart pounded with a staccato beat.

Ivy began kicking and slamming the old wooden entrance. In the woman's furious state, Reese feared she'd break it down. Unfortunately, Reese's plan required Ivy to enter through the back. Time hadn't allowed her to formulate a contingency scenario.

She and Bella would have to improvise.

"I know you bitches are in there," Ivy screamed. "When I find you, it's all over."

She kicked the door again and it made a cracking sound.

Finally, the pounding and kicking stopped. Silence descended. Reese's lips twitched, and she hoped Ivy had noticed the footsteps in the dirt heading behind the store. She prayed the woman's anger would lead her to the bait.

Peering over the countertop, she watched as the back door knob turned. The entry slowly opened with a telltale squeak. Heavy steps pounded as Ivy rushed inside.

"You two are dead," she warned.

Reese heard the whooshing sound of the net as Bella dropped it.

"Arrgh!" Ivy growled and began thrashing around. She crashed into a shelf and items slammed down onto the floor.

Reese dashed out from behind the counter to where Ivy rolled on the ground, encased in the net. Ivy shouted at her, struggling to point the gun. She wasn't successful, however, because her hand and the weapon were tangled in cords.

Ivy managed to squeeze off one shot before Reese squirted her face with the noxious chemicals. Howling with rage, Ivy tried to claw at her eyes, but her fingers became caught up in the net. Between sobs, she muttered a string of foul obscenities.

Reese lowered down to her knees, tossed aside the pepper spray, and pinned Ivy to the floor. She reached up under the edge of the netting and managed to untangle the gun. Pushing to her feet, she pointed the weapon at Ivy.

"It's over," she told her. "Face it."

By now, Bella had hustled down the stairs, her eyes wide as she stared down at the struggling woman.

"I can't believe that worked," she said breathlessly.

"This can't be happening!" Ivy screeched. "You'll pay for this!"

"You're out of luck," Reese told her. "Plan on going to jail for a long time."

"No, no, NO!" Ivy groaned and struggled to free herself, but to no avail. She looked like a camouflaged mummy stretched out on the floorboards.

Chapter Thirty-Eight

While Bella held the gun on Ivy, Reese removed the net, then secured zip ties on her wrists and ankles. Ivy wailed with outrage.

"I'll be right back," Reese told Bella. "I'm going to try calling 9-1-1 again."

Stepping outside, she searched for a spot where she might be able to pick up cell service. Jogging down the road, she entered a small clearing and scrambled on top of a rock. Thankfully, her call worked this time.

"There's an emergency at the Gray Rocks Country Store," Reese said, explaining about Ivy and her armed pursuit across the mountain.

"Where is the woman now?" The operator asked.

"In the store, secured at the moment. I got the gun away from her and the situation is under control."

"You were very brave," the operator said. She added that she'd dispatched a sheriff's cruiser and that it would be coming soon.

Reese answered more of the operator's questions as she hustled back to the store. She tried staying on the line as she approached the building, but at a certain point, she lost reception. Hurrying inside the store, she let Bella know the cavalry was on their way. Then she went out to stand on the porch, where she watched and waited.

It seemed like an eternity before a siren wail cut through the air. The sheriff's cruiser arrived, red and blue lights flashing. Reese opened the front door and stood aside as two tall, lanky law enforcement types got out of the car and came inside. Wearing light brown sheriff's department uniforms, they took stock of the situation, all while Ivy complained about the injustice of what was happening.

As the sheriff questioned Reese, she identified who the three of them were, then explained that Ivy had admitted to murdering Hunter Northwood, a Meadowlark Valley resident. She added that Ivy had also attempted to murder her and Bella.

The sheriff jotted everything in a notebook, then snapped it closed and stuffed it in his pocket.

Ivy whined and cried out, "It's not right that I'm being detained like a common criminal."

"From what I've heard, ma'am, you are one," the sheriff said.

"You haven't listened to my side," Ivy insisted.

"You'll get your day in court, ma'am."

"Thank you for your help, Sheriff Brookings," Reese said as she glanced at his name tag.

"I'm glad you're safe," he told her. To his deputy, he said, "You know what to do Roy."

"Yes, sir," the deputy responded as he cut the zip ties off of Ivy's ankles. He helped her stand, put her in handcuffs, then told her, "You're under arrest, ma'am."

"I'll have your badge for this," Ivy threatened, her face as dark as a thundercloud.

The deputy marched Ivy out of the store, reciting her Miranda rights. The entire time, Ivy continued to make outlandish threats.

Reese and Bella exchanged glances.

"Thank you," Reese told Sheriff Brookings, and Bella seconded the comment.

"You two gals were mighty lucky," he concluded.

"We were tired of being hunted," Reese said.

"Reese is a former cop," Bella said. "She knew what to do."

When another siren sounded in the distance, Brookings added, "That's the ambulance. They'll need to have a look at your leg."

"I'm fine," Bella said. "I don't need to be fussed over."

"That gash tells me otherwise," the sheriff said.

"By now, I don't even feel it," Bella said.

"You're both probably in a state of shock after being chased at gunpoint all over the damn mountain," Brookings said.

"We've had a long, long day," Reese admitted.

"I'll be back, ladies," Brookings said, tipping his hat. He stepped out of the store, no doubt to see how the deputy was faring with Ivy.

Reese walked over to a refrigerator case and pulled out two orange-colored energy drinks. Since the electricity was out, they were warm. But they'd still be good enough to wet their whistles.

"Here," she said, handing one to Bella.

"You're a lifesaver," Bella said as she opened hers and took a long drink.

Reese did the same, relishing the cool liquid rolling down her throat. She felt thankful they were both still alive and kicking. For a few seconds there, she'd been worried.

"I'd really don't need the paramedics," Bella said.

"Your leg needs to be treated. You don't want infection to set in."

"It's not that big of a deal," Bella said as she walked out onto the porch and sat down on the bench. "I'd rather go home and see my family."

"You'll see them soon enough." Reese followed her out and settled next to her.

"I thought we were done for today," Bella admitted in a weary voice. "Ivy scared me out of my wits."

"You're a survivor." Reese stood inside the open doorway, watching as the wailing ambulance drove off. "Maybe that's what courage is all about."

"What do you mean?" Bella asked.

Reese met Bella's gaze. "You might have been afraid the entire time, but despite the danger, you handled every challenge with a cool head."

"You did the same," Bella said.

"I lost my nerve a few times," Reese admitted.

"You could have fooled me."

They both laughed.

Chapter Thirty-Nine

Sheriff Brookings wanted to send Reese to the Meadowlark Valley Hospital along with Bella, but she insisted on remaining at the store. Ivy may have tossed her Bronco keys in the bushes by the cabin, but she carried a spare set in her purse. She intended to hike back to Timber Cove to collect Betty so she could drive the old girl back down the mountain.

Hopefully, the rain storm had slowed the progress of the wildfire. Still, Reese didn't want to risk leaving her truck in the path of destruction—just in case.

Finally, it seemed Brookings and his deputy accepted that they couldn't change Reese's mind. They rode off in their cruiser, following behind the ambulance. No doubt Ivy, secured in the cruiser's back seat, treated them to a litany of cussing.

When she was finally alone, Reese felt a huge weight lift off of her conscience. She was no Florence Nightingale, and she was relieved that Bella would now receive proper medical care. The wounds in Bella's mind, caused by nearly being poisoned to death by her husband, would take healing of a different kind.

Walking back inside the store, Reese straightened up the shelves Ivy had knocked over, then she found paper and a pen. As rain began to hammer the roof, she jotted down the reason she'd entered the place and offered her cell phone number so Nell and Tom could call her.

After placing the note next to the cash register where they would surely find it, she reached into her back pocket and withdrew a slim wallet. She counted out enough money and placed it on the counter to cover the items she and Bella had used, along with the energy drinks. She left some extra cash; in case any items had been damaged during Ivy's struggles.

By the time she was ready to leave, the storm had passed and the rain had faded to a drizzle. She grabbed another package from the shelves that contained a water-proof poncho. Opening it, she draped it over her shoulders.

She walked outside and locked up. After replacing the spare key in the fake rock, she tucked it securely beneath the bush. Her return hike to Timber Cove went quicker this time. As she entered the abandoned resort with its damp buildings, she headed to Bella's cabin.

Dripping wet and covered in splashes of mud, Betty waited for her.

"I'm back," Reese said as she approached her vehicle, wondering if normal people talked to inanimate objects. On the outside chance she might find her keys, she searched the bushes where Ivy had thrown them. She did not get lucky.

"Oh, well," Reese muttered. "At least Ivy didn't send me off to meet my maker today."

Grateful that she tried to be prepared for anything, a trait both her mother and grandmother had instilled in her, Reese opened the driver's door and reached for her purse. In a zipper compartment, she found her spare set of keys.

Reese climbed inside, shut the door, and buckled up. After starting the engine, she headed home, humming an old John Denver song.

• • •

Reese called Jeremy as soon as she got home to tell him everything that had transpired. Just as she'd suspected he would, he counseled her about taking unnecessary chances, then complimented her for a job well done. Though surprised by the outcome, Jeremy said he was pleased Reese had found Bella up in Timber Cove.

However, he wasn't surprised to hear that Ivy had confessed to killing Hunter for the life insurance settlement or that she'd attempted to murder Reese and Bella.

Upon investigating Ivy's background, Jeremy said he'd noted the huge policy she'd taken out on Hunter the day they were married. He suspected a potential scam, but when Reese explained Hunter and Ivy's twisted, youthful love affair that had gone wrong, he said he now understood Ivy's vengeful motive.

Reese slept soundly that night, thankfully with no nightmares. Bo curled up in his favorite spot beside her on the bed, seemingly pleased as punch to have her back home. In the morning, she went out for a jog, then returned home to shower and throw on her jeans, a top, and her boots.

She switched on the kitchen TV, fed Bo, then began making a pot of coffee. During a weather report delivered on the local station, the anchor mentioned that the recent storm had helped quench the southern wildfires. More rainstorms were predicted for the area, which would be a welcome relief not only to firefighters, but also for the parched countryside and its inhabitants.

Carrying a hot cup of java, Reese walked past Bo, who was now curled in his window seat, and headed out on her front porch. She sat in a wicker chair to enjoy the fresh morning air, which was much clearer than in previous days.

Jeremy's dark blue Trailblazer rolled up alongside the curb. He got out and shut his door, adjusted his gray corduroy blazer, then sauntered up to her porch. His dark hair gleamed in the sun, along with the detective's badge on his belt.

"You ready to head to the hospital?" he asked.

"I didn't know we were going anywhere," Reese said as she stood.

"Ford's awake," Jeremy said. "I want to talk to him." "Just a sec," Reese said. She went inside, grabbed her purse, and then walked onto the porch where she locked her front door.

"Naomi called me to let me know he'd finally come around," Jeremy said as he walked with Reese to his vehicle.

"That's great news," Reese said. "Did she say anything about how Bella is doing?"

"Along with being grateful that Bella didn't drown, Naomi mentioned her step-daughter is in good shape. The doctors wanted Bella to spend the night for observation, though."

Jeremy opened the passenger door, allowing Reese to get inside, then closed it for her.

The gentlemanly gesture was not lost on Reese, and she smiled, watching as he walked around and got in the driver's side.

As he drove toward the hospital, Jeremy added, "Naomi said she made a FaceTime call to Ian in Texas, so he could hear the good news."

"That's nice," Reese said.

At the hospital, Jeremy parked on the top level of the garage. After getting out, they walked inside and rode down in the elevator to the first floor.

"Naomi told me they are getting some fresh air in the atrium, so that's where we're headed," Jeremy said.

Once they stepped inside the plant-filled patio, which was covered with a clear roof, Reese spotted Naomi and Bella. Seated together on a bench, they talked to Ford who sat in a wheelchair wearing a white hospital bathrobe. Bandages still swathed his head.

Upon seeing Reese and Jeremy, Bella smiled and waved them over. Naomi was dressed in her scrubs, but Bella wore a white hospital bathrobe, just like her father.

Naomi stood and handed Reese a bouquet of mixed flowers, then hugged her. "What can we ever do to thank you?"

"No worries, Naomi," Reese said. "I'm glad I could help."

"We appreciate everything you did for Bella," Ford said, the color on his bruised face now giving off a healthy tint. "All the plans I had went down the toilet after Hunter attacked me and put me here."

"So, it *was* Hunter who did it," Jeremy said with a nod. "Reese and I figured as much."

"Yeah, he was pissed when he couldn't find the burner phone with his text to Ivy," Ford said. "He figured Bella had brought it to me, and when I wouldn't give it to him, he went crazy and flew into a rage."

"You must have been referring to Hunter when I found you and you muttered, 'He knows.' "

"I don't remember anything from that time," Ford said. "But I bet you're right, Reese."

"Bella told me you'd hidden Hunter's burner phone in the Diamondback Revenge diorama," Reese said to Ford. "That's why you were so desperate to get it back, right?"

"Exactly," Ford said. "That phone had evidence against Hunter that could have been used in court against him. He and his family are so powerful, I knew it would be tough to take him down, but I was willing to try. That's why I cooked up the plan for Bella to fake her death, which might not have been too bright, now that I think about it. But I was worried. Until the cops could arrest Hunter, I wanted to keep my girl safe. There's no telling what the Northwood family might have done to her if she'd lodged a complaint against that bastard."

"I get it," Jeremy said.

"Me, too," Reese said.

"That damn Hunter." Ford shook his head. "I sensed he was no good. He sure had a pair of brass balls on him. I know it's wrong to speak ill of the dead, but I'm glad he's gone."

Naomi touched Ford's knee. "There's no need to work yourself up," she said.

"Yeah, I know, but that nut job Ivy Drake could have killed Bella yesterday," Ford said. "Reese, too. That still burns me up."

"Rest assured, Ivy will most likely be locked away for life," Reese told him. "She admitted to killing Hunter after their so-called wedding in order to collect the life insurance she took out on him."

"Yep, Bella explained the whole story, from the time those two were in college and why Ivy hatched the plan to kill him," Ford said. "Including the fact that Ivy couldn't have collected the life insurance if Bella were still alive. Her marriage to Hunter wasn't legal."

"Hell hath no fury like a woman scorned," Reese said.

"Ain't that the truth," Ford agreed.

"Hunter and Ivy had one thing in common," Jeremy said. "Their love of wealth. Hunter wanted it so badly he set up his insurance scheme, poisoning his wives so he could collect."

"Obviously, he was desperate to come up with money to maintain his lavish lifestyle after his parents cut him out of their will," Reese said.

Bella gave a bitter laugh. "Apparently, he didn't want to obtain it the old-fashioned way—by hard work."

Naomi patted Bella's hand. "It's all over now, dear. It's not healthy to dwell in the past."

"I know, but Hunter put me through hell. When I found that burner phone in his SUV and discovered he was poisoning me, I was outraged. I could hardly believe it when Reese told me he's done this before. He was ruthless."

"All the murderers I've come across are that way," Jeremy said. "They have to be."

Reese remembered finding Hunter rummaging through his truck the night she'd taken him dinner. He must have been searching for his burner phone, which is why he seemed so distracted. She'd wrongly assumed it was widower's grief, when actually, he didn't want anyone to find the phone and see what he'd texted to Ivy.

"What will happen to Colton Drake, now that his mom will go to jail for murder?" Bella asked.

"I talked with Colton early this morning at the police station," Jeremy said. "It was quite a blow to him to find out his mother murdered Hunter Northwood, and that Hunter was his biological father."

"I feel sorry for the kid," Reese said.

"Fortunately, he's got a good head on his shoulders," Jeremy said. "Henry Drake was the only father Colton's ever known, so he's well grounded. The kid's got a lot to process, but I believe he's going to be okay."

"Does he know what he wants to do now?" Bella asked.

"He has an academic scholarship to the University of Wyoming," Jeremy said. "He plans to apply to a medical school once he graduates with a bachelor's degree in biology and hopes to someday become a doctor."

"Just like Henry," Reese said, pleased to hear that Ivy's son was on a good track. "Where's he going to stay until he graduates from high school in the spring?"

"Doug Marsh's family is taking him in," Jeremy said.

"That's great to hear," Reese said. "Doug seems like a good kid, too."

"Colton also said he might go up and visit with Pearl and Walt Northwood sometime," Jeremy added. "Just not yet—it's too soon."

"That's right, they are his grandparents," Reese said. "It would be nice if he decides to get in touch with them. They are, after all, family. Even if they are a different breed."

"I never liked them," Bella said. "They scared me."

"Colton doesn't seem like a person who is easily scared," Jeremy said. "One day, he might just be curious about who his relatives are. Although I doubt that he'd ever look at life the way they do."

"Which is a good thing in my opinion," Reese said. She leaned over to smell the flowers Naomi had given her, inhaling the blossoms' fresh fragrance. Turning to the Presleys, she said, "Thank you for these."

"After all you've done, they're only a small token of appreciation," Naomi said.

"Still, it was very thoughtful," Reese insisted.

Later, after they'd finished visiting with the Presleys, Reese and Jeremy headed back to the elevator and rode up to the first level of the parking garage. Outside in the bright sunshine, they walked toward Jeremy's Trailblazer.

"Thanks for emailing me Bella's accident report," he said.

"I need to update it now, after everything that's happened," Reese said.

"No worries, I'll type an addendum at the end, explaining the outcome."

"I appreciate it," Reese said.

"I'll also write the report on Ford's assault," Jeremy added.

"What's the deal? I thought you wanted me to handle that." Reese stopped walking and looked up curiously at Jeremy.

"I need you to follow up on a new case," Jeremy said. "It may be nothing or it may turn out to be something."

"What's going on?"

"There are a couple of little old ladies in town who take in homeless men and feed them for a week or so, then the old gents go missing."

"You think they're burying them in their basement or something? Like 'Arsenic and Old Lace?' Really?"

"I can't say for sure," Jeremy said with a chuckle. "Either way, I sense it's going to take a woman's touch to get them to talk. I want you to infiltrate their camp, so to speak, and try to find out what's going on."

Reese resumed walking back to the Trailblazer. "Wow, it blows my mind that something like that is happening. And if so, the ladies need to be stopped."

"Do you have the time to help on this?" Jeremy slung an arm around her shoulders as he walked alongside her.

Reese grinned up at him and said, "You can count on me, detective."

About the Author

Born in Portland, Oregon, Cindy has lived all over the United States and spent five years in Misawa, Japan. She has visited Canada, the Philippines, Samoa, Hawaii, both the western and eastern Caribbean and New Zealand.

Currently, she lives in Cheyenne, Wyoming, where Cheyenne Frontier Days is held each year. CFD's well-known rodeo is often referred to as the "Daddy of 'em all."

Over the years, she has won or placed in various writing contests. She has also written for and edited numerous newsletters. Her non-fiction magazine articles have been featured in "True West" and "Wild West." She was a book critic for Storyteller Alley and is a freelance writer/editor.

For the last 18 years, she has been a contributing editor and writer for Laramie County School District 1's Public Schools' Chronicle, which has a circulation of approximately 46,000 readers.

From baby alligators to glow worms, Cindy has seen a variety of life's wonders.

www.ingramcontent.com/pod-product-compliance
Lightning Source LLC
Chambersburg PA
CBHW011512100726
47899CB00010BD/3337